A FITTING REVENGE

CA SOLE

Helifish Books

First Published in the United Kingdom in 2016.
Second edition published in 2021 by Helifish Books

ISBN: 978-0-9954809-0-2 (Paperback)
ISBN: 978-0-9954809-2-6 (ebook-ePub)
ISBN: 978-0-9954809-3-3 (PDF)

British Library Cataloguing in Publication Data
A CIP catalogue record for this book is available from the British Library

Author's website: www.helifish.co.uk

I am indebted to my wife who added her valued suggestions early on in the project and supported me throughout.

Your vengeance is worse than murder. What does that make you?

A life, a love and a fortune hang in the balance. Sandra is a ruthless misandrist immersed in greed. No act is beyond her.

Alastair is helping his close friend, Giles, avoid a punishing divorce from Sandra. He struggles to gain the initiative in this battle as she stays one criminal step ahead the whole time.

When Alastair strays, his relationship with his long-term love, Juliet, is ripped apart. But she needs to help Giles too. With this common goal, they strive to work together, but the stress they're under widens their rift as they face appalling crimes and the ruination of both their lives.

Sandra's actions demand retribution, but Alastair stretches reason in exacting a terrible revenge for the impact they've had on his friends. In doing so, he discovers a side to himself that he never knew existed.

A Fitting Revenge is a fast, event-packed thriller in which CA Sole engrosses you in a horrific yet credible scenario that could affect any one of us.

Please visit: www.helifish.co.uk

A Fitting Revenge

By

CA Sole

1

WHEN I SAW that painting placed in such a prominent position, I should have suspected something was wrong, I should have been alert to the danger in that liaison. The work evokes so much emotion through its blood red sky and that tortured soul crying open mouthed at – at what? The future, the present or the past? To display it on a wall in a public room would invite study and admiration, but to hang it where peace and rest should prevail surely indicated a troubled mind.

SHE CAUGHT MY attention, and she certainly caught the attention of the pavement diners, a good number of whom were turned in her direction. She had positioned herself well back from the end of a short queue for the bus on the far side of the road. There was something commanding about her; perhaps an arrogance that set her on a higher plane than those who used public transport. In front of her were an elderly lady leaning on her stick, a teenage couple in identical T-shirts restraining an excited terrier, a thickset man in a leather jacket and a brown beanie, and a Rastafarian who was jigging about to whatever was coming out of his headphones. The queue was shaded from the heat by overhanging chestnut trees whose lower branches waved and parted to let the bus in. My view had been stolen, so I turned my attention back to my immediate surroundings.

Antonio ran a pretty decent restaurant he called The Mandolino. He served good, simple Italian food, good coffee and kept his wine prices low. The concept was obviously successful as it was often difficult to get a table. Those on the pavement were all occupied late on that warm August evening, but I had found one inside by the window where no one was behind me and there was an unrestricted view of the entrance, the street and most of the clientele.

A crooning Dean Martin in the background was almost drowned out by the buzz of conversation and raucous laughter from one particular table out of my sight. Even when Pavarotti took over he could barely be heard. Huge mirrors on the opposing walls provided additional vantage points for me to indulge in a favourite pastime – people watching.

Glancing out of the window, I saw the bus had departed and taken the queue away. For a short while the woman remained, though. Then, aloof from the attention, she began to cross the road towards the restaurant. Her long dark hair swished from side to side as she gave a quick glance left and right. She was tall and her strides were long, her walk determined.

She passed out of view again, and I ordered a Peroni while considering what to eat. Appetising smells of garlic and pizza and oregano hung in the air, and a comfortable anticipatory feeling settled over me. Antonio kept his choice of items small with a new menu every Monday, preferring quality rather than a large and mediocre selection. The pizza options did not change though. Which one? Procrastination over menus is a failing of mine. The Italian waiter brought my beer and stood back expectantly.

'I'll finish this first, thanks,' I said. He raised a single black eyebrow, spun on his heel and hurried over to another table, there always being a rush at that time in the evening.

The woman came into the restaurant. The task of choosing a pizza was suspended. I lowered the menu and watched her over the rim of my glass before putting it down.

The waiter was at the next table attending to a middle-aged couple. His mouth had dropped open in an expression of gormless amazement. The wife, who was facing the outside and had no idea what was going on, had to give her order twice before he snapped out of his trance, '*Mi dispiace, Senora,* repeat please.'

'It's all right,' said her greying husband, grinning at him man to man, 'quite understandable.'

'*Magnifico!*' he breathed and flashed a false smile at the wife.

The woman scanned the room looking for a table, or perhaps the person she was meeting. Her gaze eventually settled on me tucked into my corner. She eyed me for a second or two without a change in expression, then the click of her heels on the terracotta tiles came closer. My heart started to pound; there wasn't another spare seat in my corner of the room. I'm not a nervous person generally, but I'm not comfortable with strangers.

'Alastair, Alastair Forbes?' She stood over me, her voice husky and soft. I was conscious that the room was turned in our direction, which only added to my discomfort.

What the …? Who was this? She simply oozed appeal and she knew who I was! I rose awkwardly to my feet, glanced to the side and met envious male eyes.

She smiled a greeting, but there was a hint of arrogance in her look and perhaps amusement at my confusion. Her eyes were captivating. With her dark hair, they should have been black or brown, but instead they were such a deep Mediterranean blue that they forced a man to drown in them. An even row of teeth were spoilt by a slight gap between the top front pair, but it was a solitary imperfection which only added to her appeal.

'I recognised you from a photograph.' A sudden flash of doubt crossed her features as I must have still looked dumbfounded. 'You are Alastair Forbes, aren't you?'

'Yes,' I nodded, 'but, er… what photo, where?'

'I'm sorry.' She held out her hand and gripped mine firmly. 'I'm Angela Parsons and I know you're a friend of a friend from the photo. This place is crowded, may I share your table? I sort of part know you, don't I?' She gave me a coquettish smile, then spoke timidly, because I hadn't reacted, 'Of course, you're expecting someone else? I'm so sorry, I'm intruding.' She turned to go.

Her attempt at departure restored my confidence. 'No, no one's coming. You're welcome. Sorry, you took me by surprise. It's not every day that strange women join me. Please sit down. What photo? Where did you see it? I'm intrigued.'

She ignored my questions and continued as if she hadn't heard, 'What are you having?'

'I hadn't decided, may I buy you a drink first?'

I selected a bottle of Pinot Grigio for us to share and watched, amused, as the waiter struggled to write down our order while trying to get a better view down Angela's cleavage.

She started a completely different conversation when I pressed her once more about the photo and skilfully diverted my probing questions about who she was and what mutual friends we had. Eventually I asked her again, insisting on an answer.

Angela looked me straight in the eye and smiled gently, brushing her hair away from her right eye, pushing it back behind her ear in the familiar manner women use; always futile because it falls back again. 'That must remain a secret for now. Trust me.'

While she was talking, I was trying to assess her. She wasn't as young as I first thought: somewhere just in her thirties, thirty-two probably; there were tiny little crow's feet fanning from her eyes. Her trim body was dressed to emphasise gentle curves in tight navy pants, which were topped by a matching short jacket over a white, low cut shirt. Her hands were bare of jewellery.

Like so many of us, I have a tendency to initially regard attractive people with undeserved favour – how can someone so gorgeous be corrupt/untrustworthy/dishonest? It's akin to celebrity worship, even if it's undeserved. With this woman, I was trying to conquer the tendency because something was not quite right. She was teasing me, of course, but I felt there was another side to her, calculating maybe. There was no doubt that she was self assured and had the sort of confidence that is a consequence of sexuality and good looks, but she also had an air of command about her. She might ask what I wanted but, whatever I said, it was going to be her choice in the end. Did I need to trust her? I decided to make the best of the situation; it had been a while.

'This is excellent food,' she said at one point, then wrinkled her nose, 'but I'm not one for the pseudo-Italian effect in here.'

Her eyes tracked around the room taking in the decoration of dried red chillies hanging from the ceiling in our corner and the long string of garlic by the window. She did not spend time on the old pictures of Tuscany dotted around the walls, nor the photo of the ruins of Monte Cassino, but she did dwell on the mandolin itself which hung above the door. Sadly, its gloss finish had long since faded and it was in a sorry state with two of its strings broken and twisted back over the headstock.

'Well,' I countered when she turned back to me, 'it's not so pseudo. The owner is Italian, the waiters are mostly Italian, as is the chef, and the food certainly is. I find it most reminiscent of Italy.'

'I suppose so. It's just that the place has too traditional a look to it. I can't cling to the past, it's history, gone. We need to get rid of the old and the useless, we need to move on and look to the future. Contemporary is the closest we can get to the future, unless we make it ourselves of course, so we have to change our choices as society moves forward.'

This was not a view I could entirely support, but to avoid disagreement spoiling the evening I changed the subject and asked about her background. She had a younger brother, she said and had had a happy childhood. Her eyes, however, lacked any of the sparkle or softness that such emotions would normally produce. Either her story was not true, or she had shut out that part of her life and would not discuss it further for some reason.

We switched to easier and more entertaining subjects as the second bottle of wine was consumed. All the while her glances became more and more suggestive. I was toying with the stem of my glass when she made some point and stretched her long fingers to rest on my hand. In my experience, a first date might do that but would remove them soon afterwards; an initial exploratory touch. Angela kept them there, and it was certain then where this was going to end.

HER FLAT WAS on the second floor of a block that wasn't far away. I said I wanted to climb the stairs, she said she normally would but not tonight, she was 'too pissed'. We had the lift to ourselves. She was hungry and attacked me as soon as the doors closed. She had my shirt buttons undone and my belt released before we reached her floor. She ran from the lift across the landing to her door and giggled while she fumbled with the key. Inside, we stood partly undressed and breathing deeply, staring at each other in the lounge. She waved a hand at the drinks cabinet, defusing the moment. I poured us both a malt, which she downed in one go and held out her glass for another. The look on her face was pure hunger, and it wasn't for the whisky. She was using it as a prop. She had now drunk a considerable amount which only seemed to amplify her desire. It was time to act, before the whisky had the opposite effect. We rushed into her room where we fell onto the bed. The details don't matter, but it was the wildest sex I'd ever had. Her enthusiasm and athleticism more than matched my pent up levels of testosterone.

After the bout, sweating and panting, we lay back on the pillows. 'Now I feel like getting high,' she murmured.

I said nothing. Quicksand lay ahead.

'Be a sweetie, there's a bag behind the sofa, bring it here will you.'

She brought out what I later learned was a kit for hippie crack or nitrous. I was a stranger to drugs – still am. If others want to wreck their lives, that's their business, but the main reason I don't do drugs is because I want to be in control of myself, not under the influence of some foreign substance. The whole thought scares me, so when she tried to persuade me to join her on her trip, I turned her down, softly at first then more emphatically as she kept nagging me, until eventually I'd had enough. 'No, Angela. You go ahead if you like, but I won't.'

'Suit yourself.' It was a tart reply, her annoyance clear. All the time we were arguing she had been preparing her kit which involved using a 'cracker' into which she put the little nitrous oxide canister, the same type that cooks use to produce whipped cream. She screwed the cracker down onto the cylinder to pierce the seal, ready to dispense the gas under control into a balloon. That done and holding the balloon closed, she lay back on the pillows, put the neck to her mouth and breathed in the gas, alternating one breath from the balloon and one from the air. Nitrous oxide is the gas that dentists sometimes use as an anaesthetic – laughing gas. They administer it as fifty percent with pure oxygen so that it's only mild, safe and short lived. Angela was breathing the gas at a ratio of fifty percent with air from the room. Her oxygen intake was much reduced, and if she had kept it up for a long time she would have ended up with hypoxia. After a few deep breaths, she sighed happily, 'Oooh, I feel good.' She giggled and her voice rose in pitch. 'God, I love this feeling,' she squeaked and laughed hysterically for a few seconds. Almost visibly her body seemed to relax. She took another breath, then one of air, then another of the gas. 'Al, do me again,' she ordered. 'Slowly this time.'

So I did. Her dulled brain only allowed her a constant stream of oohs and aahs, not even a giggle. She laid still and just absorbed the feelings until she jerked repeatedly in a final spasm.

After that, she slept soundly for a couple of hours. I was wide awake though, kept there by my thoughts and doubts. The fucking had been free of any emotion, and I use that word deliberately in its most raw and coarse of meanings. She had been detached, satisfying herself alone; I was merely the necessary means to relieve her frustration, and I wasn't sure just which one of us was driving things.

On the other hand I had just had a fantastic bout of sex with a strange woman who refused to tell me how she knew who I was and, for all I knew, was going to con me into something or out of something. And yet another tack – guilt, because I was in a deep and meaningful relationship, even if Juliet lived a long way away. This night to remember was a stupid thing to succumb to, and it could not happen again.

The bedroom wasn't completely dark, some light from the street lamps leaked round the side of the curtains and there was a lilac nightlight at floor level near the door. There were no family photos, and no teddy bears or cushions or any other bedroom comforts. Surely someone who had a happy childhood would have some pictures of those times? There was nothing that could give a clue to who she was or where she came from, which is why the only picture in the bedroom, that large print of Edvard Munch's The Scream, was so significant. Positioned where it was, it seemed somehow to be very personal, hanging over the bed as a ghastly and torturous reminder.

I got up at one point to go to the bathroom. There was one as an en-suite and another off the living room. I didn't want to wake her, so chose to go there. The summer night was warm and a slight breeze came in the open window. I looked outside and peered down into a dark alley which butted onto the street about thirty metres away, its yellow sodium lights unable to reach into the shadows down below.

Before going back to bed, I had a quick look around. The bedroom aside, the flat as a whole was not what one would expect of a woman living alone. It was almost masculine. The lounge was sparsely furnished in a cold, contemporary style dominated by a modular sofa. In front of this was a glass and chrome coffee table set on a thick white fluffy rug. There was a computer desk in the corner, backed by the full drinks cabinet. Abstract art made its presence felt through three large paintings and the bold red, blue and yellow curtains. The place was cold and clean and tidy to the extent it was sterile, lacking any character. Did she really have a life here in this Spartan apartment?

Eventually I drifted off to sleep, but it wasn't for long as I felt Angela carefully leave the bed so as not to disturb me. It seemed a long time before she came back, but in that state of partial wakefulness there was no way to be sure. My thoughts resumed, churning around and bringing me back to consciousness. They were interrupted. 'Can we do that again, another time?' Angela murmured in her husky voice which stopped me from drifting off. 'I feel deliciously done.'

'Sounds like a good plan,' I said, 'but can I have a week's rest?'

She gave a throaty laugh which stopped when I added, 'I still need to know how you know who I am.'

'Not yet, Sweetie, not yet. It's my little secret and I'm having fun with it, but you will know, I promise, just not yet.'

There was an undertone to her words that left me feeling uncomfortable. This strange woman had seduced me after introducing herself in an unlikely manner and was either lying about her past or did not like discussing it.

Another thought struck me as I was leaving: when she had left the bed in the middle of the night, she had not gone to the en-suite bathroom, I had seen her passing the nightlight on her way to the lounge. Curious, but there was probably a simple explanation.

2

I WAS LOOKING forward to dinner at Giles's house. He had invited me about a month previously, but I had been in Chile and couldn't go. Another couple were to be there, but Giles didn't sound too enthusiastic over their attendance when he called. I suspected that he wanted me there in part to provide him with some genial company as well as having another chance for us to get together.

When I arrived at his house there was already an old and dirty silver Ford Fiesta in the drive with a pre 2001 number plate. Who were these other people? Had they been there much earlier, all afternoon, or were they staying with Giles? Their car, in stark contrast to his Aston Martin and Sandra's Porsche Cayman, looked distinctly out of place in front of the rambling old manor house.

As such places can be, the house itself was not particularly large, but the first time I went there I had counted thirty-two chimney pots for rooms on three floors. There were stables and Giles had a couple of horses that had the run of two large paddocks. The present drive was narrow and tarred and approached the house from the south, but an ancient avenue of well matured chestnut trees led towards it from the east. Giles's family, of which he was the only surviving member, had lived there since the early nineteenth century. I had not been to the house for over a year, because he and I preferred to meet out and about.

Justin Giles Collins, who loathed his first name and insisted on being called Giles, was my closest and absolutely trustworthy friend. He was dressed casually in pale jeans and a long sleeved dark blue shirt. Standing above me on the top step with his trademark highly polished shoes, he appeared even taller than his six foot two inch frame. With a broad grin, he reached down to shake my hand with both of his. 'God, it's good to see you Alastair! How long has it been? You're always swanning about the world and I can't get hold of you. Listen, before we go in, I can't promise tonight is going to be a ball of fun, the others just don't fit in, but Sandra hangs onto them, or the wife actually – can't think why, she's a bit dim frankly. But you and I, we've got some catching up to do, and we can get pissed on our own if it all becomes too boring. Come in, come in.'

Wood panelling below a dado rail lined the expansive hall. Portraits of Giles's military ancestors and others stared down with steely expressions, challenging guests. Two large oriental carpets covered most of the wooden floor, one was a Tekke-Turkoman and I recognised the other as originating somewhere in the Caucasus, but couldn't pinpoint where. A huge brass shell case held a variety of walking sticks and umbrellas, and a Chinese vase, which was incredibly valuable, sat on a table flanked by two modest flower arrangements. A further quick glance around the various other ornaments, figurines and paintings told me that nothing had changed in the last year which, in an old house like this, was utterly normal.

Giles ushered me to the right into the drawing room. A man with close-cropped yellow hair was looking at something on a table next to the far wall. He was flanked by two women, one slim with long blonde hair gathered up on top of her head, which served to emphasise her height, the other shorter, heavier and with a fair bob. Giles called out, 'Sandra, come and meet Alastair at long last.'

All three turned to face us. For a second, I could not see past the blonde hair. For what felt like an age, I couldn't respond in any way as, with an innocent, welcoming smile on her face and without any sign of recognition, came Angela Parsons. She was immaculate in skin tight black leather pants with a low cut pink top. Somehow the lapels of her leather waistcoat managed to parallel the curve of her breasts precisely, accentuating the cleavage, forcing one's eyes down into the crevasse; it was hard to look at her face.

'Alastair! I know she's beautiful, but you look really silly with your mouth half open.'

I pulled myself together, forced my lips into a smile and shook her warm, deceitful hand. There was no extra pressure, no lingering, no secret hidden in her grip. Only, 'You haven't changed a bit since that photo was taken of you two together.' There was an amused smile in her eyes as she waved her arm towards a number of frames on a table between the windows. 'That was at university, Giles tells me.'

'Yes, a long time ago now.' My mouth was dry and I needed a drink. *I had fucked my friend's wife!*

Giles's introduction to the other couple gave me a welcome break to recover. At six foot, I looked down on Tony Wiggins at about five foot seven or eight, but he was as solid as a lump of granite. The first thing I noticed about him as we shook hands was how large, calloused, hard and heavy his were; the way hands develop from a lifetime of manual labour. He didn't exert excessive pressure, but I knew he could crush my fingers with ease. His face was weaselly though, with brown eyes under pale brows, a narrow, high bridged nose and thin lips which smiled without conviction. His small head seemed incongruous, set as it was on top of those massive shoulders by a muscular neck. He struck me as more cunning than intelligent. He was slightly bow-legged, and when he sat down, his knees and thighs produced a thin outline through his jeans in comparison to his powerful torso. At a guess, he worked out regularly in a gym, but only concentrated on his top half.

Mandy however, might have been described as cuddly and sensuous but, as Giles said, she did seem to have limited intelligence. A pretty woman in her thirties carrying too much weight, she was a caricature of a buxom barmaid or the proverbial rosy cheeked farmer's daughter open to a roll in the hay. Her pink ruffled blouse topped a pair of black trousers which were stretched tight around her waist, accentuating her excess tummy. The blouse had a loose thread hanging from it and the trouser pocket edges were frayed.

Not only their car but also their rather tired clothes emphasised that while Sandra exuded wealth and taste, her friends were not so fortunate. Wasn't it a bit unusual for such different types to mix socially? Was it the girls who had been school friends, perhaps, and one made it up the ladder by collaring the wealthy husband? It wasn't the men, I would surely have known if Giles had a friend like Tony.

The others became embroiled in a conversation about the local butcher who might be getting his game meat from dodgy sources. It gave me time to try and make sense of it all. What the hell was I going to do about Sandra? Should I tell Giles, to whom I owed infinite loyalty? There was obviously something seriously wrong with his brief marriage. Would it make things worse if I told him, or would he appreciate the truth? He seemed quite happy and I could wreck that by telling him, however loyal it would be. Sometimes things are best left alone and matters die a natural death. Whatever the solution, it was far too early to make a decision. I needed to sound out what was going on in Giles's world first.

I knew he had married, of course. It was a little over a year previously and I was his natural choice for best man, but I became embroiled in an aircraft accident investigation in Chile and couldn't leave in time for the wedding. He 'made do' he told me, but in our own different ways we both felt my absence was a loss. Of course, he'd invited Juliet too, as the other part of our inseparable trio, but she was at her dying mother's bedside with her sister and couldn't go. Juliet had asked Giles not to attend the funeral because, she said, he should not disrupt and ruin his honeymoon with so sad an event. A combination of my foreign trips, Juliet's distant home, his travels and our choice of places to meet, meant that, extraordinarily, neither Juliet nor I had ever come face to face with Sandra. Now I had.

So far that evening, Sandra (I had to mentally correct myself from using Angela) and Giles had appeared to be a happy couple; why not, after only a year together? She could obviously lie and act convincingly and apparently without feeling, which vindicated my earlier suspicions. For Giles, as an honest and straightforward man, it was not so easy. His tanned face under a mop of thick and prematurely greying hair was showing signs of strain. That would not be surprising for most people involved with moving vast amounts of money on a daily basis, except that Giles was used to that and had always coped well. No, it was something more; was it a difficult marriage? It was worrying, especially since I was involved. We needed to talk, but not necessarily about everything.

I wondered how Sandra, with her strong contemporary tastes, regarded this house. It was a complete contrast to her flat. It represented a different era, and she must have hated the place. Apart from the modern amenities in the kitchen and bathrooms, everything about it, including the contents, was old and traditional. One afternoon prior to his marriage came to mind: Juliet, in her short tweed skirt and heavy house socks, was sitting on the sill in the deep window recess, her back against one side, her feet on the other and a glass of wine in her hand. 'Giles,' she had said, waving her drink at the sitting room, 'some of the rooms in this house are too gloomy and oppressive with their wood panelling, your aggressive ancestors and heavy curtains. It needs brightening up, it needs a woman's touch.'

He laughed. 'Hah! Are you volunteering? People ask me why I don't move into somewhere more manageable, but why would I change? Parts of it may be a bit dim and dark, but I was born here and it's worth something provided I keep it up. Besides, I would need an equally large place to house my things. I'll certainly never dispose of them, some are quite valuable.'

Giles did not need anyone to look after him, but he reasoned that if the house was not kept in good order and was allowed to deteriorate, it would cost more to repair than if he employed people to maintain it on an ongoing basis. There were two full time staff, Henry who was a general helper and an occasional and informal butler and Mrs Potter, the house-keeper and cook. Part-time staff and maintenance people were hired as required, but it only needed the two for this small dinner. I did not know for certain, of course, but I suspected that Giles paid Henry and Mrs Potter well over the accepted wage for their services. He was a kind man who believed in fair play, and he could afford to be generous.

We were ushered into the dining room which was always bright and cheery. On this night it glittered, and the table was immaculately laid. A warm gleam emanated from the wood, and light from the chandelier sparkled on crystal glasses. Georgian silver cutlery, cruets, salvers and candlesticks were precisely placed, not a millimetre out.

There was plenty of space at the long table, so much so that it would have been unsociable had we five occupied the whole of it. We bunched up at the one end with Giles at its head, Sandra on his left and me to his right. Mandy placed herself next to Sandra and Tony was next to me. Neither Henry nor Mrs Potter were present during the meal, thank goodness. At one end of the room were two hot trays with silver dishes on them from which the guests would serve themselves. Mrs Potter had made a delicious gazpacho soup which was followed by a main dish of venison. This re-kindled the discussion over the butcher.

Tony Wiggins didn't talk much, in fact he only responded to questions. He was, apparently, a man who fixed things. Whether that meant plumber, kitchen fitter, gardener or builder was difficult to determine, because he never gave a straight answer, but quoted what he had done for Mrs Kidd, and what for Mike Gibbons, and how old Miss Halfpenny needed him to trim her hedge. Mandy called him Anthony as did Sandra, but I followed Giles's lead with Tony, which didn't seem to please him. Maybe he simply wasn't comfortable being in affluent company. Something niggled me about Tony, but I couldn't pin it down.

Mandy had been Sandra's firm friend since school apparently. She had a high pitched and slightly musical voice which lifted in tone at the end of a sentence as if each one was a question. She would issue a silly giggle at the slightest sign of humour but also when nothing was remotely funny. I think it was mostly that characteristic that gave the impression she lacked intelligence. Nevertheless, most of what she said was of little interest to anyone. While Tony might not have been comfortable though, Mandy revelled in the display of upper-middle-class tradition. Giles, of course, thought nothing of it, he wasn't putting on a show for his guests' benefit. Giles did not put on shows, he was merely using his day to day possessions and living the way he was brought up.

The conversation shifted from one subject to another without much enthusiasm. There was talk of the Wiggins's holidays, of their park home down in Swanage and how well it had served them for cheap weekends away. Apparently Tony was always fixing it and fitting it out to incorporate new ideas. They did not seem to do anything else. Giles and I reminisced about a climb we had done together in North Wales, well it was more about the weekend than the climb really. Then we talked about what we had been up to since we last saw each other: my visits to Chile, his occasional business trips abroad, mostly to the continent and China. It was obvious that our conversation did not enthral the others, which was not surprising as the subjects were at opposite ends of the travel spectrum.

Sandra kept glancing at me throughout. Each look may only have lasted a second or two, but I could feel them prodding me. It was an uncomfortable distraction. I looked up once and caught her before she turned her attention back to Tony. In her slight smile lay our shared secret, as if we two inhabited our own hidden world.

At one point, without being asked, Tony went back to the sideboard and heaped more meat onto his plate. Giles glanced at me and raised a single eyebrow. His manners would never have allowed him to do that without a second helping first being offered.

The two women chatted a bit about the pranks they had got up to as teenagers, but Mandy became less enthusiastic when it came to the subject of boyfriends. With an engaging smile playing on her lips, Sandra started telling a story about one boy she had toyed with. She gazed over at me as if she were drawing me into her confidence and no one else was there. It was a look that lasted a moment longer than it should have done and, to me, was loaded with meaning.

My attention was diverted as the door opened slightly and Henry poked his head around, scanned the room quickly to check on progress, gave me a friendly nod of recognition and disappeared again. Mandy leaned right and whispered briefly in her friend's ear as Sandra was finishing her story. Soon she changed the subject. 'Alastair, tell us what you and Giles got up to as students. He won't let anything slip, he's so boring, but I bet you were a devil with the girls.' She leaned over the table, cupping her chin in one hand and stared at me unashamedly. 'You have a lovely one now, after all.'

Whatever this woman was up to made me suspicious. She was playing with her husband and making me part of the game. I refused to engage with her wide eyes. 'Nothing remarkable, I'm afraid. Sorry to disappoint you, but I used to be quite shy. It was Giles that got all the girls. I picked the crumbs from the big man's table.' That earned me a look of understanding from Mandy, raised a laugh from Giles, but only a shift to a more comfortable position on Wiggins's part.

'Giles?' Sandra scoffed incredulously, and I sensed him tense beside me, but she didn't add anything else.

Henry came in at that point and Giles said, 'Thank you Henry, we've finished now. Please tell Mrs Potter it was an excellent dinner as usual. It's late, you should both go home or to bed and sort this out in the morning.'

'Oh, Henry,' called Sandra, 'I just have something for you to do first.'

Giles rose quickly to his feet and strode towards the door. 'I'm sure it can wait until tomorrow, Sandra.' He touched Henry on the arm and ushered him out, returning after a few moments. 'They really need to go off now, and Mrs Potter has to get home. I've told them to go.' *Fait accompli*. The subject was closed.

Sandra stared fixedly at her coffee cup and said nothing. Her normally full lips were set in a thin line and her eyes had narrowed in anger. This was not some little disagreement to be quickly forgotten. This was another round in a battle for dominance, and she had lost it.

Mandy extended her right arm below the table top, I saw it through the movement of her shoulder. She must have nudged Sandra, but it wasn't important then and I forgot it immediately. Sandra quickly regained control and switched on her enticing eyes. 'Alastair, come on, you tell us about Giles at university. I want to hear about all those girls, what a ladies man he used to be.' There was ever so slight an emphasis on the words 'used to', and Mandy gave a silly little snigger.

'There's nothing to tell really, just typical uni high jinks. One student to whom the girls were naturally attracted and one who happily tagged along, nothing unusual at all. There were quite a lot of girls over the years, though. Giles had more than his fair share, I'd say, but nothing serious.'

Sandra was licking her spoon slowly as she listened to me, her eyes fixed on mine with an unwavering invitation. She turned it upside down and licked the inside with a deliberately slow upward sweep of her tongue, her head tilting back, but her eyes remaining fixed on mine. I looked away and she answered, 'That's hard to believe, Alastair. I'll bet it was really you that drew the girls. If anyone has a magic touch, it'll always be there, but Giles certainly doesn't have one now, even though he's still young!'

Giles banged his palm down on the heavy table. Cutlery bounced and the wine in our glasses rippled. Mandy started visibly. 'That's enough, Sandra, drop it,' he snapped. All those years and I had never heard him raise his voice in anger before.

'Sensitive about your manhood, darling? You shouldn't be, it happens to all men eventually, though not normally at your age, Just-in.' Wiggins nearly choked as he tried not to laugh out loud, and Mandy put her napkin up to her mouth to muffle her inevitable giggle. Sandra's natural prettiness had left her face, which had taken on a harsh and ugly look; seductress to witch in a few smoothly orchestrated moves. Giles had put her down, countermanded her order to Henry, and now she was taking revenge.

Abruptly, there were only two people at the table, no one else mattered. No self respecting man will tolerate implications of sexual inadequacy being broadcast to others, but Giles's reticence would not allow him to conduct an argument of this nature in public. Only the necessity of preventing an escalation of Sandra's abuse deterred him from a furious outburst. His face was flushed with anger, and he glared at her with undisguised animosity.

Not so Sandra. In Kenya once, I took a picture of two lions after mating and still have it somewhere. The male looked up at me with a stare so intense it was frightening, even from the security of my car. It was a look of death. It was the look of a predator utterly focused on its prey. It bored into me then to such an extreme that I dreamed about it for ages. Even in the photo it was disturbing. That same intense stare marked Sandra as the predator and Giles her prey. There was no hate in her eyes, only dominance backed by the confidence that she would destroy him, just as that lion would have destroyed me.

The tense atmosphere seemed to dull the glitter from the crystal, and an impossibly long silence settled over the room. It was briefly interrupted by another silly titter from Mandy.

Wiggins was grinning for the first time that evening. He was rocking his chair on the back legs and kept switching his glance between Sandra and Giles to see what would happen next. The conversation was suddenly interesting and right at his level. Mandy was looking down still trying to hide a smile behind her napkin. Were they just the props that were necessary to embarrass my friend, or were they party to some deeper plot? Sandra, meanwhile, was deliberately bending a long ladle. The destruction of the two hundred and fifty year old piece of silver would be another silent attack on Giles and his respect for his family possessions about which she only felt contempt.

I couldn't stand to see that beautiful piece destroyed on a vindictive whim. 'Sandra, please don't do that, it's valuable.'

She never took her eyes off her husband, but much to my surprise, she put the ladle down. She would never have done that if Giles had asked her to, so why did she do it for me? Was she trying to drive a wedge between him and me?

I was acutely embarrassed. The tension had to be broken before Giles did something he would regret. I had a feeling that she was about to embark on a tirade of verbal abuse which had to be stopped before it started, and that this was all for my benefit; once I had gone there would be no reason to continue the fight. 'I think it's time I left,' I said, 'I'm really not interested in family squabbles.'

'Oh no, don't go yet,' Sandra said, 'we're only playing.' In an instant she had switched to her sensuous role, and her now soft, imploring eyes tried to tempt me into more of her company, or more likely to listen to a further denigration of her husband.

I could not help him in this. 'I need to go anyway. I've a lot to do in the morning and must start early.'

Giles rose to his feet with a terse reply. 'I'll see you out.'

I said goodbye to Mandy and Tony who stayed seated, while Sandra came round the table, let her fingers touch mine without lingering, gave me a kiss on the cheek and simultaneously breathed softly into my ear. Her perfume was heady and enticing.

'Thanks, it was good to meet you at last, and that was a really great meal.' I was ashamedly acting as insincere as she was.

At the door, I looked Giles in the eye. 'Lunch tomorrow in the City. I'll call you.'

He gripped my upper arm and nodded.

3

GILES'S CHOICE OF restaurant was on the top floor of a building in the City of London with a view of the Gherkin, the Shard, St Paul's Cathedral, the London Eye and many other landmarks including a good long view up the river. The sun was shining and some smokers were enjoying the air outside when I arrived. He wasn't there ahead of me, so I chose seats that would afford us some privacy in a corner against the window. A couple arrived not long afterwards and selected the nearest table to take advantage of the sun which was beaming in on that side. They were in their early forties, but were behaving like a pair of love-struck teenagers. An illicit affair, or a very new one at least? The good thing was they were so engrossed with each other, they were not likely to notice what Giles and I were saying.

As I waited, I separated the bundle of crockery wrapped up in the napkin and rearranged it into a classic setting. At least the napkin was cotton. I used it to wipe the water stains off the fork and then reset the glasses into the correct order. There was a smell of grilled meat in the air, and the salads the cooing couple had ordered looked delicious.

Giles was doing a BSc in economics and I a degree in aerodynamics when we met. We shared digs and played rugby and climbed together, but neither understood the other's choice of subjects. He made a terrific flank forward with his height, speed and aggression. I was never as good and could not be assured of a place on the team, whereas Giles was a given. He was never short of a girl to choose and, as I had limply tried to explain to Sandra at dinner, I usually struck lucky through my association with him and not through my own rather shy efforts.

We became really good friends; in fact I would go so far as to say that I had feelings for Giles which were far deeper than anything I'd ever felt for a woman, except Juliet. It was very different, of course, more a mutual appreciation and a loyalty that was proven several times over.

A memory of the sort that never leaves the mind: an icy alpine wind, low clouds scudding past, spitting occasional drops of rain and encapsulating the higher peaks. Me, suspended in space by my climbing harness from a piton under the overhang, dazed by a falling rock, my helmet cracked, my shoulder ineffectual. Beneath me, barely visible in the failing light, a five hundred foot fall to the boulders below, and one piton had already pulled out. Giles on the face opposite, out of reach and unable to pull me in to him, was organising his rope and self belay to climb up under the overhang for a rescue. Unable to move or help, I would probably not have survived the freezing night. He got me off that cliff and down to the pastures below in a tandem abseil long after nightfall.

It's true that I and many other climbers would have done the same, but that did not diminish his achievement in saving my life. Typically, he thought nothing of his efforts. Nevertheless, another strand had been woven into the rope that bound us.

He came through the restaurant door, glanced around and spotted me immediately. He was looking drawn and tired, smartly dressed, his shoes gleaming as usual. He must have left his jacket in the office.

'I feel like something strong, but I have to go back to work,' he said, slackening his tie. There was a short silence as if neither of us could think of what to say, or perhaps where to start when there was so much to talk about.

'Last night was a little embarrassing,' I ventured.

He stared at his glass of water for a while then gave a deep sigh. 'When we call a woman a bitch or a witch, it's usually without much foundation, it's just that we don't like them.' He carried on talking slowly to his glass. 'She's neither. A witch weaves magic, a bitch is a female dog and usually quite pleasant.

'We had a great time when we were first married, plenty of fun and laughter, and we went away a lot. At first, she was enthusiastic about the house and had some quite sensible suggestions on how to improve various aspects, making a couple of rooms larger by breaking down the adjoining walls, redecorating and so on. When I agreed, she went ahead and had them done and they made a big difference. When I tried to pay, she had already done so at her own expense. She was staking a claim in the house. I see that now. Then, towards the end of last year we started to argue about things, little things. At first I took her arguments as part of her strong character rather than a deliberate plan. She would find fault in Mrs Potter's cleaning, or my dogs had left hair on her clothes. She created problems, like trying to persuade me that the fishpond should be filled in, to which she knew I would object. Then she would become difficult and retaliatory when I said no, it had been there for over a hundred and fifty years and it would bloody well stay another hundred and fifty. She pushes me in these confrontations until I reach the point where I'm about to lose my temper, then she stops, cries, apologises and becomes seductive and loving and is all over me.

'It upsets me that she orchestrates these situations when she feels like it. You know me Alastair, I hate personal arguments and would go out of my way to avoid one.'

I opened my mouth to say something, but he carried on. I don't think he had previously told anyone about what was happening and this opportunity was cathartic for him.

'She probes for weak spots and discovered that I set great value in Mrs Potter. That old lady's been in the house since before I was born. She helped bring me up, so I won't stand for Sandra blaming her or being rude to her, which she is, even though it's only to get at me. For a while, I learned to live with these ups and downs, but early this year I found myself avoiding intimate contact, I didn't want to be with this manipulating, argumentative woman. Unlike her, I can't switch my mood from anger to affection in a moment, it takes me hours. The last couple of times we "made love" (what a stupid expression for intercourse that is), I haven't been able to keep it up – you know … I was depressed for a while, then went out and found some girl in a bar and spent the night with her. It was like the old days. I was randy as hell, hard as a rock and she was drooling over me in the morning. I only did that once, but I had to prove myself and it brought home that it wasn't me that was the problem, it was that there was nothing between Sandra and me. It's not only that this beautiful creature no longer holds any attractions for me, she actually repels me. Since then our sex life has dwindled to nothing.' Giles raised his head, looked steadily at me with tired eyes and pressed his lips together in search of an answer.

The Polish waiter arrived to take our order, interrupting our thoughts. Neither of us was hungry, there was too much on our minds. I ordered a salmon salad, and Giles a bowl of soup.

'Last night,' I said. 'Why?'

'Last night was a new, extreme low. It used to be that our rows were in private, but recently she has taken delight in countermanding me in public – as you saw, when I first told Henry he could go? She tries to get the upper hand on every decision, then if I retaliate, battle is joined. She did this once before. She organised the event and invited people we both know. She embarrassed me that time, but at least it wasn't about my libido. I thought with you there last night we would have a normal pleasant dinner, especially since she had seemed so adoring and happy during the afternoon, which put me in a good mood. I never dreamed that even she would try to denigrate me in front of you. She manipulated the conversation around to my supposedly little penis and inferred erectile dysfunction. You obviously got the Just-in joke. This is in public, for heaven's sake!' He was leaning forward, his forearms on the table, embarrassed, but he had to ask, 'Alastair, you know me, we shared digs for long enough, would you say I have a little dick?'

I laughed. 'The girls you had never complained, and you were perfectly normal, as far as I noticed. I didn't spend much time inspecting it!' At least that raised a smile on his face.

'We had a monumental row last night after the others had left,' he went on. 'My humiliation at dinner was a new experience, it was a shock, it put me entirely on the back foot. It sunk home that this was not something I had previously dealt with; a rugby or a climbing challenge which I could take calmly, this was a full unprovoked assault on my emotions, and I bloody nearly lost control of myself. I told her to get out of my bedroom. She told me that if I wasn't able to keep it up and sleep with her then it was I that should move. I lost my temper then and said it was my house, my bedroom and there were plenty of others to choose from. She was livid, but she could see I wasn't going to budge. Instead, she called me a pathetic loser, asked why I couldn't be a man? She reminded me of my one night stand and asked if that girl had laughed too. She kept taunting me almost to the point of my hitting her. My arm was drawn back, for heaven's sake, my fist closed I was so angry! As I took a last step forward, I saw a glint of triumph in her eyes and stopped myself.' His voice slowed, his words clearly separated and forceful. 'She wanted me to hit her, Alastair. She wants a black eye for evidence – it took all my willpower not to give her that present. She's after a divorce, of course.'

The waiter arrived with our order and we fell silent until he went away. Outside, on the river, boats and barges ploughed their slow way up and down, and a police launch sped rapidly downstream leaving a prominent wake. It seemed an untroubled and silent world out there. Engines must be roaring, shouts must have been made unheard by us, and those labouring down there would have their own problems to cope with, some of which might also be marital struggles.

'Why did you marry her?' I said. 'She's not really your type.'

'Like you, I'm attracted to strong personalities. All those silly girls out for good times that we had, they were there for the fun, the parties and picnics, but none of them deserved serious respect, they were hangers on, followers not leaders. Eventually, I tired of all the fun and games and was wandering around at a loose end emotionally. I wanted something more substantial.' He paused, his eyes flicking from one of mine to the other, reading me. It was as if he was making a decision on what or how much he should say. 'Sandra appeared when I was feeling down, pure coincidence, even she couldn't have planned it better. Whatever else she may be, she's strong, she's a leader and she won me over very quickly. You probably noticed she doesn't wear a wedding ring? I put one on her finger when we were married, but she took it off immediately, said she's not prepared to be chained to anyone. In fact she never changed her name from Parsons to Collins. She'll only use Collins if it's convenient.'

I let him carry on without interruption. 'I fell for her looks and her sensuality, and my God, but she can turn that on and every man in town is drooling. But she's ... she's, I hesitate to say evil, but she is not a pleasant person. I thought I was the luckiest man in the world: an incredibly beautiful wife, fairly well off in her own right, the envy of every man I knew except you who had never met her. How did that happen, I wonder? Not meeting her, I mean.'

I picked at my salad without interest. There was something he wasn't telling me, but then I was wrestling with the decision whether to tell him about Sandra and me, or not. As far as Giles was concerned, I harboured no guilt. With Juliet – yes certainly, and I was avoiding confronting that, but not Giles. After all, I hadn't known who she was, she wasn't wearing a wedding ring, there was nothing to indicate that it was anything other than two people with a healthy need for sex. But would he see it that way? My friend was in a sorry emotional state. I didn't want to depress him further by adding to his troubles, and I certainly didn't want him angry with me. He didn't deserve that extra burden. On the other hand, if he didn't care for her any more, the knowledge might well give him ammunition for the inevitable fight ahead, and better to hear it from me directly than have it thrown in his face later in public. 'I've been away a lot,' I said. 'You and I have met elsewhere, you went away after you were married as you said, and of course I never made your wedding for which I'm eternally sorry. It's one of those things. There's more to it than that, though.'

He misunderstood and assumed I was waiting for him to carry on. 'Yes, sadly,' he murmured. He hadn't touched his soup, but had settled back in his chair and was stirring the bowl slowly and absent-mindedly. He stared up the river for a moment. 'One day I was talking about things to a chap I know here in London. I can't remember how it arose, but the conversation drifted around to a friend of his called Alan Parsons and then to his very acrimonious divorce from Sandra. Apparently she had walked away with a fortune. Of course David didn't realise she was my wife now. Well that was news to me. Why on earth hadn't she told me? Why withhold that kind of information? After months of this rather unpleasant existence, I began to wonder if she was making a business out of marrying rich men and then divorcing them, and it didn't take long to convince myself that was the case.'

'She wants a divorce, you said, on what grounds?'

'Anything she can drum up. Try incompatibility, supposed sexual incompetence, although surely she can't use that as a ground? Physical abuse if she can drive me to it, my infidelity. I don't know how she knew about that, but I wouldn't put it past her to have had a private detective on my tail.'

I could only brave a tentative reply. 'And she doesn't sleep around?' I had to tell him. With the marriage disintegrating under Sandra's orchestration, he needed to know what she was up to, whether he liked it or not.

'I don't know, Alastair, and I don't care. She flirts with other men in front of me; she did so with you last night, for heaven's sake. Flirts in an openly obscene manner with my best friend in front of me, and in the same breath embarrasses me in front of you and her dumb companions.' He settled back in his chair, then blurted, 'I bet she contacts you. I bet she tries to get you into bed to ruin our relationship just to spite me.'

'If she does that, she'll lose her moral high ground in a divorce.' I was still hesitating in spite of his loosely granted permission.

'No, because she's clever enough to know that I will never put you in that position. She knows what we mean to each other, and I will not have you standing up in court and admitting that you slept with the wife of your best friend. Juliet would also become involved, of course.'

Typically, Giles was thinking of me not himself. And, as each of us had always done, I reciprocated. 'Thank you for the thought, but you can you know, if you have to, you can use me as a witness.'

'We'll see. Incidentally, she came out with your 'lovely girlfriend' at dinner, remember?'

'Yes, what of it?'

'Well, I'm damn certain that I've never told her about Juliet. I wouldn't.'

This was not good, even suspicious. 'Strange, how did she know, then?' I took a deep breath. 'Giles, it's too late, I've already had that wild night. I'm so sorry, I didn't know. She picked me up in Antonio's one evening, said she recognised me from a photo, but wouldn't say where until she pointed it out at your house last night. She was dark haired then and called herself Angela Parsons. I couldn't believe my eyes when you introduced us.'

'You slept with her? For Christ's sake Alastair, she may be what she is, but she is my bloody wife!' His voice was too loud and the nearby couple looked up.

'Sssh! I said I'm sorry, I had no idea. I would never betray you. You know that. I think it's important you know the facts now if there's a divorce in the offing.'

'And what about Juliet?' He snapped back in hushed, angry tones. 'How could you do that to her? That girl absolutely adores you. You can be quite a shit at times, Alastair!'

'That's fine coming from you who's just admitted a one-nighter, yourself. And look at all the times you've done the same thing!'

'That's different. I don't love my wife and I had to prove something because of her behaviour. As for earlier times, yes

I've had a few drinks too many and ended up in bed with girls, but I've never done it when I've been in even a weak relationship. I've never two-timed any girl. I'm really annoyed with you because of Juliet. She deserves better than that from you.'

'I know and if it helps, I feel the shit you say I am.' Which was the truth.

'Well, you'd better sort it out with her and you'd better pray that she'll take it as a one-off while under the influence.'

His flash of anger evaporated as quickly as it came. His shoulders slumped. In silence he contemplated his cold soup. 'It's all right,' he said at last. 'It's unfair to blame you over Sandra. This is her, it's her scheming. When was this?'

I looked over to the nearby couple. They were holding hands across the table but not talking, probably trying to hear something else interesting from us.

'Friday.'

'Two days before you came to dinner, and she knew you were coming a month ago. Do you see how she manipulates things? It's a tactic of hers, keeping a step ahead by doing something unexpected and outrageous to provoke a response.' He took a deep breath. 'Thanks for telling me. You're right, I do need to know these things. Please don't worry on my account, but it would be wise not to do it again. Sorry I blew up, I'm a bit on edge.

'Alastair, I don't know the boundaries of hatred, when complete and utter dislike can be called hate, but it must be something close to what I feel about her. If I had the guts and was prepared to take the consequences, I'd kill her.' He paused, reflecting on what he'd said. 'I won't, of course, but it is a satisfying, vengeful thought.'

4

WOODS, FIELDS IN different shades of green and bright in the sunlight, embankments, sheep, horses and cattle rushed past the train window. I saw them, but they didn't register in my mind which was clogged with thoughts. A small child in a pink jumpsuit with something yellow round its mouth put its sticky little paw on my clean trousers for support. I gave it an evil glare, and its loving mother quickly whisked it away. She looked at me as if I was about to do it some harm. Two rows behind, a man with a loud voice was conducting his business on the phone for the entire carriage to hear, issuing instructions and not appearing to listen to the other party. He kept it up for twenty minutes, almost as far as Reading, making it difficult to concentrate on the rest of my conversation with Giles.

'Alastair,' he had moaned, 'I cannot live with her any longer, I cannot endure the continual arguments she puts me through any more; not to mention last night's humiliation …

If we divorce, then she will do her utmost to ruin me and move on to some other unsuspecting well heeled sod.'

'Why don't you divorce her immediately – get it over with?'

He sighed. 'I've thought about it, but … I know a detailed history of my ancestors over three hundred years. I know there are a few bastards in the family tree. My great aunt was one of them from her father and a mistress. I believe several of the ladies in the line had lovers too, but no one got divorced and the children were all cared for. They considered divorce as taboo, just not done. I don't want to break the tradition, even if almost half our population considers it the norm these days. It's simply not right. But then I think that it's got to happen somehow, we cannot continue to live like this. I know I'm being stupid and sticking my head in the sand over it, hoping the problem will go away, but I'd rather she initiated proceedings, not me. Plus, of course, I have no proof she has ever been unpleasant to me, so I have no grounds. I think I'm just waiting for something to happen, hoping she makes a mistake.'

I had understood. This was typical Giles: traditional values, always do the right thing, treat others as you would wish to be treated, give generously, good manners make the man and so on. There are many attributes that Giles adhered to that had a greater value in an earlier time, without considering the effect they would have on him in a world that had moved to a less refined and respectable way of life.

'When are you going back to Chile?'

'Tomorrow week,' I said. It was Monday.

The train shot through a station so quickly it was impossible to read the name. The steady song from the rails was interrupted as the wheels clattered noisily and irregularly over points. Pink-sticky-fingers was tottering down the aisle in the other direction, but the mother seemed unconcerned, which made me feel an ogre – briefly. I wasn't interested anyway, my thoughts were wrestling with an alternative and hopefully risk free strategy. I knew Giles better than he knew himself sometimes. Having let off steam by confiding in me, it would not be long before he became fired up and vengeful. He needed to stay calm while we worked out the best solution with the fewest repercussions.

If Sandra had Giles followed to find out about his single wayward night, then it was possible she had done the same for me, otherwise how did she know I was going to be in Antonio's on Friday evening? Knowing what I knew now, that meeting was surely not by chance. One thing was for certain, though, communications had to be protected if we were to plan something. I thought mobile phones could easily be hacked – it was all over the press at that time – but I didn't know how and to what extent. Was my phone how Sandra knew about my 'lovely girlfriend' that Giles had not told her about? If so how had she done it? Did they tap into the network or did they use radios to listen in? I had no idea, but I was going to find out, and if my phone was compromised then Giles's must be too. A landline only rule was one option, but an additional new mobile would be better so we could hold one to one conversations in privacy. Giles would need to be led on this, he wasn't in the best state of mind, and in any case I was better at planning than he was.

As soon as I was home, I phoned his office from the call box in the village, hoping to meet again the next day, but he said he was busy, it would have to be on Wednesday. I told him to say nothing until we were face to face, and we had agreed a modus operandi. He was glad to be moving in some direction, any direction, and I know he was comforted by sharing his situation with me. It was not that Giles was a weak or indecisive person, far from it, but he had been driven into an awful choice between, what were to him, two unacceptable situations. Unless we seized the initiative from Sandra, whatever course of action he took he was going to lose financially and emotionally. He was certain to be subject to bruising public humiliation in the divorce court, even the tabloids, she would make sure of that. Brooding on these life-wrecking possibilities, he was currently in a bit of a rut, and it needed a fresh mind to see the way clear.

Before we hung up he said, 'I know something I'm going to do.'

'What?'

'Tell you on Wednesday. Thanks for everything.'

5

WE MET ON Primrose Hill to the north of Regent's Park on Wednesday afternoon. The sun was hot on the skin and comfortingly eased its way into cooler bones. As sun-starved people tend to do, those that were not at work, and maybe some that should have been, were taking the opportunity to generate some Vitamin D from the rays. Girls exposed as much skin as they could get away with. They lay on the ground, entwined with lovers, in groups or alone absorbing the warmth. Here and there men had stripped off their shirts, others strolled or kicked a football about on the flatter ground below. It was all unhurried and relaxed. The atmosphere was clear, the sky blue, the grass and trees green, and the prominent buildings of the City were clearly outlined to the South East. Somewhere in there was Giles's office, but it seemed very remote that afternoon. Midweek, there weren't too many people about, and the scene spelt peace and calm in contrast to his inner turmoil.

'I took the afternoon off,' he said. 'Told them I wasn't well which, quite honestly, is not far from the truth.'

It had not rained for days and the ground was dry. We found an unoccupied patch on the grass near the top of the rise and set about devouring our baguettes: pesto, tomato and mozzarella for me and roast beef and mustard for him.

'I pulled myself together and did a bit of poking around after our lunch on Monday,' Giles said. 'Remember I mentioned that I spoke to this chap who told me that Sandra had been married before? Well, I checked with David again and he gave me a lead to find her first husband. I still wasn't sure, you see, and I don't want to be wrong about Sandra being a serial gold-digger, it could have disastrous consequences. One has to be fair, after all.

'It wasn't that difficult to find him, actually; a few discreet questions in the city and that was it. After work yesterday, we had a drink and continued to get ourselves silly till the wee hours, even though we have nothing in common except to cry about our misfortunes together. Apparently, he'd met her when he was withdrawing a box from safe keeping. She was a manager at the facility. She took over from the assistant that was helping him and attended to him personally. By sheer coincidence her name was also Parsons, so they never had a discussion about changing it when she married him, unlike she did with me. He was instantly smitten and pursued her with a vengeance. In retrospect, he thought she had seen his Bentley and made him a target. He'd been conned out of a great deal of money, and that was going to be my fate if I didn't do something about it. He was very willing to help, not for me particularly, but because he wanted to ruin her ambitions. A little revenge for the viciousness she had displayed in bringing him down.

'He told me some interesting stuff about Sandra. She had obviously been much more open with him than with me. Maybe she learned a different tactic from her first experience of male destruction. He said she was a misandrist, which might have stemmed from her stepfather's abuse and violence to her and her younger half brother. Apparently, when she was about twelve, she tried to protect the boy from his father's frequent beatings. This creature would take sick pleasure in removing her knickers and smacking her bare bottom before taking her to the bedroom, while her brother would cry outside the door and her mother denied anything ever happened.'

'That explains a lot,' I said. 'I can understand why she hates men after that upbringing. At that age, her little brother would not have understood what was happening to her, but he would know that it was painful and wrong and probably thought it was his own fault. No matter what their past, though, everyone knows right from wrong, and everyone's responsible for their own actions. She has no justification for what she does, in my view. It also explains her flat. You must have seen how sparse it is, as if she wants no reminders of the past. Then there's The Scream hanging over the bed. She must still be traumatised by that childhood.'

'Yes, the flat's entirely hers. I haven't been there since we were married, but when I did, it wasn't a comfortable place to be. She sometimes stays there, but won't tell me why except that she's too tired to drive home or some other weak excuse.'

'Anyway Giles, I was thinking about your dinner. Something strange was going on. The other two, Mandy and Tony Wiggins did not seem surprised at the events. I didn't think about it at the time, but they gave very little reaction, they didn't seem embarrassed or shocked. In fact, he thought it was funny, and she acted as if it was theatre she'd paid to see, fully expected.'

'Well, those two women are as thick as thieves, it wouldn't surprise me if Mandy knew in advance, and it supports my view that this is a deliberate plot to bring me down.'

I swallowed a sizeable bite of baguette. 'Mmmh! This pesto is good. We're going to devise a plan to get you out of this hole. We have to switch this around so that she comes out as the guilty party. We're aiming for no serious repercussions, something that will not cost you your fortune and, last but not least, she will be defeated and will hopefully walk away bruised and battered – figuratively speaking, of course. A little revenge is permissible isn't it?'

Giles watched me intently as he bit into his sandwich.

'Sandra is going to divorce you on certain grounds, and she will undoubtedly seek legal help with that, but I've been doing some research on the grounds that are acceptable. There are a five main headings, but only two are relevant in your case.

'There's adultery, of course, and she's got you on that one, unless … When did you have your night of debauchery? Or, more importantly, when did she learn of it?'

He thought for a moment, chewing. 'It was around the end of April, and she confronted me soon afterwards.'

'Any chance of being more specific? You see she can't give adultery as a reason if she continued to stay in your house for six months after she found out about it. It would lend a lie to her claiming that she can't bear to live with you, which it's necessary to do. It's now the beginning of September so we're getting close to the six months.'

'Surely, if she had me followed – and how else would she know – the private eye would have told her within a day or two?'

'True, but how are we going to prove that it happened so quickly? She's not going to admit to hiring a detective anyway, she'll dream up some other story.'

He put the last of his baguette into his mouth and mumbled, 'What's the other ground?'

'Unreasonable behaviour to the extent that she can no longer bear to live with you. That includes: physical violence?'

'No, absolutely not, but it's been damn difficult to resist, as I told you.'

'Verbal abuse – insults, threats and so on?'

'No.'

'Drunkenness, drugs?'

'No drugs, but I have been pissed a few times without any harm to anyone or thing.'

'Refusing to pay for housekeeping?'

'Not a chance, I pay for everything. All she's done is stake a claim by paying for the alterations to the house.'

'Is she a beneficiary on any of your insurance policies? If so, change those as soon as you can. You don't know when she's going to start proceedings and you must be ahead of that.' Silence reigned for a moment. 'Giles, you had better rewrite your will and take her out of it.'

'Good point. Why aren't I thinking like that? It's a bloody obvious thing to do, but it never occurred to me.'

We sat in silence for a while. Two girls came running up the path. One was wearing a sports bra which flattened her chest, but the other, a heavily endowed lass, obviously wasn't. Giles was also watching them. He caught my look and laughed. 'Some things never change. Two almost middle aged men can quickly put their troubles behind them for a chance to admire a pair of bloody great unrestrained boobs bouncing around!'

'It's what makes the world go round.'

'There's enough kinetic energy in that pair to substantiate your theory.' He laughed again. It was a good sound after all the gloom. Then out of the blue he said, 'How's Juliet?' Without giving me a chance to answer, he added, 'Lovely girl, simply, bloody wonderful! For all the women I've had a crack at, I'd drop the lot for a girl like her. You lucky sod!' He looked at me meaningfully. 'That's if she doesn't boot you out.'

The mention of Juliet spurred him on to try again to stop me from participating. He couldn't bear the thought of either of us suffering from the outcome of his undoubtedly acrimonious divorce. Our names would be dragged through the gutter press. Juliet would only be involved indirectly, but she and her photograph would probably make it into the tabloids as the girlfriend who I cheated on with Giles's wife.

We argued over my involvement for at least five minutes, but when faced with all the negative aspects if he emerged as the guilty party, he eventually capitulated. 'So what do you propose?'

'Well, for starters, I've bought us both a cheap smart phone with a pay-as-you-go SIM card. The numbers are not known to anyone except me. It means we can communicate without fear of being intercepted.' He agreed, took the phone and tapped my new number into the contacts list.

Sandra had a record of making unexpected moves and keeping Giles off balance, forcing him into a reactive position. What we had to do was turn that around somehow and take the initiative. We also had to try and think what her future moves could be. 'If she can't get you to give her a black eye, then she could ask Tony.'

'I wouldn't be at all surprised, but I'm not sure how to deal with it.'

'Something else occurred to me,' I said. 'What were her reasons for seducing me? She might use the episode to drive a wedge between us. To do that, you have to know it happened, so either I would have to confess to it, or she will tell you. One result of you knowing is that you would lose your temper and our friendship would be over or at least fragile, leaving you a weaker person. However, if after a time, you do not react to the knowledge of my sleeping with her, then she will assume that I haven't told you and she would then do so herself. If this happens, either she uses the episode to taunt you into violence or something rash, or she might claim that I raped her which would again drive that wedge.'

'Good point, so what do we do about it?'

We fell silent for a short while, thinking. Four young people were sitting below us. They started shoving each other about, laughing and trying to get one of the men to roll down-hill. A girl was trying to pin the victim's arms to his sides, while the others were pushing him over.

Giles said, 'Actually I know what we should do. Involves a bit of pride swallowing, but sacrifices must be made.' I carefully pulled a stalk of grass out of its base to rid my teeth of crumbs and lay back to watch the air traffic above. Giles rested on one elbow as we discussed his idea and debated the finer points to a rough conclusion. The positive effort restored his humour and lifted his spirits, and by the time we left he was quite buoyant. He could see how we were going to win this and was ready for the fight ahead. For it would be a fight; Sandra was not going to lie down and give in, it wasn't in her nature. And we both knew she was going to play very dirty indeed.

As Giles had predicted, she called me shortly after the train left Paddington. Her voice, husky and magnetic, was a siren song, but had I not known of the rocks that she was drawing me towards, I would not have had such difficulty in responding with enthusiasm. The possibility of her claiming rape would be annulled by asking for a second encounter, surely? She wanted to meet the next day, but I managed to put her off until Friday; I needed time for the extensive preparation required.

6

MY HOME WAS an old farm house a little way out of the village. The farm had been too difficult for the original owner to manage and so was sold back in the Fifties. Most of the lands were bought by a local war widow who rented them out to surrounding farmers, but the remaining two large fields and the house and buildings were taken on by a succession of owners of which I was the latest.

A tree lined gravel drive led off the lane directly to the house then skirted round it to the right and back again so that the house hid the view of the farm buildings from the road. It continued into a widened area that some occupant in the past had concreted between the two sides. To the right were stables and cow sheds with a silage pit at the end. To the left were two barns, a tractor shed and three storage rooms.

The place was much too big for me as a single man, but I rented out the larger of the barns to a woodworking business and the other outbuildings for garaging, stabling and storage.

The second and smaller of the barns was empty. I had advertised it for rent but there had been no takers so far. There was
some noise from the carpenter's shop which, due to its rather
traditional nature, didn't worry me. In any case, there were a
host of lovely smells from the different woods that wafted in
when the wind was right. It was peaceful enough and there
was a bit of security with others around when I was
travelling. Beyond the barns and the silage pit were two long
adjacent fields which belonged to me and which I rented out
under short term grazing lets. I was therefore technically a
farmer, even though I wasn't personally farming.

Shortly beyond the gate from the yard, the ground sank
away between the two fields into a shallow valley. This
became progressively steeper as it descended and left each
field on its own shoulder stretching out from the ridge. At the
top of the right hand field and sunken into a slight rise was a
WW2 pillbox. It had a commanding view over the valley, as
well as the left hand field and the wood which ran downhill
from the far end of it. I didn't own the wood, but often
walked Tina, my yellow Labrador, in it. People kept asking
me why I didn't bulldoze the pillbox flat, but I rather liked
the ugly piece of history which was now almost covered in
ivy. I took Juliet there once and we found it full of chip packets, cool drink and beer cans, glass and other junk. We
cleaned the place up, shovelling and sweeping years of muck
off the floor. We opened the access, which was almost closed
with brambles, cleared the embrasures of grass and weeds
and finally painted the inside so that it looked almost homely.
We looked it up on Wikipedia and concluded it was a type 22,
because it was hexagonal with a Y shaped internal wall for
anti ricochet purposes.

'We need some pictures up on that.' Juliet pointed. 'I think it would suit a Picasso!'

When we'd finished the decoration on the second day and a couple of showers had passed by outside, I fetched a bottle of Chablis and some cheese, and we sat on the roof and watched the sun descending past a few red-tinted clouds. Tina, meanwhile, amused herself hunting unseen wildlife in the bushes. The light had that wonderful clarity that comes after evening rain, and a rosy reflection from the clouds bathed the countryside. Halfway through the bottle, I took her hand and led her down through the entrance. With no word of agreement necessary, I pinned her up against the wall so that her head fell back into the embrasure and the light glistened off her hair. She fastened her mouth over mine, wrapped her arms round my neck and her legs round my waist while I struggled out of my shorts. It was urgent and brief but passionate and fun. When we finished, she stayed in the same position for a while, her head in my shoulder, before looking me in the eye and wordlessly smiling her love. 'I don't think Picasso,' I murmured in her ear, 'some images from the Karma Sutra would be more appropriate.'

She giggled. I became very fond of that pillbox.

In the wood which extended from my other field was a dilapidated shed. The timbers were rotten and covered in moss, and the corrugated iron walls were so rusted at the bottom that they had crumbled away, leaving a foot high gap to the outside in places where brambles tried to fight their way in. The usual rubbish was strewn across the floor, drink cans, wrappers and packets: the detritus of lazy trespassing litterbugs. The door hung on one broken hinge, threatening to fall off at any time. The floor was wooden but soft with rot, and the window was virtually opaque with mould and water stains. I said we should renovate it with the same enthusiasm as we had used on the pillbox, but Juliet said, 'Why don't we stop wasting time and you take me to a nice comfortable bed instead?' I wasn't at all fond of the hut.

In the house, the kitchen was enormous with a huge fireplace filled now with a modern oil-fired Aga, low beams which looked too old and fragile to support the ceiling above and large quarry tiles on the floor. Juliet loved it. She wasn't much of a cook but, wearing a red apron she had left in the house a long time ago, she liked using the range which was always on. The living room was sparsely furnished. My needs were few, and a couple of comfortable arm chairs, a book shelf, an old military chest, a TV and a pair of speakers for the iPod dock were all there was. I had built up a small collection of oriental carpets and tribal rugs from my time in the Middle East, and some served to softened the noise from the creaking wooden floor. There was another small room off to the side that I used as an office with an iMac which made the best of an unbearably slow internet connection.

Upstairs were four bedrooms with a common bathroom for two of them, both of which were small and crammed under the slope of the roof. I used a much larger room to which some owner had added an en-suite bathroom and shower, and there was also the main spare room which had a small shower attached to it. The house was warm, comfortable and felt homely to me, though it was probably too Spartan for some. A lady from the village, Janet, helped me keep the place clean and looked after Tina when I wasn't there. I suspected that she looked after my Scotch as well, but didn't mind and couldn't be bothered as long as the tendency didn't stretch to other things. What the rest of the village knew about my life I had no idea, but Janet did have an active, although kindly, tongue.

As soon as I was home, and after an extensive and playful greeting with Tina, I threw the ball for her for the last time and went to my desk. Computer warming up, I poured a Dalwhinnie, tempered it with a little water and began the search. Tina, named after an old girlfriend called Bettina who would not have seen the funny side, lay contentedly beside the desk.

The number of 'spy' cameras on the market surprised me, and it took a long time to decide on which model would best suit the options available for a hidden installation. Cameras disguised as light switches, smoke alarms, wall clocks, bedside clocks, table lamps, room sanitisers, tissue holders and many other options could be found. The video needed to be recorded, of course, and other units were available for this, although some cameras could do it themselves. Combined units tended to have a limited battery life however, so I settled on a pack of two cameras with a separate recording device which had a 500GB memory, which was more than enough for this purpose. The digital recorder could be stored well out of sight, but hiding the cameras, small though they were, was going to be a challenge.

Delivery from an on-line order was going to take four days. That was absurd, it would be quicker to drive to Bristol and collect it direct from the factory shop. They had two left in stock so I asked them to reserve one for me and left the next morning at seven. I was back home by eleven, eager to install the equipment.

My normal bedroom had a wonderful view, good lighting and the spacious bathroom. It was a place that always reminded me of Juliet, where we had some of our most precious moments. There were always plenty of her things in there. There was no possibility I was going to infect that room, but the ideal bedroom was the one adjacent with its own small shower and importantly, it had a bookcase. While this was a classic hide for a miniature camera, the first place anyone searching would look, it was the only available option.

I put the recorder in a cupboard outside the bedroom, set it up using the instructions to record immediately, ensured the date and time would be displayed on the film and selected the highest definition; there was going to be no point to all this if the players could not be recognised. Then I drilled a hole through the wall to take the leads. The first camera went on the second highest shelf, just above head height. I pushed it to the back and placed a large book on either side reducing the light in that area and diminishing its presence. A walk around the room and a couple of casual glances in its direction reassured me that it wasn't easy to see. It was time for a walk test. I went out of the room and came back in again. Then I lay down on the bed and tried to see the camera. I played back the recording, which was on an SD card, on my computer. The definition was good as was the arc stretching from the door around the room, but the bed was not visible in its entirety. I readjusted it and tried again, but there was no way to have the camera see the bed and keep it out of sight. Leaving that camera set in the original position, I set the other model to view the bed as a reflection in the full length mirror on the opposite wall. Running the walk and bed test again proved a success, so I set about disguising the cameras with ornaments between the books and then added some personal items that made the room look as if it was in permanent use.

Finally, I took some still pictures of the bedroom that identified it within the house for possible use in court to verify the video results. I had just finished and was doing a final check of my handiwork, when my phone rang. Juliet called cheerfully, 'Hello, you. What and who are you doing?' Women and their sixth sense!

'Hello Jules, how are you? Sorry, I can't talk now, but I'll call you back immediately,' I sort of lied. I didn't give her a chance to reply and stopped the call. I had mixed feelings about her calling me though, I needed to tell her what was going on, but not now. She usually had such good ideas and it would be worth having another brain on the case. From the pay-as-you-go, I asked her to call me back to save the minutes. 'Where are you? I need to talk to you, Jules, but it's best not to use my main mobile. It's a difficult story and we need to think.'

'I can only come down on Sunday, I have to meet a buyer for the neighbour's horse on Saturday afternoon.'

'Perfect.' I breathed a sigh of relief. The last thing I wanted was Sandra and Juliet too close together. 'Can you stay for a few days? I'm leaving for Chile on Tuesday night.'

'I'll take you to the airport and then go home.'

'You are the world's very best, you know, the very best.' I meant every word.

She laughed with pleasure. 'I adore you too. I'll see you on Sunday, I'm intrigued.'

You may be intrigued, my love, but you won't be happy when you hear what's happening. Unfortunately there was no way to avoid Juliet being involved. I wasn't sure what her reaction was going to be when it came to telling her what I had done, and it was worrying me with increasing intensity as the hours went by. I had to tell her because we were always honest with each other, and that was not something I was prepared to destroy. I knew she would never forgive me if I kept the secret from her. There was no doubt she would eventually find out, especially if this divorce went to court.

First, there was my night with 'Angela' Parsons; I had been unfaithful to Juliet and there were no excuses for that at all. Would I be able to justify my alcohol fuelled stupidity in her eyes? I didn't know, probably not, and I didn't know where that would leave us. It scared me. Second, there was the plan to help Giles which involved yet another night with his wife. How would Juliet see that? In a better light, hope-fully, but it was still going to hurt her. So should I stop this whole thing now? To do that would let Giles down, and I had my loyalty to him to consider. Surely Juliet would see this as an unavoidable and honourable action to protect someone who was her friend too? When I think back on those opinions now, I realise how naively optimistic I was.

My house was for Juliet, to have Sandra there was a necessary abomination. It was a job, nothing more than a job that had to be done in a place where I would have control over the evidence we needed, and it had to be done as quickly as possible. Given that businesslike attitude, I was hoping I would be up to the task when it came to Friday night, as I was beginning to understand how Giles had lost his desire for his beautiful wife.

Juliet had made contact at the worst moment, it had brought her too close to what was going to happen. The house would need to be sanitised somehow and my soul cleansed before she came to stay.

FROM THE VERY start our relationship had been an absolute treasure. I was passing through a village near Oxford and was looking right while waiting at a stop sign for traffic to pass, when there was a bang on the left front wing of my Land Rover. I looked round just in time to see an arm come up in the air as the rider fell off her bicycle and out of sight behind my bonnet. By the time I had run round the front of the car, she was already picking herself up. 'Are you hurt?'

'I'm so sorry,' she said. 'I don't know why I did that, so stupid. My mind was elsewhere. Have I scratched your car? I'm fine but for a dented ego.'

We looked at the wing together, but there was nothing there. She must have hit the wheel, not the light aluminium bodywork. 'Not only your ego, your wheel's buckled' Head down, trying unsuccessfully to turn it, all I could see were black jeans and suede country boots. I asked, 'Do you have far to go?'

I looked up to hear her answer and saw her face properly for the first time. Her thick auburn hair was tied up in a pony tail and her hazel eyes had a hopeful expression beneath unplucked brows. A light sprinkling of freckles was barely visible across her nose and cheeks. Her complexion was fresh and naturally creamy, my impression was that she spent a lot of time outdoors and seldom bothered with make up. She exuded energy and charisma, was short, perhaps five foot five, but appeared smaller in a heavy olive shooting jacket.

'I do rather,' she said, 'but I'll get a bus. There's a stop not far down the road.' There was a slight hint of Scots in her accent.

'Nonsense, I've time on my hands. Let's find a repair shop for your bike, then I'll drop you off.'

'You don't have to do that, it was my own stupid fault.'

'Not entirely, if I hadn't been there, it wouldn't have happened.'

She laughed and that was it. She had a broad smile which lit up her whole face and was easy to summon. We dropped off her bike, explored each other over a pub lunch and at once became inseparable. The first time I said goodbye to her on her way back north, it felt as if my life was on hold until I saw her again. The moment she was out of sight, I looked at the calendar to count the days to our next meeting, and first thing every morning I ticked them off.

Although we lived apart, Juliet and I saw each other about every three to four weeks in addition to weekends away and taking holidays together. She worked for herself as a landscape designer and stabled some horses for local riders. With the help she had, her life was pretty flexible and she could easily accommodate my relaxed schedule, which was usually two weeks away every quarter, and I could vary the trips as I chose within reason. We respected each other's privacy and I kept my feelings under control by trying not to think of any other relationships she might have, if any. I was confident that she had similar thoughts. We never broached the subject of marriage, each of us seemingly content with the way things were. Deep down though, I knew that I would step to the fore very quickly to prevent any other man from claiming her for life.

Once we were together, I couldn't wait to introduce Juliet to Giles. I was so proud of her, I wanted to show her off to my friend, but for weeks we never managed to meet. When we eventually did, they took to each other immediately. Why would they not? I was their greatest friend, the common link between them. I have an enduring yet purely fictitious image of a scene which symbolised our relationship at that time, an image of us walking down the street: big, tall Giles on one side, a smaller me on the other, with little Juliet almost dancing between us, happy with her friends and her arm linked tightly through mine. She had a deep affection for Giles, I knew that, but she always came home with me. She asked Giles why he never brought a girlfriend to join us. His answer was that there was no one he was serious about at that moment, and he didn't think having a bimbo along was good enough for his friends.

A picnic right on the bank of the river: we had spread a blanket down and Giles, who had carried the hamper from the car, opened it to reveal Juliet's preparations for the day, while I filled our glasses and settled them into the turf so they wouldn't topple. She brought out cheese: a stilton, a really mature cheddar, I remember, and a red Leicester. She had made some bread, a heavy country loaf that smelt delicious, but wasn't. Giles broke off a lump and was weighing it in his hand with exaggerated effort. 'Don't throw that,' I warned him, 'you'll give someone concussion!'

So he did. I stepped back in trying to catch it. A sod on the bank gave way and I slithered sideways into the river with a lasting vision of the others shying away from the splash. When I surfaced, Giles was rolling about and Juliet was clutching her sides with laughter. I splashed them, so it became a full on fight. Tina thought this was a great game and jumped in to join me. Giles was throwing hard lumps of Juliet's loaf at me, while I tried to fend them off and make those two as wet as possible. When he ran out of ammunition, I struggled out followed by Tina who shook herself over us all to joint human protest. I collapsed on my back on the blanket. Juliet promptly sat on my stomach. 'Serves you right for being rude about my cooking. And now you've given me a wet bum!'

'Jules, I love you dearly, but I have to be truthful about your culinary expertise.'

She made a face and pretended to be hurt, muttering something about us being cruel and not appreciating her efforts. We all laughed, though. Her glass had fallen over, so she paraphrased Coriolanus imperiously, 'By Jupiter! I am weary; yea my body is tired from laughter. Have we no wine here?'

I remember that picnic from others particularly, because it was the last time I saw Giles before he married a few months later.

7

SWAMPED WITH SELF-reproach over Juliet and nervous that I would not be able to perform with a woman that was in the process of extorting my friend, I knew I had to get in the mood. What was needed was some foreplay before the foreplay. Sandra could handle her alcohol well, indeed she could match me drink for drink. If we both had just the right amount, a good meal and a heavy dose of her sensuality, my whole mood might change – hopefully.

I had to be better prepared for what was to come, I had to consider what Sandra wanted out of this night. Was she just using me to get at Giles out of spite or was it pure misandry? If both, to bring him to his financial and emotional knees would be a satisfying reward, but to humiliate his best friend as well would be a double triumph. Or, heaven forbid, after Giles was she intent on marrying me to go through the whole money making racket again? If so, she would be disappointed with the prize; I was comfortably off, but hardly in Giles's league. No, it had to be the first option. From her perspective, chasing after financial kittens was not worth the effort when there were plenty of fat cats to be had.

Having reached that conclusion, I felt a little less under pressure. A little. This was not about me, it was about humiliating Giles. I was just a pawn and did not have to be so conscious about watching my back. But I was very aware that she would be alert to any attempt on my part to protect him. I had to be seen as less than the true friend she had been led to believe I was. The fact that, to her knowledge at least, I had not told Giles about our first night was surely proof of a less than true loyalty.

Sandra arrived on time, seven o'clock as we'd agreed. A throaty exhaust heralded her black Porsche Cayman S outside the front door. I provided a welcome grin on the step and tried to look sincere. She had reverted to her natural dark brown hair colour and kissed me with open lips, her arm round my shoulder, her hand on the back of my head, pressing her whole body into mine. I could feel myself getting aroused; it was going to be all right!

A whisky later I was definitely more in the mood and was chatting cheerfully over the second one while making a puttanesca sauce for the spaghetti. There was a touch of unintentional irony in this. According to urban legend, the sauce was popular with *puttane*, whores, as it takes little time to make, leaving more time to attend to customers.

She wanted to explore the house while the pasta was cooking. Upstairs, I showed her the two little spare rooms and the one we would use. 'What's in there?' She pointed to my own room when I turned away from it.

'Oh, it's supposed to be another bedroom, but the bathroom plumbing leaks and the water's turned off, so I use it for storage.'

'I'd still like to look.'

'I keep it locked because I don't want the cleaning lady in there. I've actually mislaid the key as well. I think I'll have to get a locksmith before I get a plumber.'

'I'll ask Anthony to come round. He'll open the door and fix the plumbing too. He's good at that sort of thing.'

'I'm sure he is,' I said with more meaning than I intended.

She gave me an odd look. 'I insist, I'll ask him to come over tomorrow, you'll be home?'

'Actually no, and I really don't need to open the room that urgently. It can wait,' I said with finality. It was only a little thing, but this was the second time I had refused to do what she wanted, the first being over the nitrous oxide. The force of her will was palpable and she didn't like the disobedience, but she didn't take it any further.

She stopped halfway down the stairs, turned to face me and said, 'I thought you were Giles's most loyal friend?' This probe led to dangerous ground. I didn't answer immediately, because I had to give a reply that would convince her that I wasn't a threat.

'Did you tell Giles about us?'

'Good God, no!' I answered, hopefully sounding shocked. 'That wouldn't be very sensible, would it?'

'Why are you doing this?' She looked up at me, a step above her, and teased, 'Why are you going to shag your best friend's wife?'

I laughed. 'Why is my best friend's wife intent on shagging his best friend? Perhaps we both have pressing needs.'

She laughed too, a genuine, husky, throaty sound, and the potential for difficulty subsided.

Scotches consumed and the pasta ready, we progressed to a humble bottle of Chianti. Sandra had the capacity to transform a situation to the way she wanted it to be. I found myself pushing my concerns and guilt into the background and relaxing into the mood. My final reservations melted away.

'You put chillies in this, it's hot,' she said and made a mock blowing sound.

'Only a bit, just to give it a little kick. Too much?'

Her blue eyes narrowed, 'You'll feel the heat on my tongue later.'

ON THE LANDING, she turned around to look over the living room for a moment. I touched her shoulder. We kissed again. Her hand slid down to my belt and deftly released it. A little fumbling and she had my cock in her hand. She laughed delightedly and used it to pull me into the bedroom, while I tottered after her, holding my trousers up and entirely at her mercy.

I was more than ready now. 'I think a shower's in order.' My voice sounded croaked, my tongue dry.

'Brilliant!' She began to strip. Not slowly and enticingly, her clothes came off in a hurry. She didn't need to tease me, just wanted to get on with it.

There was no room in the little cubicle for both of us to bend down at the same time. Sandra lathered the soap and started at my feet, rubbing her way up to my thighs but stopping there. Then she worked from the top down: face, shoulders, 'Arms up!' Chest. 'Turn around!' Back and but-tocks. She stopped again and handed me the soap. 'My chance, Sweetie.'

My God, but this woman had a beautiful body! I soaped and stroked her creamy skin following the same pattern as she had, relishing her perfect form. I didn't stop though, my hand rubbed up between her legs spreading the lather from back to front. She was breathing rapidly and deeply, thrusting her hips forward repeatedly in response to my fingers. I held her with the other arm and whispered, 'The soap is yours.'

'Beast!' She laughed and began to ensure that the rest of my body was as clean as hers with fingers that lingered over every millimetre of skin.

Dried, we piled through into the bedroom, Sandra in the lead, diving onto the bed then quickly rolling over in about as open an invitation as the camera could capture.

8

THE EARLY MORNING sun streamed in the window at an angle. I watched its light track slowly across the wall and head towards the mirror opposite the bed. It is always fascinating to see how rapid that earthly movement is when you consider that it takes so many hours for the sun to reach the western horizon.

Coffee was in order. Pulling on a pair of trousers, I went down to the kitchen to get some. First though, I went straight to the cupboard where the recorder was and removed the memory card. If the recording was good, Sandra would be seen to lead me into the bedroom, into the shower and then to be a more than willing partner in the acts that followed. Suddenly, the realisation that someone else, maybe a host of other people, would watch this performance sunk home, and a flush of future embarrassment left my mouth dry. Hopefully, if our plan worked, it wouldn't be necessary. I hid the card with my car keys to take with me when I left.

Tina came to say good morning as the coffee machine hissed. She nuzzled my hand and wagged her tail while watching me prepare her breakfast. Cupboard love at that moment, of course, but I spent some time thinking how loyal and loveable dogs are, unlike some other devious bitches, one of which was waking up above me. Now that she had well and truly 'had' me, I understood better what Giles had said, that she took the initiative and orchestrated people to play the tune her way. Having involved me in her sordid game, what was she going to do now? The only thing we had in our favour was the recording of her infidelity. Would that be enough to force her off her planned course?

I reflected on the athletic night and how damn good it had been; unbelievable. I never thought I had it in me; all credit to her, I suppose. Then thoughts of Juliet, ever close to the surface, swam up and remorse set in again. How the hell was I going to tell her, even though I still believed it was a necessary 'job'? That's what it was, I told myself yet again, it was just a job, even if I had lost myself in primeval lust for a few hours.

Tina crunched her biscuits while I poured the coffee, then she followed me up the stairs and into the room. I put Sandra's mug on the bedside table, expecting the dog to stick her nose on the bed in a good morning greeting to my guest, but she didn't even go to that side – unusual and thus interesting. Sandra said thanks and sat up. Even on waking she looked good, but there was a change in her mood. Her features had hardened and they reminded me of that night at dinner when Giles had overridden her attempt to get Henry to do something before he went to bed. She smiled now, but it was forced and without feeling. I was instantly suspicious.

Why? Had she seen something, the camera perhaps? Or, her act now over, her own 'job' done, could she now revert to her true self?

We said nothing, sipping coffee, and I noticed that the light had progressed further round the room. *Damn!* The sun had shone on the mirror which had reflected its light directly at the bookcase. It must have penetrated into the dark cavity I had created, illuminating the camera in its depths and made it visible in the mirror from the bed, the very area under scrutiny.

With the change in atmosphere, there was nothing other than idle conversation as we got up and dressed. I had no choice but to leave her alone while I went to the bathroom, so she would have ample opportunity to examine the cameras. Thank goodness the separate recorder was in another room, so she couldn't mess with that.

She seemed to be undergoing an internal struggle, appearing to be nice, yet having to suppress her fury at my taking the initiative with the recording. Sourly, she initially turned down the offer of breakfast and made to leave. Then abruptly her mood swung and she had herself under control once more, opting for a simple slice of toast and more coffee. Giles was right, what should I expect next? She put her hand on mine and said, 'That was good Sweetie, but I must go. I'll call you soon.'

'I must go too. I've a meeting at Farnborough that will last all of today, Saturday if you please. Some people have no respect.'

I saw her out of the door and watched as she slithered down into her Porsche. She left slowly, the car purring down the drive, but she stopped before entering the lane. It wasn't far away, and I stepped back from the window so as not to be seen. She dialled a number into her phone with angry little stabs of her finger. The car's Bluetooth system would have allowed her to continue driving, but she stayed there and an animated conversation took place. Her hands were gesticulating furiously and her head was moving back and forth in anger. She must be furious about the cameras and even angrier about having lost control of the situation, while someone, some confidant, was listening.

9

THE PORSCHE ENGINE howled and the car fishtailed on the loose surface with a scattering of gravel before gripping the tarmac of the lane. I listened to its angry receding roar for a moment then tried to phone Giles with the news. His phone was off, so I prepared my stuff for the day, teased Tina with a dog treat before giving it to her and locked the house.

The sun was climbing steadily up into a clear sky. It was a beautiful morning, but my mind was full of the night, wondering what Sandra was going to do next, whether our plan had been thwarted with her seeing the camera and more particularly, how I was going to explain it all to Juliet. It was a jumble of thoughts so I put on the radio and listened to that without hearing anything of what was said. Farnborough was only an hour away and I made good time, arriving early. I left the Land Rover in TAG's large parking area, which wasn't strictly the correct place since I wasn't going there, and took the opportunity to walk to my client who had limited parking further along the road. He too was early and we agreed we could probably complete our work sooner than planned.

Later, after the day's discussions had given the other part of my brain a chance to think more rationally about events, I drove home in a calmer manner than in the morning. Cloud cover had begun to creep across the sky at about midday, gradually reducing the sun from a bright ghost behind a translucent screen to an unobtrusive and dimmer source of light. The ceiling dropped lower and lower as I drove and it was obvious that a stormy night was in store. By the time I was home, dark rolls of cloud were tumbling over and over in the rising wind, and the slab-sided Land Rover rocked to every gust.

I put my key to the lock, but stopped short. My heart accelerated, thumping. My mouth went dry. I had locked the front door when I left. Now it was almost closed. Almost, just half an inch of the jamb was showing. It open slowly and quietly to a gentle push. No sound could be heard over the storm and the odd creak from the old house. Precious little light entered through the small windows from that darkening sky; it was impossible to make out any detail in the room. I stood motionless until my eyes adjusted, the door pulled to behind me, listening for the slightest odd sound amidst the patter of the rain on the tiles and the rumble of the weather rolling in.

Every drawer and cupboard door was open, the contents strewn over the floor. Chair cushions had been ripped open and tossed to the side, one chair was on its back, the TV was on the floor, but intact. The kitchen did not look as if it had been touched. All this I took in at a glance. Was he still here? That was vital. Anger tried to surface. I forced it down; emotion could wait. I quietly crossed the room to my office. It was trashed. Files were ripped open and paper lay everywhere. Sellotape, scissors, paper clips and pens were strewn across the floor. The bookshelf had been tipped over, and my laptop had been given a stomping.

Lightning flashed, illuminating the room for a second, the devastation stark. An immediate crack of thunder showed how close the strike had been. The shock was distracting, but a little noise behind me wasn't right. A rustle of clothes, a breath close by, I don't know, but it shouldn't have been there. I ducked and turned. Something clipped my ear and glanced off my left shoulder dropping me to the floor. A broad, dark, hooded figure stood over me, a jemmy high above his head, the curved end silhouetted by the window. It swept down again, seemingly in slow motion. I rolled away just in time. It thudded into the floor, then up again above his head for the next blow. He wasn't going to miss another time. Hooking my left foot behind his to jam it, I stabbed at the front of his knee with my right one. He grunted in pain and fell over backwards. I tried to get up, but my shoulder wouldn't support the move. I rolled over to use the other side, but he had already clambered to his feet and limped out. Sometimes it's satisfying to cause pain.

He half ran and half hopped down the drive, disappearing in the rain before he reached the gate. He was in no state to continue the fight, thank goodness; I certainly wasn't. The whole episode had probably lasted no more than ten seconds, less, but it felt an age. Talking of age, I poured a twelve year old malt down my throat and then added a touch of water to the next one.

Where was Tina? If he'd hurt her, I'd kill him. Angrily, I searched around the house, then out into the yard from barn to barn, calling her name. She was normally very obedient, so I became increasingly concerned. Eventually, immensely relieved, I found her gnawing on a huge fleshy bone in the tractor shed, oblivious to the storm.

The recorder had been found and had also received a stomping, but the memory card was in my pocket if that was the cause of this mess. In the bedroom the cameras were ripped off their leads, and one had been used to shatter the mirror, it lay amongst shards of glass on the floor. My temper rose. Why do they have to wreak so much wanton destruction, why not just take what they want and go? This mess was going to take forever to sort out. I stared at my image in what remained of the mirror in the frame. There was a bruise forming on my left cheek and that ear was bleeding. There were marks on the door jamb of my bedroom, but no force had been applied. I must have disturbed him at that point.

The first call I made was to the police who would send a car round in ten minutes; that was good. The second call was to Giles and this time he answered. 'Bloody hell, Alastair. Are you all right? Who did this? Any idea? Was it just an ordinary burglary?'

'I'm fine. Shoulder's a bit sore, but that will get better, and the house and my things will get better eventually too. My bet is that this is the work of your lovely wife, or someone she hired. I told her I would be out all day, but I came back early and caught him in the house. He used the front door, probably because anyone in the wood shop would be able to see him round the back. And he didn't latch the door which tells me that he thought I wouldn't be back till later, but maybe not.'

'Tony, I'll bet. It'll be Tony, the jack of all trades who seems devoted to the bloody woman.'

'Jack of all trades? Is burglary a trade? But you could well be right, he was about the same size and weight and he was very strong and, come to think of it, he was slightly bow legged. If you see him, he'll be limping for a while.'

A car drew up outside. 'Giles I'm going to have to go, the police are here already.'

They were very sympathetic, on the surface anyway, and asked all the right questions, even if I wanted an ambulance. They said someone would be round in the evening to take fingerprints, they were busy with a possible suicide right then. I told them there was no need, he wore gloves, but they replied that as it was also an assault they had to investigate further and I should touch as little as possible.

Back in my office after they'd left, and searching for what might be missing, I realised that my e-ticket to Chile had gone. I would not be able to print another as there was now no computer. No matter, they only need a passport to check in. I'd have to buy another laptop quickly, though.

On the phone to Giles again, I reminded him that the six months was nearly up and that Sandra had to file for divorce before it was. 'This woman is going to stop at nothing to get her hands on your money now that her case of adultery on your part has been nullified by her own.'

'You're not wrong,' he said. 'It had occurred to me.'

'You need to be ultra suspicious of her. Try to anticipate her surprise tactics and stay out of arguments, just walk away.

Come Tuesday, I'll be off to Chile for a week. When I'm back we can put our heads together over future plans.'

No sooner had I put the phone down than there was a demanding knock on the door. I peered cautiously through the window to see a large man with a heavy belly standing with his thumbs hooked into his belt, back to the door and staring out at the rain which had lessened by then. ''Ullo, Mr Forbes?' he said when I opened the door a crack. I didn't want prying eyes looking at that mess. He put a heavy tattooed forearm up to the door frame. 'You've a barn to rent?'

'Yes, that's right. Do you want to see it now?' I reached for a large umbrella, handed it to him and took a second one for myself.

'A spot o' rain don' bother me. I'm 'Arry Burbage, by the way.' He grabbed my hand with a massive paw, and the movement shook his fleshy jowls. He took the umbrella and continued talking as we walked around the house and towards the barns. 'Me passion's old MG sports cars, y'know. Me MG TC is a truly beautiful motor. I've also got a TB (that's a rare 'un), a TA, a TF and I'm after a TD to complete the set. I've also got a Series 1 Land Rover. Although that's not a sports car you understand?'

'I have a Defender,' I said as we trudged through the rain. 'I love it so I understand what you mean.'

'Not the same, these modern ones, not the same. Too complicated. Anyway, I've only got a small garridge where I'm workin' on the TB at the moment, and there's no room for nuffin' else. So I want your barn for the others until the TB's done, then I'll swop. Reckon I'll do the TF next.'

Inside the barn, it was dark thanks to the weather, but there was enough light to see it was empty. 'Perfect.' Harry pointed at a steel door in the back wall, 'What's behind there?'

'There's a small store, but I can't find the key. I was looking for it when I advertised and then forgot about it. I don't want to cut the padlock, so I'll try to find it again. The room's about ten foot square, will that do you?'

'Perfect,' he said again, 'it's just to 'old some tools and spares in case I want to work 'ere.'

'Good. Let's go and discuss the contract over a beer.'

We sat in the kitchen, which hadn't been ransacked, to go over the rental agreement. Harry proved to be a talker and he seemed genuinely shocked at the devastation in the lounge. Eventually I managed to show him out the door with a signed agreement in place. He said he could not move his cars for another week as he had other things to do. I replied that the place was his now, and he could do what he wanted, but I'd try and find the key to the store before he moved in.

As I drifted off to sleep that night and my thoughts ran over the afternoon's dramatic events, the image of a silhouette standing over me with the raised jemmy kept looming into view. That had been very close, too damned close, then realised there was something odd about that jemmy. Unsurprisingly, I had not noticed it at the time, but the recurring image showed the unmistakable curved end to the weapon in silhouette distorted by something else, something straight as if he was wielding two things together in the same hand. Odd, but not worth bothering about, the end result was the same, and it ached.

10

JULIET ARRIVED LATE on Sunday afternoon, glad to be there. The rain had passed in the early morning and left a cooler, cloudless day which did little to remove my apprehension over her visit. I heard the car and went out to meet her. She stared at my bandaged ear with an unspoken question in her eyes. We kissed and I held her tightly for an unusually long time, my lips buried in the hair on top of her head. She was good to hug, her trim little body allowed me to feel all her curves through her tan jeans and green woollen jersey. 'Am I glad to see you?' I whispered in her ear.

'It would appear so, you're squashing me! What's the matter?' Tenderly, she put a hand up to my ear when I released her. 'Tell me.'

I led her inside and she stood still in the doorway, stunned at the scene. She wandered around, shaking her head in disbelief as she examined the wreckage in the lounge then in my office which, if anything, was even more of a mess. Then she turned and looked up at me wordlessly, her hazel eyes switching from one of mine to the other and back repeatedly, searching for an answer.

'You had better sit down and have a drink, if it's not too early. This is a long story. I'm going to tell you everything and you're not going to like it, I'm afraid. Jules, please, do not fly off the handle until I'm finished. I need your understanding and help, and so does Giles.'

The only chairs not slashed open were at the dining table. She pulled one out and accepted the scotch, sliding it across the table towards her with two hands. 'You know I'll help, anything. Shall we clear up this mess?'

'Don't make promises you may not keep. I'll clear later, it's not important right now.' Nervously, I began and left nothing out except the details of my sexual adventures. Deliberately, I switched the order around, so that the two bouts with Sandra were left to the end. I wanted Juliet to listen to what was driving Giles's and my decisions before she became so jealous and angry, that she wouldn't want to hear anymore or couldn't concentrate on what I was saying. When I had reached the end of the reasoning, she got up and wandered round the room again, taking in the shambles. She picked up a book and put it on the window sill, then found my small wooden Buddha on the floor, which she cradled in both hands. 'But why this destruction? Why would someone want to do this? What do you want me to do? How can I help?'

'Giles and I both think it's his wife that's behind it, probably using her friend's husband, Tony Wiggins who's a bit thuggish. Sandra must be paying him, otherwise why would he trash this place and try to kill me if there wasn't some reward for it?'

Her brow furrowed with concern. 'It's awful, lover. But why? What are you going to do?'

'I haven't finished, and this is the bit where I'm honestly petrified of your reaction, but please listen to the end.' I had thought long and hard whether to tell her about the first episode with Sandra, as I had no excuse for that, but honesty had never been doubted in our relationship. There may have been omissions on both our parts, and I didn't doubt that she had been out with others far away in Yorkshire, she was far too attractive not to be pestered by men. If we come through this intact and together, I will commit, I promised myself.

Her eyelids sagged and her mouth turned down as it became obvious what I was going to say about the first epis- ode. She was struggling to contain herself, her lips tight and trembling. Then, when it came to Friday night, she became really angry, her eyes glinting with moisture. 'Alastair, how could you?' She jumped up and strode to the window, passing the Buddha from one hand to the other repeatedly. Loudly, she demanded, 'How could you let me come here and then tell me this?'

'I've tried to explain that.' My words were guilty and timid. 'Jules, I'm so sorry, really sorry, but it was just a job, something that had to be done to help save Giles.'

'It wasn't a 'job' as you put it, on the first occasion. *Was it?*' Tears ran freely down her cheeks as she slumped down into a chair again. 'How could you? Everything we've built up, the trust, the love, the honesty between us – in one stupid drunken night you've destroyed us! Oh Alastair, *how could you?*' she stood and suddenly hurled the Buddha at me. 'You bastard! You absolute bloody sod!' I dodged, and the symbol of peace smashed into the wall and fell to the floor.

I could do nothing, it was as she said. Everything we had I had single-handedly destroyed. I watched her pacing up and down the room, my misery matching hers, not knowing what to say. Tina was worried, she had never experienced even raised voices between us before. She pushed her nose against my thigh, so I put a hand on her head; at least I could comfort someone.

More quietly Juliet said, 'Giles won't have told you this, but at that picnic when you fell in the river, and you went to the car to get a towel for Tina, he stood next to me and put his hand on my shoulder. He often touched me in a friendly, firm and supporting fashion, but this was different. It was a tentative touch loaded with feeling. He knew it and I knew it. I don't think he set out to touch me like that, I think it was meant to be his usual reassuring gesture, but it emerged as it did from some deep rooted emotion. I moved away from him then and told him that I truly loved him dearly, but I loved you more and I had made my choice and asked him not to complicate our relationship and possibly ruin his friendship with you. I told him I was not prepared to come between you two and that my mind was made up. I felt I had to do that immediately, before he got any more ideas. I did that for you, I could have succumbed to a temptation from the second most wonderful man in the world for me, but I didn't because of loyalty to you, because I loved you more. And now you do this.'

She stopped and leant on the back of a chair, breathing deeply. I put out my hand to her, to put my fingers on hers, but she shook them off angrily. 'Don't touch me with those hands! It's too late to drive home now. I'm going to bed in the little room.' Tina followed her up the stairs. On the landing, Juliet knelt down to the dog and, holding her head in two hands, kissed it. The bedroom door was shut very firmly.

There was a vacuum in my belly and bile stung my throat. The void in me could only be filled by her understanding and forgiveness. There was no possibility of sleep, so I set about clearing up. Tina responded to the tension by following me around the room. She was getting under my feet, so I shepherded her to bed, gave her a cuddle and carried on until after midnight. At the top of the stairs, near the door to the little room, I could hear muffled sobbing. It only served to reinforce my shame and bring tears to my eyes too. I had hurt her terribly, how could I ease that pain? What could I do to make it right? Was there anything? The Buddha was in my hand. I must have carried it upstairs. It was split along the grain from a shoulder to the opposite thigh. It was symbolic; split but not separated. If I seamlessly glued the two pieces back together, would that restore the bond between us?

In bed, anguishing over our future, I still couldn't sleep, but it must have caught up with me at some point because I woke to the smell of coffee wafting up the stairs. Partly dressed and with trepidation, I went down to the lounge then watched her at the counter. She was facing the other way and hadn't heard my bare feet. Her long auburn hair, normally held up in a pony tail, was slightly tousled and cascaded down her back in a shining tumble of waves. She had a gymnastic figure. It was hidden now in a silk dressing gown with the belt pulled tight around her waist. God, but I loved this woman! We were such a perfect pair. Please Jules, please forgive me.

She turned around and started. 'Don't creep up on me like that!' Waving a hand to the machine, she said without any semblance of warmth, 'I've made coffee.' Her eyes were red and swollen. I wondered if she had slept at all.

'Thanks. Jules, I …'

'Don't Alastair, don't say anything. I need time. I understand why you did what you did on Friday, you've explained that very well, and maybe in time I can forgive you that. What I cannot forgive, maybe not ever, is your infidelity the first time.'

I opened my mouth to speak.

'No! Don't say anything. I'm going to have a slice of toast, then I'll go home. I can't bear to be in this house any longer. I will contact you, I promise, but I'm not sure when. In the meantime, please don't call me.' She glared at me, forcing my reluctant and nodded acceptance, then added, 'At least you maintained your honesty. Thank you for that.'

11

SO GILES HAD made a tentative approach to Juliet. He must have held his feelings for her in check for a long time. Dammed them, until that touch with its unintended feeling opened the sluices and his emotions poured out. How, with Juliet present, could he have ever invited another girl to make up a foursome?

It was no wonder that, after Juliet put him off, Giles could not bring himself to be in our company. He would have been severely embarrassed over the threat to our relationship that he had almost created. When he and I had lunch in the City, he had hesitated too long, debating whether to tell me of his desire for her, before declaring that he had been searching for someone intelligent. I had known he thought Juliet was wonderful, but I hadn't realised he had loved her to the extent that her rejection had set him adrift, blinding him to Sandra's dark side.

Had Giles betrayed me by approaching Juliet? Yes, of course, and that too smarted, but was it any worse than what I had done to her? Yes it was, because his action was for love, mine was only temporary lust. It didn't matter now though, it was over a year ago. Or did it matter? It showed how fragile a relationship could be. One stupid wrong move could drive the injured party into the arms of another treasured friend. It would be so easy for Juliet to turn to Giles for help and understanding. Would she seek him out in revenge? No, that sort of tactic was not in her character. If she never forgave me and walked away from our relationship, she would go into hibernation, she would not want anything to do with either of us, wouldn't she? If she took up with Giles, her proximity would kill me. I would have to go away, disappear off the planet, it would be too painful. I again reminded myself that it happened well over a year ago and he had done the honourable thing and walked away. It was my duty now to continue to support him, but I wasn't going to tell him about Juliet and me. He was too decent a man to interfere in any way but, being the person he was, he would be distracted by his concern for his friends when he needed to focus on his own problem.

Monday went by in slow motion. Juliet's misery dominated my thoughts and refused to leave. I hardly ate, worried sick that this break might be final. Tina seemed to understand and followed me around far more closely than normal. In the morning, I went to town and sent the memory card with its valuable, almost toxic, information to Giles's office address by special delivery. I replaced my crushed laptop and spent the rest of the day restoring the information from a separate hard drive which hadn't been damaged, thank goodness. I also listed everything for which I could claim and spent another age talking to the insurance company.

A lousy day, except that later in the evening I repaired the little Buddha. It was split, but the two pieces clung fast to each other with wood fibres which had stretched. It couldn't be repaired seamlessly as the fibres now had more bulk than before. I could not bear to tear the pieces apart and remove the excess so that the repair would be invisible. In my weak emotional state that would be akin to creating a permanent rift. Instead, I fed some glue into the gap, wrapped the figure in a thick cloth and gently squeezed the two halves together in a vice. The glue's instructions claimed it was more powerful than the wood. If so, then although our relationship would have a slight battle scar, it would be the stronger for it. Superstition or hope?

Giles and I had been speaking almost daily, usually around lunch time and using our pay-as-you-go phones. On Tuesday morning the call came earlier, while I was packing.

I said, 'Giles, I've been thinking. You must file for divorce yourself before she does. Although it may not make any difference to the outcome, at least it gives you the high ground. Then you have to assemble all your evidence and present it to her. Hopefully, she will see that she cannot win and accepts a reduced settlement.'

'Well, I've been thinking too,' he said .'I don't stop thinking. It's not going to be so simple. Sandra is going to deny the first encounter with you and she'll get the Wiggins to provide her with an alibi. We have the film of the second night, but she can say that was just revenge for my indiscretion or something; anyway, we'll be even. I need more ammunition and I'm going to ask her last husband if he'll state that she treated him in a similar way. That, at least, will provide evidence of her character and a plot. I reckon he'll be itching for revenge, he'd love to see her defeated.'

'Good idea. Speed is essential, though, she could even file today. What I don't understand is why it's taking her so long?'

'I suppose she's trying to build a stronger case. If she could just get me to hit her, it would be a major success.'

THE FLIGHT I had chosen left Heathrow at just after six that evening with Iberia on a British Airways ticket. It meant a layover in Madrid of some seven hours, but that could not be helped. The whole trip to Santiago took around eighteen hours which, even in business class, was exhausting. At least there was a lounge available in Madrid, because it wasn't worth checking into a hotel.

I barely rested on the long haul. I watched a movie without seeing it and have no idea what it was called. I drank too much and ate too little. The cabin attendant was very pretty and charming, but I couldn't respond. My left shoulder and ear were still painful preventing me from sleeping on that side, and the ear bled too easily if I lay on it, even under the dressing. Of course, there were also far too many confusing thoughts in my mind. Juliet, Giles, Sandra, Wiggins, they all had their part to play in contributing to my unease. Juliet dominated them. How was I going to win her back? Had she actually left, was she considering breaking with me permanently? Every morning for the entire trip I woke with a feeling of hunger but never felt like food. I managed to push it into the background during the day and force myself to eat properly, but it would return at night and give me a troubled sleep.

Our agony aside, I really needed her opinion on this whole business with Giles. She was very good at analysing situations and, although I knew I could do it, it would be a real bonus to have her thoughts as a woman dealing with a woman.

My thoughts also strayed to Tony Wiggins, undoubtedly the man who had almost killed me with a jemmy. I had been sure I'd seen him before that dinner at Giles's house, and it came to me out of the blue while I was half asleep. He had been standing at the bus stop across the road from Antonio's restaurant the night Sandra had walked in and messed up my life. I had taken no notice at the time of course, because he wasn't the only person at the stop. The fact that he had been wearing a leather jacket and a beanie on a warm August evening was what stuck in my mind, and he had been staring into the restaurant. With hindsight, he must have followed me and reported my position to Sandra. It had always seemed more than a little odd that she could just walk up to me as she did, 'recognising me from a photo'.

VERTILIFT WAS A helicopter operator with its headquarters in Santiago, but with operating bases at strategic places in the country. Although they would undertake all kinds of work, they specialised in tasks that required their helicopters to carry loads on a cargo sling underneath the machine, often high in the Andes mountains. It was risky work which required good training, reliable equipment, a dedication to proven procedures and a healthy respect for the mountains and their weather.

The company was formed and owned by a General Manager who was willing to pay for what he believed in. To people like me, who make a living from helping aircraft operators put Safety and Quality Management Systems in place, someone who was unequivocally prepared to fund the changes these systems required and put his full and enthusiastic support behind the programmes was a fantastic bonus. No profit would come of the expense, but Mario Montano knew that the work his crews did incurred a great deal of risk, so he adopted the philosophy that things had to be done the correct way, risk had to be reduced to the absolute minimum with every decision analysed for safety, and the highest level of quality had to be attained. He charged his clients accordingly which put off some potential customers, but there were enough that would pay to get the best service. Managers as supportive as Mario are a rarity, and it was a pleasure working with him as there was immense satisfaction to be had from seeing my ideas and systems put into practice and accepted by the staff, most of whom added valuable contributions. Mario had many business interests and was an extremely rich man. I did not know how rich, of course, but I certainly benefited from his largesse. I counted him as a true friend, and I liked to think he felt the same way; certainly trust and goodwill were present on both sides.

After an initial year of regular visits every six weeks, I now only had to go there once a quarter. Mario saw to the business class air travel and a five star hotel when I was in Santiago. Out in the camps, I took whatever accommodation and food were offered. My role as a safety consultant had grown in the last year to include the position of a roaming flight standards instructor. I had no legal authority under Chilean aviation regulations, but Mario wanted an independent person to ensure that all the pilots were adhering to the same standards. This was an excellent position, as my flying rate had been falling away as the consultancy grew. In this instructor role I was able to keep flying and help the young pilots mature in their work at the same time. Two of the older men harboured a slight resentment towards me as a foreigner, although they were too polite to be unpleasant about it. Most of the others accepted me because that's what Mario wanted, but all three of the younger ones, who felt that the older pilots were too domineering and stuck in their ways, welcomed my input. I became good friends with two of them, Humberto and Felipe, and it was Felipe, Mario's nephew, who inadvertently shaped my future.

Vertilift's camp was in northern Patagonia, two hours drive from Puerto Montt, past the impressive Volcan Calbuco and in the Cochamo region. It was composed of a number of mobile cabins which gave every occupant his or her own room together with a common mess hall and kitchen. In another cabin was a lounge with a TV and some board games. The crews ran a book swapping club and there was always something new to read, but many would retire to their rooms after supper and use their computers. In addition to the pilots, there were helicopter engineers, a couple of surveyors, a geologist and a medic. I had him change the dressing on my ear to something thin enough so that I could get a flying helmet on my head.

On the second day, we had a good afternoon's flight, practicing approaches to a high altitude landing pad, feeling for the updrafts of rising air that would boost the helicopter's lift and learning to be wary of the downdrafts that could pull it down the mountainside towards the valley floor. Felipe had been working well since I had been there, but I felt that his mind was not fully on the task. With Humberto out of earshot at some point I asked if something was bothering him, but he brushed it aside and merely muttered about a headache. Later, when we had finished the evening meal and the others had drifted off to their rooms, Felipe and I sat and talked. When the last person had left, he got up and walked slowly round the room, his tall, strong frame upright and proud. As was often the case, he had not shaved for a few days resulting in a thick black stubble. Usually he had no problem talking, but he seemed troubled as if he was trying to make up his mind about something. Then in a low voice, even though there was no one else to hear, he leant forward, his long hair falling over his ears and said, 'Alastair, I must talk with you, I want to confess something, but you must not tell anyone. You must swear not to tell anyone.'

'Felipe, you know I won't tell, but why don't you go to confession?'

'Tsah!' His disgust came from deep within him. 'Those priests, they give forgiveness away like sweets to kids. Every week they take a bucket of forgiveness and throw a handful through the screen of the confessional. And to make them-selves feel better, they give punishment; twenty "Hail Marys". Is nonsense! No Alastair, for this I don't want for-giveness, but I need to tell someone, one I can trust, for my self help. I trust you, you are foreigner and will not tell any-one, and you are my big brother!' His swarthy features broke into an ever-easy grin, which faded quickly. 'I don't want you to do anything, only to listen to me and to keep the secret, please.'

'I'm listening, Felipe.'

'I killed a man.'

I stared at him. He had my full attention. No wonder he was distracted. There had to be a long explanation coming, so I went to the fridge for another couple of beers and signed the bar book. 'Go on,' I prompted him.

'Alastair, this man – he touching my sister. She very upset, I think also that he rape her, but she not speaking of that. For a long time he touching her and getting very close. She not fighting it, in the beginning she like the attention, she only fifteen, but very ....' He flapped his arms as if he wanted to shape a buxom woman but thought it was disrespectful to be that descriptive about his little sister. 'She look older, you understand? After a time of this touching, always getting more sexual, you know? He stroking her arm and sometime her leg, then later he start feeling her breasts. When he do that she say "No" and try to stay away from him, but one day he sit next to her and start again. She very afraid and not move, so he feel up her leg. It disgusting, Alastair. Do they do that in UK?'

'They do. They do it all over the world. Sick people. There's something wrong in their heads that they have to try this with children. Who was this man?'

Felipe leapt up and started pacing around the cabin again, weaving in and out of the chairs and to the door and back. I wanted to tell him to sit down, to calm himself, but could not bring myself to interrupt.

'I not tell you that, but he was good friend of my father and like an uncle to Cristina and me, but not an uncle, you understand?' He didn't wait for a reply but went on, his face earnest. 'He always being friendly to my mother, more than he should be, but not for sex. Now I know why he acting nice; to get to my sister.'

I knew his father was dead. 'Go on, Felipe.'

'My mother she very angry about my sister, of course. She make many threats into the air, but she not know who to blame, Cristina not tell her, only me. Anyway, my sister she is crying and crying, and my mother she is trying to give comfort, but Cristina is too upset and cannot find words to say what is wrong. Is very dramatic, Alastair, I also want to cry, but don't know what about. Only for sympathy with her.

'My mother go out to make *maté* and I ask Cristina if this man touch her again, because that is all I can think that could be wrong. She not answer me, but she nod her head. Now I angry, Alastair, very angry, but I have sense to make sure of the facts before I do something stupid. I ask if he raped her. Again she not answer, but she make a noise like a wolf and cry even more, so I know it true.

'We people from Chile, from Brazil, from Peru, from all over South America, we can be … How you did you say it? 'Hot head' when we angry. I know this, and I know what you teach us in the safety training and I try to cool down. In a few days I cool off, but I still angry inside.' He held his closed fist up to his chest and thumped it twice. 'It is burning like a fire in me and I have to do something. This man is important, he rich and he political, and I know that if I go to the police, he will bribe them and it will all go away. So I must do something myself, and I make the plan.' Suddenly he laughed, a short, sharp, humourless sound. 'Alastair, I do like you tell us, I make a risk assessment! You think I joke, but no, is true. I think of all the ways to take revenge, I think of all the risks and I think of ways to make them small.'

'What did you do?'

'He kill himself,' he said quietly and at last sat down.

Now that he had spoken about it, Felipe relaxed and was keen to tell me what he had done and the care he had taken to cover it up. All in line with my teaching, he told me proudly. It took another hour, and a few more beers, but by then I think I knew every detail. The way he had gone about the murder, the devising and the execution (his unintended pun) of his plan was admirable, and I was pleased that even though the subject was hardly my intended goal, he would not have done so well if I hadn't shown him how.

Felipe leaned forward with an earnest look in his eyes. 'Alastair, you think I did right?'

He needed me to ease his conscience, but what could I say? I could not lie to him. Part of me claimed it was a just solution, another said it was too great a punishment – did a rape where the victim was left alive justify the death of the perpetrator? 'You got rid of a paedophile and a corrupt person who would otherwise have tried it on another girl,' I said. 'You satisfied your family's honour, and I hope gave some comfort to your sister. But you still killed a man. People will say that you should not have taken the law into your own hands but, as you explained to me, he would have got away with it and that would not have been right. But to kill him? Maybe that's a bit excessive, Felipe. Anyway, I'm not going to judge you right or wrong, I cannot. I don't know, Felipe, but you made the world a better place in a little way.'

'What else could I do?' He looked at me, opening his hands to the ceiling. He was desperate for my blessing, 'Cut off his cojones?'

'Felipe, that might have been a better solution; 'an eye for an eye'. You would have no lasting conscience about killing him as you do now, and will have for the rest of your life.

And, you would have great satisfaction in knowing that he would not be able to rape anyone else, and that he would be tortured with regret until he died.'

'But, Alastair, if he lived, he would know it was me and take terrible revenge on me and my sister and my mother; that is the way it works! You not have a little sister, Alastair, maybe you not understand how this will affect Cristina? Will she ever marry? Will she ever trust a man after this? Will her life ever be normal? I don't know the answers, Alastair, but I know he did terrible damage to her.'

I stared at him with sympathy and sighed. What a position to be put in. What I would have done if faced with the same situation I couldn't think, but 'an eye for an eye' has a lot of merit in my vision.

BACK IN SANTIAGO with decent internet in the hotel, I picked up an email from Juliet. I hesitated to read it at first, petrified that she had written to tell me it was all over. No, she would never do it that way, she would never take the easy way out of something so important, not through a letter. She would get in her car when I was back, drive for four and a half hours and confront me face to face before driving back again. Comforted by that thought, I opened the mail with curiosity.

The tone was matter of fact. It started and ended without any term of endearment, not even my name (could she not bring herself to say it?). It was closed with a simple 'Juliet' as opposed to her usual 'Jules'. She said she had traced Tony Wiggins's roots and discovered he was Sandra's half brother; she was born Parsons from the first father and he, Wiggins, from the second.

Tony was the half brother, the little boy who was frequently beaten by his father and who cried outside the door when his big sister was being raped. She had tried to protect him, no wonder he was loyal to her, why he would commit crimes for her, it wasn't only about money. Doubtless he would be in for a share of what she could get out of her scheming though, which gave him considerable incentive.

The early morning sun climbed above the snow capped Andean peaks to the east and tried to force its way through the net curtains of my room. I opened them to let the natural warmth combat the air conditioning. The view of the mountains was, as always, calming, their solid immobility a symbol of order above the chaotic world that humans have created for themselves.

At around eight thirty, just before I had to check out of the hotel, I called Giles using FaceTime. His image on the phone was good enough for me to see how drawn and worried he looked, but he seemed in good health. Although I had only been away a week on this trip, I was looking forward to moving on with our plan. We needed to end this situation soon, it was telling on him, and I was concerned over what Sandra's next unexpected move would be.

First, I told him the relationship between Tony and Sandra. He said he wasn't surprised, it explained a lot, then changed the subject, 'This situation is now beyond a joke. They've been through my things, mostly files in the office at home. It's not obvious, just a few little things out of place or not how I left them.'

'Sandra? What would she be looking for, the memory card, I suppose?'

'It must be her, probably aided and abetted by that bloody man, Tony; no one else would take the trouble to hide the search, surely? Insurance policies, my will perhaps. The card's in the safe at work.'

'Did you change it? The will, I mean.' The phone in one hand, I checked around the room for items that had escaped my packing.

'Done,' he said with some satisfaction. 'I did it freehand yesterday afternoon, signed it with my solicitor's tea lady and a client as witnesses and left it with him to formalise.' He paused for a moment. 'We had another serious row last night, and I told her that I was thinking of taking her out of my will. I didn't say I'd already done it, though. *Stupid* – I should have kept my mouth shut, I tend to say things I don't want to when I get heated.'

'You're not alone in that. Sandra will react to this in some way, be careful.' I changed the subject. 'What about your computer?'

'There's nothing on the computer that's relevant to my will; only my insurance policies and fortunately she doesn't have the password.'

'Are you sure?'

'Well, I've never given it to her. I suppose some IT wiz could crack it easily enough, though. I left everything to you and Juliet. I've no one else to leave it to, and we go back a long way.'

'Giles, please! That's very good of you, but you're far too generous, I don't need the money or the house. Thank you, my friend. I can't speak for Jules, but please leave my share to Mrs Potter and Henry or the RSPCA, RNLI or something, but not me. I'm going to put myself on the line on this, so it's got to be clean, and if I'm a beneficiary then it puts me in a very difficult position, Jules too.'

'I've already made provision for my servants, and I haven't the time to change it again, not right now anyway.'

THE CONNECTING FLIGHT from Madrid landed at Heathrow at nine fifty on Monday morning having broken through a layer of scattered cloud. While waiting for the bags to reach the carousel, I switched on my phone. Immediately, the message tone sounded. It was the usual blurb from the phone company welcoming me back to the UK, which was quite unnecessary as I certainly wasn't interested in welcoming them. The bags were slow to arrive and by the time I had collected mine and walked out into the arrivals hall it was ten forty five. The limousine drivers were clutching capped paper mugs of coffee and holding up cards or tablets with big bold names. People waiting for their friends or family to arrive eagerly scanned the steady stream of passengers coming through the doors. There would be no one to meet me, so I fought my way through the throng as quickly as possible. The message tone sounded again. It was from Giles which was unusual as he hated texting. He said it was impersonal and fiddly to do and thoroughly irritating; a view that I echoed, which is why we talked more than typed.

'Something's up,' it read, 'meet me at the field entrance off the lane as soon as you can. Give notice this wretched way. G.' Typically, he had laboured through the keys to express himself in English rather than textish. He must have been busy and couldn't talk. And what was he doing at home on a Monday? And why had he used the phone we agreed was insecure? I replied with an estimate for the lane.

Preoccupation with the matter meant that I failed to pay much attention to the crowd around me, but a woman seated at a table as I passed Costa Coffee caught my eye, probably because her lipstick was bright red and glossy and stood out, reminiscent of that picture of Marilyn Monroe pouting. She was blonde, wearing dark glasses and head down playing with her mobile phone; in fact she looked a bit like Marilyn.

12

THE LANE LEADING towards Giles's house was not the only way of reaching it from the motorway, but it was the prettiest and carried far less traffic than the B road did. Beyond the flat ground where the lane left the main road, less than half a mile away, a wooded ridge rose steeply out of the valley. From the top, where the lane disappeared down the other side, you could see for at least ten miles to the south. Roe deer were sometimes on the lane itself or watching you from the adjacent fields. Rabbits scurried for cover in places and, sadly, there were often badgers that had been too adventurous at night lying dead to the side. It was too narrow for cars to pass, but had widened places into which folk would tuck themselves to allow the other vehicle by. Fields lay behind the hedges that bordered the lane and several had entrance gates off it, but I knew which one Giles meant. It was bigger than the rest and the steel gate was set further back, allowing probably three cars to park there, certainly two.

All the way from Heathrow I had felt uneasy for no discernible reason, but I put it behind me as I turned into the lane. It would be good to see Giles again and put our heads together to make some progress.

It had been raining the night before, there were puddles in the road and, off the tar, the dirt to the side of the passing places was churned to a soft mud from the impact of tyres. The early morning cloud layer was breaking up, and the sun shone through periodically. Another car appeared ahead and I pulled over to let it by. Her head barely above the steering wheel, the blue-rinsed driver was fiercely attentive to the clearance she had and seemed reluctant to get too close to her hedge, so I folded my mirror to create more space and she squeezed past, flapped her hand once as a wave and gave me a smile before quickly returning her intense concentration to navigating her car.

The nose of Giles's Aston Martin was visible, sticking out from the gate some time before I reached it. He wasn't in the driver's seat; he must have walked into the field. The clatter of the Land Rover's diesel would bring him back soon enough. I peered into the Aston – nothing, so I went through the gate and into the field which held broad beans so tall I couldn't see over them.

Rough grass formed a border about two metres wide along the left side of the field between the hedge and the plants. In my light travelling shoes it was an ankle twisting exercise. There was no sign of him, so I went back to try the side to the right of the gate. What the hell was he doing? Where had he gone? A massive tractor roared along the lane.

I could just see the top of the cab and the driver's head over the hedge. It was followed by another car which was invisible to me.

Trudging on over the rough ground, I saw a gap just ahead where the beans had been flattened. I was almost upon it when I saw the highly polished brown shoes.

He lay on his back, his head facing to the right. I rushed forward and knelt beside him, put a finger to his neck and found a pulse. It was weak and rapid, but it was there. He was alive! Though his face was pale and waxy, his chest rose and fell, but with a worrying lack of regularity. I stabbed 999 into my phone, my hand sticky with blood which oozed from his head and pooled in the soft ground. I ran back to the car, grabbed the first aid kit and yanked out a bandage and dressing. 'Ambulance and Police, a man's been attacked,' I shouted on the run, then more calmly gave directions.

Carefully lifting his head, I tried to stem the flow and protect the wound. His scalp had parted, and through the mess of bloodied hair broken bone was evident, like a cracked egg shell. I turned him into the recovery position, on his side and with the injury off the ground. I couldn't think what else to do, he was breathing for himself and his heart was beating, albeit weakly. His hands were cold. I didn't have a blanket, but there was a jacket in my vehicle. I ran to get it. Where was that bloody ambulance? It was taking an incredibly long time. How far did they have to come? I looked at my watch, only about five minutes had passed since I'd arrived – *Calm down, Forbes!*

He didn't seem to have any other wounds than that to his head. The cold damp ground wet my trousers when I sat next to him. I held his hand in a gesture of support, knowing it did more for me than for him. It seemed an age before the noise of the siren drifted across from the main road. 'Stick with me Giles,' I kept saying. 'Fight to stay with me, they're nearly here. They won't be long.' He couldn't hear me, of course, but it made me more comfortable knowing that I was trying to do something, even if it was pathetically useless. Up to then I had had no time to think but, during the wait, while agonising over my friend, I realised that this attack was actually an attempt to murder him.

Juliet. Her support was essential. Her strength must have been buried in my subconscious for years. I had always solved my own problems without the help of another, but this was bigger and more traumatic to me than anything else I'd experienced, and I had to share it with her. She would be even more angry if I didn't ring, in spite of her telling me not to, especially about Giles. But, as I keyed in her number, the ambulance arrived at the gate and there wasn't time to talk. I stood so they could see me and shouted. The men in green came running and dumped their cases on the ground. Standing back out of the way, I called Juliet, but only got the answering service. I left a message that something dreadful had happened and asked her to call back as soon as she could. There was nothing else I could do but wait for the police. I hate being useless.

Another siren whooped close by and wound down. Two uniformed officers came over, looked at the medics busy with Giles and then at me. 'Good morning, sir. What happened here?'

Before I could answer, a paramedic turned to the police and said, 'He needs a helicopter, NOW!' and started talking on his radio. One of the policemen ran back to his car to organise things. They would have to find a clear landing area and keep any onlookers away. The field on the other side of the lane was only grazing, and there was a gate directly opposite. That would do as a landing zone, I told them. More uniformed police arrived. There were suddenly a lot of people about and activity intensified.

'Can we start with your name and address, please.' The constable was trying to do his job in the midst of the excitement and preparation for a helicopter. There wasn't much point in telling him a long story, so I kept it to the bit which started when Giles had sent me a message on my arrival.

It looked as if they were ready to move him, as one medic went back to the ambulance and fetched a scoop stretcher. I left the constable in mid sentence and offered to help them, but they asked me nicely to move away, they could manage. 'We'll wait for the helicopter,' he said, 'It shouldn't be too long.' Two other men appeared behind me, but I ignored them. 'Is he going to be all right?' was a pretty stupid question at that stage, but it came out of worry not sense. 'Where will they take him?'

'The doctors will do their best, sir,' one said, as he arranged the scoop around my friend. 'He has a depressed and open fracture of the skull which needs surgery, urgently. They'll most probably take him to Oxford. The John Radcliffe Hospital has a major trauma centre, but if not then it'll be Southampton.'

'May we have a word, sir? Mr Alastair Forbes, is that correct?' A tall thin man was regarding me with dark brown eyes. He was dressed smartly in a grey suit with a navy tie decorated with little red diamond shaped icons. He held up a warrant card, and behind him the other man waved his above his boss's shoulder. 'I'm Detective Chief Inspector Carter and this is Detective Sergeant Vale. If you would just confirm your name and address for starters.'

I was worried and couldn't be bothered with this detail. But I was probably going to see quite a bit of these two, so I curbed my impatience.

DS Vale had the complexion of someone in his mid thirties, but already his light brown hair was thinning and receding. His suit was shiny and ill fitting on his tall, wiry frame. It was tight across the shoulders, but hung sack-like below there, giving the impression that he was ordered to be smart, but he didn't know how, it wasn't in his nature. He had his note book out and carefully wrote down my details. Once again, I went through what had happened that morning, leaving out nothing that I could remember.

'What I've just told you is a fraction of the story behind this, and I would like to relate the whole thing and tell you who I think is responsible.'

'We'd very much like to hear that, sir,' said Vale pleasantly, tapping his pencil on the cover of the notebook, 'but we'd be more comfortable down at the station.' He turned to lead the way back to the gate, but I wanted to remain close to Giles for as long as I could and stayed put.

'Look,' I said, 'I've been travelling for nearly 24 hours. I'm very tired and I feel very dirty, and I'm covered in my friend's blood. However, all I need is a shower and a change of clothes and then I'll be happy to help.'

'Er, I think it would be best if we took possession of your clothes,' said Carter. 'You don't live far away, we'll follow you home, then you can give us your clothes immediately and we can conduct an initial interview there.'

My suspicions rose, then subsided. Of course, I would be their first suspect. I was at the scene and was covered in blood. There was nothing for me to fear though, as I would not have tried to murder Giles in a million years. 'I want to wait for the helicopter,' I said. 'I want to see him go.'

The two detectives glanced at each other. Carter said, 'Time is important, Mr Forbes, so if we can start talking while we wait, that'll help.'

'I'll start by telling you who's who. That's better than introducing them as they feature. First there's Sandra, his wife.' I explained who everyone in the saga was, their relationship to each other and what they did, as well as managing to give a brief personal opinion of their characters before we heard the helicopter approaching. Back at the gate, we could see into the opposite field.

The pilot circled the area once, inspecting the landing ground before making a careful approach. The fuselage disappeared behind the hedge, but the rotors were still visible and the roar of the engines was hardly dimmed. I wasn't really watching from a professional perspective, but could not help analysing it. The landing was quick, he wouldn't have wanted to dwell in the hover, being worried about damage from the debris thrown up by the downwash. It was mostly grass, though, which quickly fell out of sight. The engines whined down to silence and two men in flight suits rushed over to Giles. They checked the work of the ambulance medics and made sure he was ready to be transported. He was carried, strapped to a stretcher, through the gate, out of my sight and into the next field. It wasn't long before the familiar sound of a turbine engine starting wound up from a low pitch through a higher whine and into a constant roar, covering the noise of the second engine's start. We watched as the machine rose amid another smattering of grass and quickly left the scene. When it turned north, I knew it was going to be Oxford.

I took a deep breath – so much energy left my body with that exhalation. I was tired from travelling anyway and probably had been running on adrenalin while everything was going on, but now it had subsided and the shock was beginning to set in. 'Thank you, Chief Inspector. Shall we go?'

The lane was now full of vehicles and more people were coming into the field, SOCOs I supposed, Scene Of Crime Officers in their protective overalls. Carter climbed up into the passenger seat of the Defender. They obviously weren't going to let me loose on my own. I glanced at him as I looked left for traffic. He had a distinct roman nose and a pale face topped by thick, mouse coloured hair formed in a widow's peak. He appeared to be about forty five, older than I was anyway. He caught me looking at him before I turned away, which was embarrassing, my being in a disadvantageous position.

Several vehicles were pulled well into the passing places along the route so getting out of the lane back onto the main road didn't take too long. At home, I greeted Tina who jumped up enthusiastically and sniffed the blood on my shirt. Janet, the cleaning lady, was upstairs judging by the noise of the vacuum cleaner. Vale drove the police car in behind mine, and when he was inside I offered them coffee and waved a hand towards the stairs. 'I'll get Janet to make it.'

'Mind if we look around, sir?' said Vale, but he was already nosing about the lounge and was moving towards my office.

'Feel free,' I said, 'but the place is still disorganised after the burglary. I reported it and your people came out straight away. It was just over a week ago, on the eighth.'

Janet took one look at me and went white at the sight of all the blood. I calmed her down and, without saying what it was all about, asked her to make some coffee for everyone. A shower never felt better. Teeth cleaned and body refreshed, I bundled up my stained clothes and shoes and handed them over to Vale who checked that everything was there and put it in a large plastic bag. Janet hovered around in the kitchen, pottering about and doing nothing. Her curiosity was so obvious, it was almost amusing.

'Am I going to have to leave here?' I asked Carter.

'That depends, Mr Forbes. Did you assault Mr Collins?'

He had to ask that. If I had admitted it, he would have had to arrest me and my own question would be answered. 'No, I didn't. It's just that I'd like to ask Janet there if she could finish for the day and go home.'

When she had left, probably to tell the entire village that I was in some kind of trouble with the police, we sat down and I told the detectives an abbreviated version of the whole story from the very start. Vale was taking notes furiously. Carter said, 'This is developing into a long and complicated story. We'll have to do this more formally down at the station, Mr Forbes. It incriminates other people in a conspiracy – we need to get it on tape and get a written statement from you.'

'I understand, but do we have to do that now? Quite frankly, I don't feel up to it. I'm dog tired and am worried sick about my friend.'

He looked at me for a long moment, sizing me up, then said, 'Time is of the essence in solving crimes, Mr Forbes. I'd really appreciate it if you could come to the station within the next two hours?' He put it as a request, but it felt more like an order. 'We'll treat you to a late lunch in the canteen,' he added with a slight smile.

'Two hours, I'll be there.'

As soon as they left, I phoned the hospital in Oxford, but they could only tell me that Giles was in surgery and there was no news. Then I called Juliet again, but still got the answering service. It was difficult to get to sleep, but eventually I went down into some abyss for forty minutes, disturbed by images of broken skulls and blood and sticky hair.

I was about to get into the Land Rover when the house phone rang. Juliet had the no-nonsense voice of a strict teacher. 'Alastair, it's me. What's the matter?'

'Jules! I'm sorry to call you when you asked me not to, but you'll want to know this. Someone's tried to kill Giles!'

'Oh God! Is he all right? What happened?'

I told her briefly and was adding that it was certainly Tony Wiggins that had done it when she interrupted, 'Oh God, this is awful! Poor Giles.' She sounded angry, and from her tone was controlling her tears.

'I'm coming down. Two of us will be better than one,' she said and put the phone down. That was a surprise. I was delighted but worried, she had not given me a chance to explain the situation I was in, nor that I was bound to be the prime suspect for a while at least.

13

I ASKED THE policeman at the front desk for DCI Carter and gave my name. Vale appeared a few minutes later, said good afternoon rather curtly and led the way to an interview room. He asked if I wanted tea.

'Black please, no sugar – thanks.'

I was left alone. The room was Spartan, about ten foot square with a Formica topped table and four chairs, which weren't comfortable. There was a tape recorder at the end next to the wall which had a No Smoking sign on it and a window higher up, which was closed. It didn't look as if it had been opened in years. It was hot and airless. There was a fan in the corner which spluttered still after a weak attempt to turn when I switched it on. A large clock on the wall ticked every second off loudly. About ten minutes later the door opened and Carter came in followed by Vale with my tea and a paper cup of his own.

'Rested?' said Carter without any noticeable interest. He had a glass of water in his hand, and I wished I'd taken that option. 'I'm sorry about the temperature in this room,' he said taking off his jacket, 'but the other one is occupied.'

'I tried the fan.'

He gave a brief thin smile. 'Budget cuts.' He sat down opposite me, and Vale took the chair next to him and closest to the tape recorder.

'Have you heard from the hospital? I tried to get an answer before I left home, but they said he was still in surgery.'

'Mr Collins is suffering from a serious head injury,' Carter said. 'He's now in an induced coma. It could be months before they can bring him out of it.' His eyes were steady on mine as they searched my reactions – or was I being paranoid? I glanced at Vale. He too was observing me closely – well, that's what they did, wasn't it? Nevertheless, they made me feel guilty, even if I wasn't.

Carter stood a file on its end and tapped it on the table top to align the papers. 'What condition he'll be in when they bring him out of the coma is uncertain, I understand.'

Vale switched on the tape recorder, checked it was running and said, 'Interview of Alastair Andrew Forbes started at 1412 hours on the seventeenth of September. Detective Chief Inspector James Carter and Detective Sergeant Harry Vale.' He looked at me dispassionately. 'For the tape. State your name and address, please.'

I started my story from the beginning, following the chronological order and leaving nothing out except for the details of my time in Chile. I explained my relationship with Giles and tried to make them understand the depth of my feelings for him as a friend. Then I went back to the first meeting with Sandra as Angela Parsons and gave my suspicions of how she knew I would be there, drawing attention to Tony Wiggins for following me. When it came to the second escapade with her, I told them how her attitude had changed, that there was a hidden and vindictive side to her that was certainly not there on the first occasion, although she had showed it at dinner. Then I pointed out my torn ear and showed them the now yellowing bruise on my shoulder.

There was a subtle change in the attitude of these two detectives that afternoon compared with the morning at the scene and in my house, when they had been businesslike but still displayed a touch of sympathy. Now, there was an element of suspicion in their questions. Carter smiled occasionally and inclined his head as if in understanding, but Vale was almost antagonistic. I had the feeling he would like to bully me if he had the chance. I instinctively liked Carter and it was important to me that he felt the same way, even though he would certainly be far too professional to let such a factor influence his conclusions. I wiped the sweat off my forehead with a handkerchief. Were the hot and stuffy conditions a deliberate part of their interrogation technique? Why was I being treated as more of a suspect than in the morning? Something had changed while I'd been asleep. I had to retain the confidence that I was innocent, and the truth would inevitably win.

'Let's go back over a number of points, if you don't mind.' Always polite, Carter, appearing to ask for my approval. 'You say that Mr Collins sent you a text for the meeting in the lane?'

'Yes, but I tend to take unnecessary stuff off my phone. I deleted it.'

'That's unfortunate, because there's no record on Mr Collins' phone of his message to you or your reply.'

'I had to have some arrangement in order to meet him, so I suspect Sandra sent that text on Giles's phone and then deleted it.' I was tired and not thinking properly, so the obvious answer took a moment. 'Hang on a minute; Giles would not have sent that message on his usual phone. I told you we agreed to use the pay-as-you-go ones between us, but Sandra couldn't have known that, and she would use the one she knows about. Can't you check with the mobile operator?'

He nodded. 'We will.' They both began asking questions to which I had already supplied answers, 'just to be sure. I felt that they were trying to have me contradict myself, which wasn't going to happen because I was telling them the truth. There was a cobweb in the corner of the shelf above the tape recorder. A fly struggled vainly to extricate itself, rested and tried again, but the web held fast. Hopefully, that wasn't symbolic.

'You claim that Mr Collins told you he had an argument with his wife the night before, in which he told her he was thinking of taking her out of his will, but that he already had and left everything to you and Miss Meredith.'

'Yes.' It was obvious where this was going. 'If Sandra thought he would take her out of the will, then she had a strong motive to kill him before he did so, but she would have to be quick about it.'

'Well, because we can't waste time in an investigation of this nature, while you were resting we interviewed Mrs Collins. She claims that her husband told her that he had already left his entire estate to you. If that was the case, then she had no motive for his assault. She is devastated, by the way.'

I shrugged, 'Well, that's not what he told me on two counts. First, it was that the estate was left to both Miss Meredith and myself, not me alone, so she's mistaken there. Second is that he definitely told her that he had not yet changed the will. I'm sorry, I can only tell you what I know is correct and what I believe to be true. If she contradicts some things then it's in your hands to determine who is telling the truth. And, Chief Inspector, if Giles took her out of his will, that is surely evidence of the bad feelings between them that would hardly have left her 'devastated', as you put it. That woman is more likely to be devastated over being deprived of his estate.'

Irritatingly, Vale was lightly and rapidly drumming his fingers on the desk. 'Just what is your relationship with Ms Meredith, how strong is it?' he asked, using the neutral title rather than the older man's more defining, 'Miss'.

'Up until a week ago it was about as strong as it could possibly be. That was until I told her about Sandra Collins. What's that got to do with it?' I knew the reason the moment I asked the question.

'It means that Ms Meredith could be part of a scheme between you, of course.'

'You can leave her out of this, she has nothing to do with it.' I was feeling increasingly hot and short of breath in the stuffy atmosphere and was conscious that my irritation at all this was beginning to show in my answers.

Carter interrupted, 'Mrs Collins also claims that the first encounter you say you had with her never occurred, and she has an alibi for that evening.'

'Provided, no doubt, by both Tony and Mandy Wiggins'. I needed to get a better grip of myself, I was giving sour, adverse reactions to this line of questioning which seemed to me to favour Sandra's view. 'I'd like to make another point, which I forgot earlier, please.' I paused until Carter glanced up with a questioning look and went on, 'Giles told me that Sandra was married to another wealthy man before. Giles met him once and he told my friend that she was a vicious gold-digger who took him for almost everything he had. You can verify that if you find a man called Parsons who works in the City. You'll recall that Sandra first introduced herself to me as Angela Parsons, which happens to be her maiden name as well. She never officially changed it to Collins.'

Carter made a note in his book then motioned to Vale who briefly left the room to returned with a long transparent bag. He placed it on the table between us, his eyes never leaving me. Closest to me was the end of a stick, but light from the window glinted off the plastic at the other end and I couldn't see clearly what it was. I picked it up to avoid the reflection and take a closer look.

It was my knobkerrie, and the head was smeared with blood.

'You recognise this club.' It was a statement from Vale not a question. 'It has your initials on the shaft under the head. Is it yours?'

I set it down, making sure it was lying at precisely ninety degrees to the table, taking my time. 'Yes, it's mine. Where did you get it?' *Bloody hell!* They had a motive and they had a weapon and both were mine. This was serious. To calm myself, I gave them an explanation. 'Technically, it's a knob-kerrie, a club used by mainly Southern African tribes, particularly Zulus, as a weapon along with a short spear and a cow hide shield. The image of a Zulu warrior dressed like that is common.'

'It was thrown into the hedgerow not far from the scene,' said Carter. His words were matter of fact and lacked any emotion in contrast to Vale's obvious dislike of me.

I took a deep breath and swallowed. 'It must have been stolen during that robbery, but I didn't miss it. Thinking about it later, I'd seen something else in his hand before he tried to hit me the second time.' A positive clue at last. 'This means that the same person who broke into my house hit Giles.'

'Possibly.' Vale again, continuing his irritating tap on the desk. Without a word Carter touched the Sergeant's offending arm. Vale quickly withdrew his hand to below the table and said, 'But you could have dropped in at home and picked it up before going to meet your friend, or had it in your car already.'

'I could not have taken that to Chile with me because I had no reason to and there's airport security, and I hand my car over to parking attendants. I remove all items of value, obviously, and that has some sentimental value. Also, I went straight from the airport to the field. There would not be enough time for me to go home first. You can work it out if you want.' I was thinking out loud so my reply was scattered and confused.

'We will, you can be assured of that,' Vale said. Carter was letting him continue with his accusatory nature and keeping quiet. They weren't quite playing 'good cop, bad cop' but it seemed to me that Vale was less experienced and thought he had an arrest in the offing whereas Carter was a thinker with more years behind him, and was prepared to look for additional evidence before holding me.

Unwillingly, I found myself captured by the clock's incessant clicks. It was two hours and forty three minutes slow. Only the gravity of my situation prevented me from getting up and putting it right.

'I can see that this is not looking good for me at the moment,' I said, talking my way through my concerns and appealing to Carter's hopefully open mind, 'but Giles Collins was a very close friend. We climbed together, we shared bivouacs on sheer cliff faces together, he saved my life once. We were at varsity together, sharing digs. We got drunk and, I'm ashamed to say, annoyed the police sometimes. Our lives have been more closely intertwined than most siblings. I don't mind saying that what we feel for each other is probably more akin to love than you'll find in most marriages.' Vale's expression of disgust was blatant, and it annoyed me. 'And when I say 'love', Sergeant Vale, I don't mean homosexuality, quite the opposite, so you can take that look off your face!' He dropped the sneer and glared angrily. Carter had his head down, and I'm sure he was masking his expression.

'Look,' I went on, 'why would I kill my friend for his money? I'm certainly not as wealthy as Giles, but I earn enough to live without financial restraint and provide for my eventual retirement in comfort. You can check my accounts as I'm sure you will, I've nothing to hide, I've not got myself into debt nor made any investments I can't afford. I don't gamble. I own my house outright; no mortgage. I tried to get Giles not to leave me anything, as I told you. And why would I hit him over the head and throw the knobkerrie away so close to the scene? I'd be stupid to do something like that – and then call 999.'

Carter watched me rant without any apparent feeling. 'You'd be surprised at the number of double bluffs that criminals try on us.'

They had me worried. 'Do I need a solicitor? I don't have one.'

'Not yet, Mr Forbes, but I suggest you alert one. You are currently under suspicion for attempted murder. You should not leave the country and should remain available for further questioning, and I would like you to hand in your passport, please. I'll send an officer to follow you to your house to collect it. When is your next trip to Chile planned?'

'About four weeks time, but I can shift it as long as I give them enough notice.'

They gathered their stuff together on the table. 'Thank you Mr Forbes, you've been most helpful,' said Carter.

'I can't say it was a pleasure, but nevertheless I'll continue to give you my full cooperation.'

As I walked down the corridor ahead of them, I heard Vale say, 'Why don't we arrest him now, sir?' Carter's reply was inaudible.

Driving home with the police car never out of my rear view mirror, I tried to work out what was going on. If I was Carter with the evidence that he had against me, I would have myself arrested and charged. The fact that he didn't meant that there was an element of doubt I wasn't aware of. The trouble was that in spite of watching all sorts of crime drama on television, I really didn't know how the police worked at all and felt well out of my depth. What I did realise was that there was limited time left to prove Wiggins's involvement in the robbery and the attack before I was arrested. With Wiggins would follow Sandra, the composer, the conductor and the driving force. Giles had commented how she was always one step ahead, well now it was another two: a false alibi and a lie about the will.

I WAS EVEN more tired after that experience, but I had to go and see how Giles's servants were coping. They were both a significant part of his life, having worked on the estate for decades, and were entitled to know what was going on. I could not visit them if Sandra was there, but from the gate I could see that her garage door was open and no Porsche was inside.

Mrs Potter was a round, matronly woman with a cheery disposition – normally. She looked terrible when she opened the door, her eyes red-rimmed and her mouth downturned. 'Oh Mr Alastair,' she cried, and promptly burst into tears while I was still standing on the step. I put my arm around her and drew her close. Her head only came up to my shoulder. She pulled out a little lace trimmed handkerchief, blew her nose and sniffed. Henry appeared in the hall looking just as grim. He came over and took Mrs Potter from me.

'Terrible, terrible, Mr Alastair, sir. Why, why? He was such a good man.' He was shaking his head in utter incomprehension.

'Is, Henry,' I said, 'is. He's not dead and he may have a full recovery, but it will take a long time. Are you busy? I would like to talk to both of you. May we go to the kitchen, and I'm sure you'll make us some tea, Mrs Potter?'

'Of course, sir.' She brightened a little, glad to have something to do.

Seated at the kitchen table, we clasped mugs of tea, but none of us felt like the biscuits that Mrs Potter put out. It was interesting that she would serve me tea from a pot into cups in the living room, but we had mugs in the kitchen. It was always warm in there with the Aga going, and I shed my jacket.

'I'd better tell you that I'm a suspect for this attack,' I said.

'No, sir. Not you. You're his very best mate, you're like brothers you two. They've got that wrong, very wrong,' Henry replied.

Mrs Potter just sat there shaking her head in disbelief and muttering, 'Very wrong, very wrong.'

'Well, I didn't do it, just to reassure you, and I'm sure it will be cleared up in the end. Anyway, the reason I came is to find out how you're getting along and to discuss the future. Mr Giles might not recover to a normal state for a long time, possibly a couple of years, and we need to think about that.'

Mrs Potter gasped, and Henry shook his head again. He was hunched over the table and holding his mug in two hands as if trying to warm them.

'While he does recover, he's going to need a lot of looking after, and I want to know if you'll be comfortable with a part in that process?'

'Of course, Mr Alastair.'

'Of course, sir.' Mrs Potter repeated.

'But,' Henry added, 'Mrs Collins told us there was no need for us to stay on now that this "accident", as she put it, had happened. She said that if he recovered then he would not need a house like this, and therefore she was going to sell it straight away and there would be no need for us to continue, and she did that this afternoon. He was only attacked this morning. Mr Alastair, neither of us can understand this. People don't do things like this, not normal people. She gave us a month's notice. This has been my home for over thirty years.'

'Forty years I've had here,' Mrs Potter added in support. 'I still remember when young Giles was born.'

My mind raced over the options, these two had been at the house long enough to have a moral right to at least pass an opinion on the future of it. 'All right, Henry. I must admit that attitude is pretty unbelievable, but please don't worry. Firstly, I'm sure that she'll not be able to sack you just like that, there are laws about dismissal. Also, I'll go and see Giles's solicitor and discuss it with him. I'll see if he can provide money to continue to pay you both a retainer until this is sorted out. If I had power of attorney over Giles's estate I would do just that, but I don't, and I wouldn't get it under the present circumstances. If that's not possible then I will loan you both some money to stay on, but it will only be the bare minimum, I'm afraid.'

'That's very good of you sir,' Henry said, 'but speaking for myself, I've money put away for a rainy day.'

Mrs Potter followed him, 'Very good of you, sir, but I won't be relying on anyone else.'

'The offer is there and won't be withdrawn.'

'I have to say Mr Alastair, sir.' Henry was hesitant. He was speaking with his head bent over and staring into his mug. 'I shouldn't speak ill of people, but I never took to Mrs Collins at all. She was always offhand to us, rude sometimes, like we're beneath her. Seldom a "good morning", never a good word.'

Mrs Potter shook her head. 'No, never a good word.'

'You know what I say, Mr Alastair, I think she was born working class like us, but she's made some money and she thinks that puts her above us now. And she was always fighting with Mr Giles. It was her that picked the fights, not him. He was far too forgiving. I don't think she's a nice person, sir. And to just turf us out after all these years without so much as a kind word … It's not right, sir.'

'Like Henry says, she's no manners, never a good word. It's not right.'

'No, it's not right, but we'll sort it out. Fortunately you both have other homes to go to, but you still have a month here, and I believe we'll know what Giles's future will be before that time is up.'

I left them alone amid profuse thanks and good wishes, and drove slowly home. If there had been anything more which was necessary to endorse my already rock-bottom opinion of Sandra's character, the last half hour had been it. An ever-present threat lurking in the background, she would be calculating and refining her next unexpected and appalling move for personal gain. So far, her reach had touched Giles, Mrs Potter, Henry and me; Juliet too, although that was my doing more than Sandra's. Thank goodness Juliet had been up north over the past week. For a brief moment I wished she would stay out of harm's way.

14

'IT'S THAT SAME man again about Collins,' the ward sister said, apparently lowering the phone but failing to cover the mouthpiece. 'Won't you talk to him?'

There was some muffled exchange, then a doctor who was obviously harassed and did not want to take the time to talk to interfering friends of the injured took the phone. He was blunt. 'Look Mr Forbes, I understand your concern, but Mr Collins is in an induced coma to lower the pressure in his brain. It may be many weeks before we can very slowly bring him out of it. In the meantime there is not going to be any quick or dramatic improvement. To be frank, and I'm sorry to have to put it like this, for you to call in so often when we know there will be no change is not only frustrating for you, but it is also disruptive for the staff here who need to get on with caring for a lot of very traumatised people.'

That was a telling off. 'Oh, I'm sorry,' I said. 'I didn't think, I'm worried. Stupid. Sorry.'

Juliet came in the front door at that moment. She put her case down, hung up her jacket and came straight over to me. Her familiar black jeans and leather boots were topped by a deep green polo shirt. She never seemed able to get all the mud off those boots. I liked that in a way, it showed she was not concerned with fashion as much as with practicality. Without a word she put both her hands around my upper arm. Her head was close to my shoulder. The physical contact banished my anxiety over what attitude she might have, and I dropped my chin into the cool raindrops on her hair. She quickly dropped her hands – they had merely been a gesture of support – and stepped away. Nothing had changed.

The doctor was still talking, and I held the phone off my ear so that Juliet could hear. 'Never mind, Mr Forbes. If you will just give me your phone number, I'll ensure that it's put down as a primary contact in the event of a change; after his wife and the police, of course.'

After the police. Of course, what else? 'Are we able to visit him?'

In the background we could hear another phone ringing and the bustle and voices of busy staff. 'I understand from Inspector er......'

'Carter.'

'Carter, yes. ....in charge of the case, that visitors will be allowed when we think he's stable enough, and only with his permission. There's been an attempt on his life, so there's a level of security regarding Mr Collins. In the meantime we are monitoring him continuously.'

'I think Inspector Carter will allow me in,' I said. 'May I just come to see him? I know he'll be unconscious, but he's more than a brother to me. I'll stay outside the room if that's necessary.'

The doctor gave an audible sigh. 'It will be necessary, but please wait until next week. You can ask Inspector Carter, and he can let the ward sister know. Now, please excuse me I have patients.' He put the phone down without waiting for my answer.

Juliet's voice was filled with anguish. 'Poor Giles. Why? He's such a lovely man! He's good and kind and fun. Why would anyone do this?'

There was no point in explaining, it was a rhetorical question to which she already knew the answer. At that point I was fretting because she had moved away. The pause in conversation dragged on. A bit later, she went back to the door and removed her boots.

'I need to update you,' I said, as much to keep a dialogue flowing as to the necessity for an explanation. 'Things have changed.' I outlined the situation I was in as the prime suspect for the attack and why. 'I'm afraid that you're also involved. Giles rewrote his will and divided his estate into portions for the servants and the substantial remainder split between you and I. That has already raised questions from the police about our relationship and whether there might be collusion between us in the attempt on Giles's life.'

'God, what a mess,' she said, staring out of the window. She knelt down to Tina curled up in her basket and stroked the dog's ears. 'It's all over your head, isn't it? You lucky thing.'

The following silence was tense; it wasn't the comfort of two people in agreement maintaining their peace. Juliet was looking around the room. In the past I would have imagined she was surveying the things she liked and disliked and suggested how they should be changed. That interest was wasted now, she seemed to be thinking, it's all gone, thrown away, discarded. Eventually, I summoned the courage to ask the question burning its way through my mind. 'Jules, where do we stand? I need to know – now.'

Her eyes were sad, but her tone hardened. 'You have hurt me, Alastair. You've betrayed my trust in you. You had me miles high on a pinnacle of happiness, then you pushed me off. A mere week passes and you want my forgiveness?' She was shaking her head slowly in bafflement. 'Have you no sense of what you've done, of how I feel? If all you're thinking about is your own misery and loss, then you have at last shown your true selfish nature, and we are finished.'

I couldn't meet her eyes, I had never seen her so upset. For a moment I really didn't know what to say or do. Eventually, I stopped staring at my feet and looked up into her face. 'Jules, I do understand what I've done to you. We've been so close that your feelings were my feelings too. It's been your hurt that has stopped me sleeping, not mine. My mind has been in a turmoil as I've tried to think how to make it better for you, to regain what I've ripped apart. I'm sorry for asking you now, I didn't think about the short time that's passed. So much has happened in the last week that time has been distorted. It's just that I'm desperate to see you happy and have you back again.

'I can't summon the words to express how stupid I was to get drunk and fall for that woman. The only argument I have is that it was pure lust, certainly there was no feeling there. I let you down and I have to live with the guilt of that for the rest of my life. It can't be undone and it won't go away. All I can say is that, if you let me back in your life it will never happen again. It's just too painful for us both. Beyond endless repetitions of regret and "I'm sorry", please tell me what I can do to regain your trust.'

In the lengthy pause that followed I despaired of righting this wrong. It stifled my ability to breathe. I tried to prepare myself for the words she would use to end everything there was between us, everything we had spent in building what I had thought was an unbreakable partnership; and we hadn't even had to put any effort into it, it had seemed as natural as an oak growing – big and strong.

Her voice was softer, she sounded exhausted, and I wondered how much she had slept recently. 'Right now Alastair, there's nothing. I'm living in what feels like a capsule of shock that is floating around in space without direction. I feel isolated from the rest of the world, I'm numb and not thinking a full range of thoughts about anything, not even on how to escape from it. I'm staying with my sister. Mary says time will sort it out, and she's probably right. I don't know how long it's going to be, but you know me, I will eventually be quite clear about what we'll do. I can't forgive you yet, and maybe not ever.'

'You know I love you,' I said. There was no point in trying to reinforce my position.

She was oblivious to my words. 'I came down here again for the two men who made my life so rich for a while, particularly for Giles who is the greater victim of all this. I felt so bad after I told him I was with you. It hurt him, I know, so I came here because I felt I had to give him support somehow, as well as to honour past loyalties. Now you tell me that I'm a beneficiary, so I have a more tangible reason to be involved. That's why I'm here. Understand that.'

The anger left her face and we stared miserably at each other across a great divide.

The jangling ring of the telephone broke our mood. ''Ullo, mate. It's 'Arry 'ere. You got into that storeroom yet?'

'Oh God! I'm sorry Harry, I haven't tried. There's been an accident and I'm a bit preoccupied at the moment, but I'll go there right now and call you back. I did sort all my keys out, so here's hoping. If I haven't the key, I promise I'll go and get another lock tomorrow.'

'Orl right, but I really need to put my stuff in there as soon as possible.'

'I'll ring you back in fifteen minutes.'

'Enough.' Juliet stood up suddenly. 'We've a job on our hands, and we have to put our heads together over what to do. What's happened between us must not interfere with that.'

'Come and see Harry's cars, you'll enjoy that.'

She was a country girl whose father had dragged her round shows and fairs exhibiting old machinery of various sorts: traction engines, steam engines and cars of which she had driven various odd specimens. Hopefully the cars would detract from her misery for a while.

With an umbrella each and a yard separating us, we walked past the big barn with its joinery and its wonderful smells of freshly cut timber and from where we had a cheery wave from John Knott, the artisan.

I unlocked the doors to the smaller barn and stood back for Juliet to enter.

'Oh wow! MGs. Almost all the old models must be here – and a Series One. How fabulous.'

I left Juliet admiring them and went to the heavy steel door at the back of the barn. None of the keys fitted, and it would not be a simple job to get the door open without a cutting torch or bolt croppers.

Harry Burbage answered the phone on the first ring from my mobile; I wanted to let him know well inside the fifteen minutes I'd promised, just to show I was better at my word than he was probably thinking. 'I'll go into town and get some bolt croppers and another lock tomorrow. Can we meet in the afternoon?'

''Bout four?' he suggested. 'I've also got fings to do, an' it'll give me time to get my stuff together and bring it over.'

Back in the house, Juliet made tea while I explained how helpless I felt and couldn't understand why the police hadn't arrested me. 'The trouble is, I have no way of knowing what's going on. Carter won't tell me anything, of course, and I have no idea how the police operate. It's so frustrating, not being able to do anything and not knowing what progress the police are making. They might be here tonight and take me away, for all I know.'

She rummaged through empty tins in the cupboard before pushing a cup of tea across the table to me. 'You've no biscuits. We must get the papers and listen to the news at every opportunity. The police make statements to the media and that will be the only source of information available to us. Did the case get into this morning's paper?'

'I don't know, I don't normally read them, but you're right, we will from now on. All I can think of is exacting revenge, making sure that Sandra and her brother are shown to be guilty.

'Giles kept saying how Sandra was always a step ahead, how she orchestrated arguments and set up situations to her advantage. She's sure to employ the same tactics with us, and we have no idea what she'll try next. Somehow we have to seize the initiative from her and have her responding to what we do, not the other way around.'

Juliet was angry and frustrated too. I could see from her pursed lips and the intensity in her eyes that she was now on a mission. She desperately wanted to punish the culprits who had hurt her friend, but didn't know how to. She was an incredibly positive person and usually had several ideas at once to solve a problem. She would come up with a daft one on the spur of the moment then settle into analysing a more sensible and practical solution.

'We should send them a note, one of those ones made of newspaper cuttings stuck on a sheet of paper. Or better, I've a friend with an old typewriter. We could use that and they would never trace it to us.'

I sighed inwardly, this was going to be one of her daft notions. 'And say what? In any case, they would know it came from me. I'm the only other person who knows the truth, and it would just encourage Wiggins to more violence.'

'The idea,' she said, as if talking to an imbecile, 'would be to spook them into making a mistake and bring them out into the open. We would then be confident that it was them and not some other bloody awful person.' She perked up as her idea developed. 'Aunt Alice could say she was watching birds up on the hill with her binoculars, when she saw him hit Giles with a club and then run away. She could say that she could identify him and would go to the police, but needs money for an operation or something, and he must give her, er..... fifty thousand by the end of the week, or something like that?'

I played along. The last thing I wanted to do was destroy the partnership that would hopefully build through our co-operation. 'Jules, what if they ignore the letter and bluff it out? We won't be able to do anything because you can't identify Wiggins in a line up, you're biased, and in any case the police will find out you were never there but in Yorkshire at the time. And, what do we do if they fall for it and pay the blackmail? We need to have answers to both those questions before we decide on this or any other plan like it.

'I could break into his house and burn it down.' My grumbling was stupid, but I carried on anyway. 'I could also give him a severe beating, but all that would achieve is a great deal of satisfaction and it would be criminal. I can't afford to do anything illegal, I'm already standing on melting ice with my legs either side of a razor's edge.'

Juliet ignored the pitiful attempt at humour. 'I could make the letter sound as if it was written by an elderly lady twitcher. We could do it now, put it on a flash drive and have it printed in an internet cafe, avoiding use of your printer which might be identified. I don't know, can they identify printers?'

I suddenly saw that this might not be such a silly idea after all. 'It will only be worthwhile if we can hack all their mobile phones: Sandra's, Tony's and Mandy's, because their reaction to the letter is bound to be discussed and we might be able to get Wiggins's location.'

'Hacking's illegal, don't you pay attention to anything in the news?' Her curtness was wounding.

'Sandra knew that you existed, and Giles swears he never mentioned you to her, so I have a strong feeling that my phone is being monitored. I'll bet we can find a private sleuth that will do it for enough money and keep quiet about it. With the information from telephone calls it'll be worthwhile and there's no reason for the details to come out in court. I'll do some research now while you work on the letter.'

I made us a salad to share and we munched on that as Detective Chief Inspector Carter gave a briefing on the lunch-time news. He said what a shocking and savage attack it was and that the police were doing everything in their power to bring the culprit to justice. Already they had interviewed two persons and their inquiries were continuing. It was still early in the investigation, but they were confident that an arrest would be made in the near future. He made the usual plea for any witnesses to come forward, and I thought of the old lady that had squeezed her car past mine in the lane.

'Interviewed two persons?' I said. 'Why only two, we know that was Sandra and me, why haven't they talked to Wiggins?'

'He must be hiding.'

'I know why I haven't been arrested!' We were then looking at the video footage of the reporter in the bean field where the attack had taken place, and could see how the whole area outside the police tape behind him had been trampled down by the ambulance crew, all the police activity and the press now that the SOCOs had finished. 'His feet left impressions in the ground before mine and everyone else's. Carter knows there was another person involved before I got there. Great! Once they eventually find him they can connect him through the footprints.

'I think we should hand deliver this letter of yours to be absolutely certain it gets there when we want it to. The trouble is we don't even know where he lives.'

'I do,' she said with only a trace of smugness. 'I found out while I was researching his relationship to Sandra.'

In the end, after half an hour composing the letter, Juliet decided that we should not have the phones hacked. She pointed out that the police could do it better with their resources as well as legally with a warrant and, given that Anthony Wiggins had gone missing, they would almost certainly be doing it already.

I disagreed. 'The letter will have no benefit to us on its own. We may stir up a hornets' nest and not know about it. Tapping the phones will forewarn us of any adverse reaction from them and hopefully help us find the man. We can't guarantee that Carter will tap the phones, and I want to know as soon as possible where Wiggins is. I want to get to him before the police do.'

'That's a silly attitude,' she said. 'Being focused on revenge is detracting from solving this, and it will lead you into all sorts of trouble.'

I didn't respond to that. In any case, after an age of research, I eventually had to give in and drop the idea of hacking. 'It seems easy enough to buy software that you can use to monitor someone's phone for messages, but what we want is to listen to the actual conversations, and you can't do that without installing an app on the target phone. That then links to your computer and you can listen in to the recording it leaves. That's almost impossible to do as we would never get to all their phones. It is, as you pointed out, illegal, and it would be daft to tempt fate considering that it's possible for the authorities to trace the origin of the spying.'

Juliet followed me when I went to the kitchen to make coffee. 'So,' I said, 'let's look at how we can get the best out of this letter. In simple terms, if they fall for it, then Aunt Alice will have to give instructions on where and when to drop the money. We can be sure that their aim will be to identify Alice and then get rid of her, and there will be at least three of them watching. I mean that Wiggins might have another bloke he could call on to help as well as Sandra and his wife, Mandy.'

'Then we have to make sure that Alice is protected when she picks up the money.'

'I've already got an idea on that. I wouldn't mind betting that they won't leave real money, though, they'll leave a bag of newspaper or something. Their aim will be to get to Alice and they won't need to use money for that. They only need to identify her.'

'What happens if they ignore the threat and come after you?'

'Well in that case, there's not much we can do. Alice can send them another letter, a final warning, but in the end we're powerless and will have to trust the police to do their job.

'Unlike her thuggish brother, Sandra is anything but stupid, and if she is directing operations she'll know that every move they make will be yet another opportunity for clues to be left, clues that the police will eventually put to-gether. She'll realise it's a downward spiral, so I don't think they'll take any action with me until they're sure that Alice doesn't exist and has not gone to the police. And that will be after an amount of time. Also, why would they have a go at me when I'm a leading suspect? They would reduce my profile of guilt. I don't think they can afford to ignore the letter, though, do you?'

Juliet finalised the note and agreed with me that it needed to be hand delivered to be read as early as possible. She had done a convincing job of emulating an ageing female twitcher, and we felt it looked authentic:

"Hello.

On Monday morning I was out on the ridge amongst the chestnut trees, trying to spot a turtle dove that frequents the area at this time of year, and my friend is convinced she's seen it there. It will soon migrate south as the weather cools, so it was important to me that I went out now while the weather is good to try and see it. Anyway, I was sitting in the grass in a spot where there were no nettles (don't you think that the population of nettles is growing every year? Blasted things!) I was looking down into the trees below me on the slope through my binoculars. I've a lovely pair that were given to me by my late husband, they are made by Zeiss and very powerful. Germans are so good at that sort of thing, are they not?

I was looking for the bird when just at the edge of my view I saw a silver sports car drive into the field below me. Being curious as to why someone would stop there in such a car, I focused on it. I saw you hit another man over the head with some sort of club. It was a vicious blow and I gasped in shock and surprise and dropped the binoculars. When I had them again and looked down to the car once more, I was trembling and could hardly see properly, but I soon had a clear view of you, and the other man was lying in the beans, I could just see his feet sticking out. You threw the club away and ran off. Then another man came along in a Jeep and found the body. He used his phone, for the police I suppose. I was frightened as I wasn't sure where you were so I left as fast as I could.

The thing is that I know you, and I would recognise you again. I know where you live, it's near me, and I've seen you about, but I don't know your name. I could ask the postman, and he'd tell me, but I don't think that would be a problem for the police either, do you?

I haven't told the police yet because I have some debt that my dear husband left me with that has to be settled, but I don't have the money for it. I don't want much, because I don't want to be greedy, I just need help. Let us say £20,000. If you pay me this within a week, I will not say a word. That's a promise.

You gather the money together by Friday and I'll let you know how to pay me later on. I won't tell you where to find me because you're plainly a murderer and you might try to kill me! I may be elderly but I'm not stupid.

Alice"

'Well done Miss Alice, well done. Very nicely put. Let's hope they fall for it and start talking to one another.'

She didn't respond to my tone. 'Have you organised a solicitor?'

'No, I meant to, but there hasn't been time. I've no idea who, so I'll have to call the chap Giles was using for his will, Julian Brady, and ask him to recommend someone.'

'Call him now,' she said. 'It's only just gone five and he should still be in the office, unless he's playing golf or something.'

Julian Brady listened to my sorry story. He knew me and knew how close Giles and I were. It was important to me to have some support, for someone other than Juliet to believe me, but he was involved in Giles's affairs and was not going to offer any opinions. He suggested two names, but by the time we had finished talking both of them had left the office. First thing in morning it would have to be.

15

JULIET TYPED THE letter onto a memory stick that contained a portable, open-source word processing programme. We reckoned that by doing that there would be no trace of the letter left on her laptop, although whether that was true, we really didn't know. Then, to protect against fingerprints by wearing a pair of white cotton gloves, she went into an internet cafe and printed it. To the assistant's inquiring look at her gloves, she merely said 'eczema' and put the sheet of paper into an equally sterile envelope.

The previous day's rain had vanished, but pale grey clouds hung overhead as we drove to the area of the Wiggins's house while it was still light. They lived in No. 13, a modest semi-detached place in a long row of similar buildings on Willow Street, which did not have, nor ever likely to have, any willows on it. The road led off Forest Avenue and was situated about half way up a small hill, curving gently around it before joining the main road. Two other, progressively longer streets did the same thing below it. All the odd numbered houses were on the uphill side of the streets. Behind the house was woodland stretching to the hilltop on which sat a mobile phone mast and a large concrete water reservoir.

We were in Juliet's Volvo, because my Land Rover would have been far too obvious and recognisable. She was keeping her eyes out for police in any shape or form who might be watching the house for Wiggins. I was looking for CCTV cameras that might be strategically placed on the street and only found one at the junction where Willow Street met the main road.

Juliet's mood had improved slightly, probably as a result of doing something positive. Nevertheless, I kept my distance, difficult though it was. She wanted little to do with me, yet I wanted everything to do with her and the resulting tension was uncomfortable.

'I can't see anybody who looks like a copper in disguise,' she said, 'whatever they may look like.'

'Let's go round the other crescents just to lose a bit of time, then back round Willow the other way. The reflection is stopping us seeing through some of the windscreens on these parked vehicles. This time check the wing mirrors for any sign of a driver.'

Juliet said, 'If Wiggins does come home occasionally, he's going to use the woods and come in the back. The police must surely have that area under surveillance.'

'It's the obvious thing for them to do and it makes things difficult, because we'll never spot a watcher in the woods. I'm going to have to get to the house via a neighbour once it gets dark.'

There was a small white van parked about fifty metres up the road from Wiggins's house. As we drove past, Juliet exclaimed, 'There's a man in that one. He's sitting very low in his seat, I only just made him out in his mirror because he moved.'

'Keep looking, there might be others or he's not the one.'

Darkness was descending and I felt that the sun was long over the yardarm. 'We could retire to the pub for a quick one while we wait.' It was an attempt to inject some light-heartedness into the conversation. 'It would be silly to dull the senses at this stage, though. We'll just have to suffer.'

Instead, we parked on the edge of Trident Park next to a soccer pitch and discussed what to do. Even though the light was fading, some youths were kicking a ball around accompanied by a lot of shouting and swearing. We watched them until they eventually gave up. Apart from an occasional siren from an emergency vehicle and the rise and fall of engine noise in the town below, it became quite dark and peaceful.

'This is the ideal place for them to drop the money,' I said. 'Beyond these playing fields, this park is pretty big with plenty of trees, and they're all spaced well apart from each other so we can see right across the area. Do you see that telephone box under the street lamp on the far side? That can serve as one reference point. The other thing is that Wiggins lives nearby and therefore so does Auntie Alice, so she would know it well and it's a place close to home that she would choose. Let's have a quick drive around it for a preliminary recce, we can look at it in more detail in daylight tomorrow.' Although it was then dark and difficult to see, there were no obvious impediments to using Trident Park for our purposes.

Avoiding the junction with the CCTV camera, Juliet drove into the crescent below Willow and parked. We walked together until we had reached the road and then Juliet walked on, past the white van, past Wiggins's house to No. 17, two doors further on. I followed until I reached No. 5, four houses before Wiggins's and behind the van. The entrances to most of the houses were lit by porch lights or more dimly from the street lighting, but between the buildings it was dark. I pulled on my gloves and hopped over the low hedge of No. 5 to disappear into the shadows separating it from No. 7, hope-fully while the man in the white van was watching Juliet knock on the door of No. 17.

I always have difficulty in knowing what to say to strangers, but she was perfectly capable of striking up a conversation and asking where so-and-so lived, and was it the right street, and what a lovely cat and generally wasting their time. I went to the back of No. 5 and could see past several houses over the low fences. I had a sudden vision of all the women ensuring that the hanging of their washing on the line was a simultaneous act so that rich gossip could be ex-changed across the boundaries of several houses. A bonus was that neither Mrs 7 nor Mrs 9 had taken their washing in that day, which gave me good cover as I scrambled over these barriers.

Mrs 11, however, had a six foot fence enclosing her garden which would give me better cover, but I had to get over both sides without a sound. I wondered where the police watcher was placed at the back. If it were me, depending on the arc of visibility and the cover, I would have been in the trees directly opposite the back fence. If he were there, then he would not see me in No. 11 because of the high fence panels. Alternatively, he might be positioned with a line of sight directly along the row of back fences, in which case he wasn't likely to see me at all. Wherever he was, I had to consider the situation with the greatest risk.

I looked around for something substantial to stand on. There was a bicycle at the back door. That would have to do, so I took it and leaned it against the fence in the dark gap between the houses. Carefully, so as not to have a noisy accident, I climbed up the bike and was able to slither over the fence and drop down the other side. The smell of dog mess was very strong, and I had images of a vicious beast leaping on me, or many little yappers raising the dead with their shrieks.

I kept below the light from the kitchen window of No. 11 and moved back into the dark gap that separated it from Wiggins's house. One more high fence and I would be at his back door. This time there was a tree stump to step on and I climbed quickly over the top having peered around his yard. If someone was watching from the woods, he might have seen me, but it was dark enough to make that difficult, unless he had night vision goggles, of course. Once over the fence and between the buildings, I dropped to my belly and went round the front of the house towards the porch. Too low to be visible to the van behind Wiggins's hedge, I reached up and pushed the envelope into his letter box. Job done, now to get out.

Secure in the darkness at the back of the house, I paused. Low down, lower than the fence, I glimpsed the faint passing of a shadow through the bars of the back gate. A fox? A badger? A dog? Or a man on his knees? Movement gives the quarry away, movement is what alerts the hunter. Only my eyes moved as I searched for the source of the shadow. Nothing. I had to take the risk and leave immediately. If that was Wiggins, the police would be moving into position, and I could be in the way. Once again, keeping below the kitchen lights, I wormed my way round to Wiggins's far fence and slithered over it. Fortunately, the hedges between the next two properties at the back were low. Then, in full view of anyone, I stood up and walked round the front of No. 19 and out onto the road.

I heard an engine start behind me, glanced round and saw the lights of the van come on. As it pulled out into the road and the lights swung away from me, I dived over the nearest hedge and lay still. Had I been spotted by the watcher at the back who had radioed to the van, or had he seen Wiggins? The vehicle moved slowly along the road, the driver obviously looking closely for something. As it drew abreast of my position, it stopped. So did my heart. The driver got out. My breathing was too noisy. Between the thin trunks at the base of the hedge, my one eye, the other pressed against the damp ground, could just make out his legs. He walked down the road a few paces. There was a brief radio conversation that I couldn't hear. Then he returned and got back in the van. He drove down the road a little way, turned around and parked in his original spot. I breathed normally again.

Juliet was sitting in the car when I reached it. 'I was getting worried.'

'Actually, it went well, but I think I've trodden in dog poo!'

'Oh phoof! I suppose you've left a trail of doggy-do stamped with your shoe print all the way down the road.'

'Probably, but it's too late now. Just think of the fun that forensics could have with your car, identifying the type of dog, the brand of food and …'

'You're disgusting.'

Any attempt at levity in the current state of our relationship was plainly out of the question. I kept quiet after that.

16

IT WAS WEDNESDAY morning and the sun was out again. The letter had been delivered, and, with a bit of luck, there would be consternation in the Wiggins clan. He was probably not at home, so Mandy would be on the phone to him or to Sandra with the news. There would be heated discussions and possibly a face to face meeting between them, but given that the police were looking for Tony Wiggins, they would probably restrict themselves to the telephone. They would blame me immediately of course, but the possibility that the letter was genuinely from 'Alice' could not be ruled out. Or so we supposed.

We had to wait until Friday before 'Alice' sent Wiggins an instruction on how to deliver the money. If we didn't tempt fate by repeating the previous night's exercise but sent it first class mail instead, it would arrive on Saturday morning, the day we wanted the drop.

There was nothing new about the attack in the morning news on the TV. I went into town and bought a new padlock and some bolt croppers, because Harry Burbage was coming at four to store his stuff in the barn. I bought a newspaper at the same time and flicked through it in the car, but there was no mention of the crime in there either, which was very frustrating. Juliet had stayed at the farm to do a bit of work on her business, she said.

With nothing else to do and both of us needing some exercise, we decided to go for a walk and take a sandwich. I suggested the pillbox, which was stupid; there were too many happy memories attached to it. She vetoed that strongly, so we just sat on the ridge and looked at the view and barely spoke. Tina was happy again, happier than Juliet and I were with the dark cloud of Giles's condition hanging in the air. Would he live, and if he did, would he recover? Would he return to be the same 'lovely man', as Juliet had so aptly described him? Awful, unanswerable questions that left huge doubts in our minds and, together with our own problems, dragged us down.

We wandered down into the valley and Tina rummaged around in the bushes and hedges on the way. She would fetch her ball from a throw or became possessive and carried it for ages. When we reached the stream, she dived straight in with a huge splash, 'grinned' up at us as if to say 'Come on in, the water's fine' and was totally oblivious to her ball floating away on the current. She was fun to watch, her playfulness the catalyst needed to lift our spirits, and we started to talk again.

As we walked we schemed about our next move, decided on the form of the instructions and whether an eccentric twitcher would lead Wiggins from one possible drop to another to see whether there were any others following. 'She would if she was Miss Marple,' said Juliet, thinking of Agatha Christie's ageing heroine.

'True, but she was exceptional.'

'The world is full of exceptions. Let's do it. Anyway it'll be more fun.'

'Given the reasons, none of this is fun,' I said, conscious of the grumble in my voice.

'I know, and really, I'm angry as hell. Only two things are going to satisfy me: to see Giles well again and to see this bunch in jail for the rest of their lives. But,' she added in a lighter tone, 'I can't help but be stimulated by the action.'

'Agreed, and it's good to be doing something towards a happy ending. I am unhappy that we are bumbling about like a couple of amateurs, though.'

'Well we are amateurs, but at least we're trying to do something.'

'I feel uncomfortable because I want to be more professional, but don't know how without obstructing the police. Back to Alice – you. If we give Wiggins several legs around the park before he drops the money, it will make it more secure for Alice to pick up the parcel, because if we give them a good run around, we might gain a better idea on the size of the opposition; how many are involved.'

'And how are we going to collect the money?'

'I've an idea for that, and it includes not doing so. I don't want you exposed to danger, you need to stay out of sight. I'm not sure that Sandra knows whether you're here or at home. Let's go to the park and drive around and see if what we've thought about will work. We'll do that as soon as we're back, and we can still be back in time to meet Harry.'

'What's your idea? Stop being secretive.'

'Well, either we let the council cleaners collect it and we retrieve it from them, or I dress up like a tramp and fish around in several dustbins as a decoy, eventually collecting the bag. That would be on Sunday morning very early, before dawn.'

Without thinking, we took a route back to the house via the pillbox, approaching it from the front. From a distance we could see the boards that I had installed over the embrasures to try and protect the interior as much as possible. We walked round the back and stared at the new door that I had spent a great deal of time fitting. It was closed, but the heavy padlock I had used was missing. Cautiously we entered, but it was empty and was still clean with the same smell of fresh paint. In fact there was no change inside at all. So, what the hell....? Who had cut the lock?

I called the county council, being shuttled from one department to another until I eventually got the information I wanted. The dustbins in the park were emptied every Monday and Friday. It was going to be too long from Saturday to Monday to leave a parcel of money in the park for the refuse men to collect so, if it came to it, I'd have to dig out my tramp outfit.

After that we drove into town and stopped at the soccer pitch close to the Wiggins's house where we had watched the noisy youths. The field was part of the much larger green area of Trident Park. We chose a place for Wiggins to leave the money, and we chose a route that he should take before he did so. We came to see that when you start planning for something like this, you realise that there are so many options to choose from, that picking the least risky is not always as straightforward as fiction would let you believe. There were so many 'what ifs?'. It was part of my work to continually ask such questions, so I was able to deal with them rationally. Usually though, I was catering for a hypothetical situation, 'What to do if the weather deteriorates to below minima and you, the pilot, are on the wrong side of the mountain in freezing conditions?', or 'What risks are associated with equipment failure when …?' In this case, the situation was real, a potential murderer was staring us in the face, and I was a leading suspect.

HARRY BURBAGE COULDN'T contain his admiration for Juliet. He obviously thought she was the best woman he'd seen in a long time, maybe ever. Even when he was talking to me, his eyes kept drawing back to her. After saying hello to us at the house, he drove his van to the barn so he could unload his stuff, and we walked there.

The bolt croppers made short work of the padlock and the heavy door swung open with a loud and prolonged creaking sound when Harry pulled it. We all filed inside, Juliet in the lead. I found the light switch behind the big man's shoulder and flicked it on. The store was completely bare. It smelt musty, but had a swept-clean look to it and was otherwise perfectly suitable for Harry's purpose, which he confirmed enthusiastically, adding, 'Any chance of some shelving, then?'

'It's as-is Harry, I'm afraid. If you want to put shelves in here then go ahead, and if you leave them here when you've finished, I'll pay you for them. Here's a new padlock and two keys. If you don't object, I'll hang on to the third key just in case there's a fire or some other reason to open it in an emergency. Is that fine with you?'

He nodded. 'That's OK mate, good idea. I might take you up on the shelves – let y'know.' He walked back to his van and returned with some oil for the door hinges while Juliet and I were again looking at his cars. We left him working the door back and forth until the creaking went away.

CHIEF INSPECTOR CARTER held another news conference on the television. He said they were following a number of leads and were anxious to interview another person, but he still appealed for any witnesses to come forward. I had a feeling that the investigation had stalled without Wiggins being found. Why didn't they put his face on the TV and show who they were looking for? Then self-doubt intruded. What if I was wrong and that maybe Wiggins was not involved? What if it was Sandra herself that had attacked Giles? Or even someone unknown to us? I had nothing driving me but a gut feeling based on the wrecking of my house by an unknown person that I automatically assumed was Tony Wiggins. Were we just making a mess of things? If that was the case, then what if Wiggins took the letter to the police?

'No, you're right,' Juliet said. 'It all fits together, and if Wiggins wasn't under suspicion why was someone watching his house the other night?'

'We don't really know if they were. They might have been there for some other reason, and maybe it wasn't the police at all. It might have been a drug related thing, anything. All along, I've made the evidence fit the situation.

I've done it with the presumption that it was Sandra and her brother from the start, and made the evidence of their involvement fit. I haven't looked at it objectively, unlike Carter.'

'Yours is the most likely scenario. I know I'm looking at this half through your eyes, but I've tried to find fault with the reasoning and can't. I think we're on the right track. In any case, what harm are we doing by continuing with it? We've nothing else to do and neither of us is going to sit back and wait. If Sandra and Tony are really innocent and get upset by this, it's just tough frankly, because they're not nice people to start with!'

I had to laugh at that, so I poured us both a malt. She took hers and retreated to perch on a kitchen stool.

ON THURSDAY I called Avis and booked a cheap car for use on Saturday. We did not want to have Juliet's car seen while critical events were taking place, and mine was out of the question. I printed out the page from Google maps which showed Trident Park, and with that in hand we took another drive to look at the area. There were four cul-de-sacs leading off the road that ran around the outside of the park, and one of them offered an excellent view across it, another was not so good but would do.

To Tina's delight we went for another long walk, this time returning through the woods. We had our sandwiches at their edge with a good view over the fields and my pillbox in the distance. There was a cool breeze just strong enough to make the trees sway. Juliet shivered, she was only wearing a brown polo shirt over her jeans because it had been warm earlier. I stood up to go and pointed.'Look where the pillbox is sited, these woods are well within its field of fire. Any invading Germans hiding in here would have to stay under cover or be cut down.'

'It's hard to imagine what this was like during the war,' she said. 'It's all so long ago, and we just don't think as they had to to defend themselves.'

The wind was rising and, with a thin cloud layer, the sun had lost its warmth. A branch cracked behind us and, turning involuntarily, I caught a glimpse of movement in the trees before it was gone. A roe deer in its daytime cover of the wood probably, but it gave me a sudden sense of unease. 'Come on, let's go. You're getting cold.'

Our route took us back past the old broken shed. Of course we stopped to look inside again, and at first glance nothing seemed to have changed. The rotten floor still had the same broken planks, the walls had holes, the place stank of damp, and the same litter was collected in a corner; a Fanta can, an energy drink bottle, sweet packets, chip packets, and chocolate wrappers that were so old the colouring had faded away. Something was wrong, though. It wasn't the same as before, but I couldn't pin down what the difference was.

Juliet pointed. 'The rubbish has been pushed to one side. It used to be strewn all over the floor, and I don't remember cigarette ends before, they look new. See how the moss has been flattened over there, as if something's been laid on top of it.'

'You're right. Probably kids having an illegal smoke and a bit of fun in the woods.'

'Maybe, but kids won't have cut the padlock off the pillbox.'

17

SATURDAY, AND THE forecast was for rain most of the day. Juliet had called Royal Mail and found that the post was delivered to Willow Street usually between eleven and twelve every day except Sunday, of course.

Alice had instructed Wiggins to be at the phone box in Trident Park at four o'clock sharp.

"It must only be you because I'll recognise you. Don't have your wife do it, because I'm not sure I'll know her. You, young man, are stamped in my memory," wrote Alice.

In the morning we drove into town taking a roundabout route in case we were followed. Once we were sure that none of the Parsons/Wiggins clan were on our tail, we collected the hire car, a nondescript Vauxhall Corsa. They offered me a red one, but that stood out too much.

'I hate red cars,' I said to the sales lady. 'I had an accident in one once, my only accident. Have you a blue or black one, or anything else?'

'Ah, my daughter's superstitious as well, awfully difficult it can be … There's a blue one, will that do?'

'That'll be fine, thank you.'

We had left home early and fully equipped for the day. We did not take the hire car back home in case anyone watching the farm could link it to us. Instead, we laid the trail of clues in Trident Park that would take Wiggins on a circuitous route to the spot where he would drop the money. The non-stop drizzle that promised to become heavier as the afternoon approached made the whole exercise miserable, but it did keep curious eyes from watching some odd actions on my part, such as hammering a nail into a tree root.

Juliet had been silent for much of the time. Over a lunch-time pie and without warning, she gave me another stern look. 'You're obsessed with getting to Tony Wiggins before the police do. Just what is that going to achieve?'

'I've a score to settle and a friend in a critical condition thanks to him.'

'What are you going to do with him? Put him in hospital with an assault? I think you should forget trying to take revenge and let the police handle it.'

'What are you saying, that we should drop this right here and now?'

'No. I'm saying that when we see Wiggins you phone Inspector Carter and tell him where he is. Let the system take the lead.'

Merely mentioning the man raised my hackles. 'It had occurred to me, but I'll hand him over when I've finished with him. Where is the satisfaction in just putting the police onto him?'

'Have it your own way, but when you're also arrested for the short lived satisfaction of physically attacking him, you'll be sorry. That's if you win.'

We didn't talk on the way back to Trident Park, each of us wrapped up in our own thoughts. She was right, of course. I should phone Carter when we had sight of Wiggins, but I simply could not relinquish the idea of a physical confrontation with the bloody man. At the very least I wanted to be able march him into the police station myself. I was still wrestling with the decision when we reached the park just after two o'clock. We reckoned that if Wiggins's movements were to be observed by Sandra or Mandy, then their best position would be one from where they could see the whole park, and probably have a second place on the other side so as to cover the area better. One of them would then have the most advantageous position to spot Alice when she picked up the money. We had to leave those locations to them and find another place almost as good and from where we could see where they were likely to be.

Leading away from the park on the eastern side, the land sloped gently upwards. All the streets that led down towards the green were the cul-de-sacs we had seen during our reconnaissance earlier in the week. Of these, Tilbury Close had the best view, so I reversed the car uphill into the adjacent street so that it faced the park, and we waited with an hour and a half to go. I switched on the car radio to help pass the time, but after listening for a few minutes Juliet switched it off. I, the culprit, wasn't prepared to argue over it, so said nothing and stared out at the rain, which was getting heavier by the minute.

'Are you sure you're okay with this?' I said after an hour had gone by in uncomfortable silence, 'I don't see any danger until after he's dropped the money. They can't afford to strike at Alice until they're sure it's the right woman.'

'I'm fine. Don't worry about me, but I'll be thankful for some gluhwein after being soaked in this rain while you relax in the dry warmth of the car,' she said without humour and sounding almost as dank as the weather.

Juliet wriggled her way into her raincoat while in her seat and wrapped a heather coloured scarf high up around her face. Nothing happened until about twenty to four, when a silver Ford Fiesta drove slowly down the road that bordered the park. When it was out of sight around the corner, I said, 'That was it, time to go.'

She leaned over and for a moment I thought she was going to kiss me, but she only put a hand on my arm, and my bubble of hope popped again. 'Carter,' she said.

I watched her walk away with quick steps as anyone would take in unrelenting rain. 'Take care of yourself, Jules, great care.'

Her coat swayed with her hips, but her bouncing pony tail was hidden beneath the umbrella. She strode purposefully, no one could think she was an Aunt Alice. She did not look around when she reached the phone box, but went straight inside and shook off the umbrella. I glanced about to make sure I was not being observed and took out the binoculars. Juliet was counting change out into her hand. She opened the directory and flicked to the common name of Jones, where she would stick a note giving him the next instruction. Then, using her change, she apparently keyed the numbers from the directory into the phone, but in reality called me on my pay-as-you-go. It was mainly for the cover, to prove her inno-cence to a watching Wiggins.

'The Fiesta is parked in the next cul-de-sac,' she said. 'It's also facing outwards.'

'How many people in it?' I let the handbrake off, and the car rolled slowly forward until I could just see the front of Wiggins's Ford in the next street.

'I can't see.' Juliet left the booth, opened her umbrella and strode off round the park in a clockwise direction. She stepped off the grass and waited for a car to pass before crossing the road to a coffee shop on the far side. The car stopped for her, however. She gave a brief wave of thanks as she hurried over the road.

My phone rang. 'I think that was Sandra in the car that stopped for me.'

'Damn! Keep your phone ready, in case you need to call me urgently.'

That was not good news. Maybe it was pure coincidence, their paths crossing like that, but with Sandra it was just as likely to be deliberate. She could not possibly have recog-nised Juliet dressed as she was, especially as she had never seen her before. Could they have picked on Juliet because she used the telephone directory?

At three minutes to four, Wiggins appeared on the main road to my left. He was dressed in old blue jeans and a black rain jacket. A pair of blue Adidas trainers were on his feet; the three stripes were clearly visible. Were those the guilty shoes? His head was uncovered and getting wet. He pulled the hood of his jacket up, and immediately there was nothing that would distinguish him from any other man except for the orange supermarket bag in his left hand. He looked at his watch and went straight to the phone box. A church clock somewhere nearby confirmed it was four o'clock.

Inside the booth, he opened the directory, paged to 'Jones' as instructed and ripped out the pink Post-It note that Juliet had left for him. He looked out across the park to the opposite side, then to the left and right before leaving. Striding out across the grass, he headed to the right of the small lake in the middle of the area before turning towards the far corner. The diversion he was going to be led would take about ten minutes.

Decision, Forbes, it's decision time! Sandra was close to Juliet; there was no option. I picked up my phone and dialled. 'Chief Inspector Carter, it's Alastair Forbes here.'

'Yes, Mr Forbes, what can I do for you?'

'You'll be looking for Tony Wiggins.'

'What makes you think that?'

'Elementary deduction, Inspector. Anyway, I'm looking at him right now. He's crossing Trident Park towards the coffee shop on the corner. Oh, and his car is a silver Fiesta that's parked in Tilbury Close on the opposite side of the park. It's how I recognised him.' I told Carter how Wiggins was dressed and hung up as he snapped orders before covering the microphone.

Wiggins had reached the five chestnut trees on the far side. He looked around each one before going on to the next, starting on the left. At the fourth tree, he reached down to pick up something, but had to tear it free, because the second instruction, safe out of the rain inside a clear sandwich bag and prevented from blowing away, was what I had nailed to the root.

I lowered the binoculars to cheek level for a moment and noticed an old lady progressing slowly downhill past my car. She turned and stared at me for a long time as I sat there with the glasses in my hands. She looked out at the park from under the brim of her dripping hat, trying to identify what I was watching, looked back at me again and then walked on.

Wiggins set off for the next corner of the park where the playing fields were; about four hundred metres away and some four minutes walk at his pace. I could just imagine his rising anger at the way he was being led around in the rain which was falling more heavily now and reducing the visibility. I put the wipers on and scanned the roads all around the edge as well as the parked vehicles, but could not see a head in any of the cars. Sandra might have been in the one that stopped for Juliet, but I hadn't taken notice of what it was, so I didn't know whether I could see it or not. One thing was certain, they would want to use as many eyes as they could to identify Alice. Mandy was probably in the Fiesta on this side, but where was Sandra? Most likely on the other side with some binoculars. Was she even in the coffee shop where Juliet was? Or was this activity beneath her, and she was leaving her brother to the dirty work?

Wiggins reached the football pitch. There was a rubbish bin at the end. He stopped and reached in for another water-proofed note, flinging back the lid as if it was to blame for this run-around by some bloody old woman who had the better of him.

'Good boy,' I muttered to myself. 'Have you been dreaming of what to do to Alice when you get hold of her? Will you use the old lady as a punch bag before you dispose of her, or will you just take her to some deserted spot and kill her?'

Wiggins was reading the note when I saw a police car approach the far edge of the park near the coffee shop. Wiggins yanked his phone out of his pocket, listened, and then looked towards it. Sandra had to be over there somewhere. He watched the patrol car as it cruised slowly in his direction, must have decided it was innocent after all and set off back towards the phone box below me; another three hundred metres or so.

A second police vehicle was approaching from my left. It stopped short of Tilbury Close where Wiggins's car was parked. Mandy, if she was inside, could not have seen it, she was too far back behind the nearest hedge. Wiggins's phone must have rung again, because he stopped and listened while watching the new car. He was now directly off the end of the road where I was parked. The first car was still coming along behind him and had nearly drawn level. The second car in front of him moved forward and blocked Tilbury Close.

Wiggins ran. Not across the park, but up the close towards me. Car doors slammed. The police were after him, but they were not as fast. I unlatched my door. He was almost level. I kicked the door open hard. It hit him with a solid thump and he staggered back. I was out of my seat and landed a hard kick to his chest as he scrambled to his feet. He grunted and fell backwards. The police were close and could see, but it still took all I had to resist having another go at him. He looked up with pure hatred. 'You!' was all he managed to spit out before the first officer pounced.

The constables were most grateful for my help. I said it was an absolute pleasure and meant it. They asked me how I had stopped him. I said it was an accident, he had run into the door when I opened it and must have hurt himself. They nodded and one grinned.

I called Juliet and asked her if Sandra was there. She said no. Still, I wanted her out of Sandra's reach as quickly as possible, and we knew the woman was somewhere on that side of the park. 'Come back here along the outside pavement. I'll pick you up along the way.'

As Juliet walked back beside the road, a car slowed on the opposite side. I saw her turn and talk to the driver and then walk on. The car accelerated away.

'I'll bet that was Sandra,' Juliet said as she struggled to shed her raincoat inside the car. 'She offered me a lift out of the rain. She's certainly beautiful.'

'So she knows you. I don't like that. I wonder if you would have ever come back if you had got in that car.'

CARTER RANG ABOUT two hours later. 'Mr Forbes, thank you for the information leading to the apprehension of Mr Wiggins. I strongly suspect that it was you who so ably assisted my officers in arresting him. Is that the case?'

There was no point in denying that. 'Yes, it was me.'

'Thank you again. Wiggins was originally in some pain, however, and is claiming that one of the officers assaulted him. Could you clarify what happened, please?'

Was this a trap, was Carter trying to trick me into admitting I kicked Wiggins? Surely not, he had better things to do, but he might be trying to protect his men from a false accusation.

'Your officers did not use any violence whatsoever, at least not while I was present, Chief Inspector.'

'Thank you, I thought as much, but I should warn you that should he suffer from any lasting damage you might have to answer for it. By the way, he was carrying a Sainsbury's shopping bag full of stacked newspaper tied up with a rubber band. Rather like a wad of notes, only worthless. Odd, do you have any ideas on that?'

Time to lie. 'That is odd. No, no ideas at all, sorry.'

Half an hour later, while Juliet was heating some soup, Carter rang again. 'I'm embarrassed, Mr Forbes, very embarrassed, because I have to tell you that Anthony Wiggins escaped from custody a little earlier. I've just been informed.'

'Bloody Hell!'

'Exactly. I can only apologise and assure you that we will do all we can to rearrest him. However, as you well know, he's a violent man and he may try to take revenge on you. I would put a watch on your farm tonight, but I'm completely out of manpower – these cuts have made our work very difficult.'

'That's all right, Chief Inspector, we'll take precautions and I'll have the dog sleep close by. She'll warn us if anything unusual happens.'

Except for the confirmation that the Wiggins were involved, our attempt to take the initiative from Sandra had been nullified. Instead of being on the run as the guilty party, she remained an invisible menace who had us putting out fires as they occurred.

AROUND TWO IN the morning, Tina started barking. My senses were acute after Carter's warning. I went out onto the landing, listening for anything unusual. Tina went quiet.

Juliet, in her claret silk pyjamas, answered my knocking immediately.

'You should spend the rest of the night in my room,' I said. 'I'll sleep on the floor and get Tina in with us.'

Her eyes narrowed. 'I'll be fine where I am.'

'Please Jules, don't be silly. This is not a time for sticking to your guns, it's a time for common sense.'

So she slept in my bed and I slept on the floor, and the night remained peaceful with no sign of what had excited Tina.

18

CONVERSATION WITH JULIET was becoming increasingly strained. The distance between us seemed to be widening. If something was funny, she might laugh, but it would be as if she was sitting in an audience with no close connection to the act, she wasn't sharing her amusement with me. If I said something pertinent to our crisis, she might nod her agreement or simply shake her head. She did not want to talk unless it was necessary. She was remote and becoming more so. Previously, one of us would have made breakfast for two, but she settled for a slice of toast and cheese which she made for herself. I had a bowl of porridge.

We watched the morning news in silence, coffees (made by me) in hand. Carter did not appear on camera, but the news reader said that the police were interviewing another person in connection with the case. They were obviously not going to admit that they had let Wiggins escape just yet.

Carter rang before the news recording ended. He asked if I was going to be in, he needed to ask me some questions on detail. I replied that I had to come into town to buy some hardware and could stop past the station. I tried to persuade Juliet to come with me, but she had business to do on her computer, needed to speak to her colleagues at home, organise horses and perform other quasi-agricultural activities from afar. Time alone without me interfering would allow her to do that, I was told. I had the impression that she was annoyed at following my instructions to spend half the night in my room.

For my part, I was becoming annoyed by her antagonism. Yes, I was to blame, but why couldn't she differentiate between an act of affection and another of raw lust? Not that it was an excuse, I knew that, but still, she was being unnecessarily difficult when we were working to a common cause. Because I was a little irritated with her attitude, I brushed over the concerns I'd had during the night. 'I don't know what time I'll be back, it depends on Carter.'

'I'm quite capable of coping. Go and do what you have to do.'

On the way into town I pulled into a lay-by and did something I had been thinking about for a while and with some trepidation. Juliet's sister Mary and I had always got on well. We had a joking and teasing relationship which amused both Juliet and David, Mary's husband.

'Mary, it's Alastair,' I shouted as a big truck roared past.

'Oh, you,' she said without any of the usual warmth, not that I had expected any. 'I wondered if you might ring.'

I opened up to her on a scale I had never intended. I told her how it pained me to see Juliet's agony, how I knew we were right for each other if only she would forgive my stupid drunken crime. I expected Mary to tell me to stop being pathetic, to grow up and live with the hurt that I had created for both of us, but she didn't. Instead, she told me quietly that David had had a brief affair once and that she had kicked him out. However, after a while she had missed him and realised that their future lay in forgiveness and reconciliation, not recrimination. She added that had he done it again, she would definitely have left him, but he hadn't and they were now happy, the episode long behind them. Compared with David's affair, I had only had one regrettable night to which I had readily confessed. Juliet might eventually appreciate the difference and follow her sister's example, but it would take time. Mary would do her best, she said, because she knew how Juliet had thrived on our relationship, but was making no promises.

'Whether you succeed or not, I'll be eternally grateful,' I said. 'Mary, you won't tell her I called, will you?'

'Alastair, sometimes you can be incredibly stupid. I promise I'll only tell her if I think it will help. But,' she added with no small measure of menace, 'if you do this again, if you hurt her a second time for whatever reason, I personally will cut off your knackers!'

There would be no chance of it ever happening again, so I was a bit more hopeful.

My mood changed abruptly though, when a red light stopped the traffic at some road works. The car three behind me was a silver Ford Fiesta. Yanking on the handbrake, I jumped out and strode quickly back down the queue, very ready for a confrontation. The reflection on the windscreen blocked my view of the driver. Not so the side window, but it was only a young man in paint spattered overalls and a baseball cap on back to front. He looked back nervously at my aggressive face. I was being ridiculous, on edge about a silver Fiesta; how many had Ford made, for heaven's sake? I waved an apology at the poor chap and went back to my car breathing deeply. Pull yourself together, Sandra's getting to you!

Armed with two teas, Carter ushered me into a different interview room that time. The same type of clock ticked loudly on the wall, but otherwise it was in a slightly better condition. Vale didn't join us, but I saw him watching me go down the passage. Carter wanted to clarify some details about the first night I had spent with Sandra, he wanted precise timings. I gave them as best I could remember, and he told me that Anthony Wiggins answered the description of a man who had left another with some quite severe injuries in a bar fight the same night.

'Interesting,' I said, 'Sandra had claimed that both Mandy and Tony Wiggins had been with her all evening.'

He inclined his head, put a faint smile on his hawkish face and thanked me for my time. Vale was talking to other officers, but glanced over at me without acknowledgement as I left.

I CALLED OUT that I was back as I went in the front door. No answer. I called Tina, but she didn't come either. They must have gone for a walk. I pottered about for a while, tidied up the kitchen and then my office, and made myself a cup of coffee. It was clear Juliet wanted to be left alone, so I didn't go out to find her. Instead I took out the recycling as it would be collected the next day.

With an arm wrapped around a wad of paper and gripping a couple of bottles, I opened the back door. I couldn't even take a single step. Tina lay at my feet. Blood seeped over the paving from her head. Bile surged into my throat. My precious dog, my faithful friend who listened to all my moans and chats when we were alone. Then – Juliet, where's Juliet? I forced down my panic and called her again. No answer. I ran through the house. Nothing. Both her raincoat and her sheepskin jacket were still hanging by the front door.

Tina's head was a dead weight to lift, and one look at the back of it was enough to know that it had been a vicious blow. There was an envelope under her head, sodden with blood. Fingers trembling, I fumbled the note out from inside. It had been prepared well beforehand, for it was done with newspaper cuttings stuck to the sheet.

"1, 2 ...3? £1.5m by Saturday – Police = no 3"

1, 2…..3? – Giles, Tina … Juliet? is how I read it. That bloody man, I'm going to kill him – painfully! I'll force Sandra to watch her brother suffer before I rid the world of her too!

Juliet! God, I hope she's all right! I didn't think about the money or where it would come from, I just raged for five minutes and stared down at Tina's lifeless body with tears welling up in my eyes.

Anger and loss and fear for Juliet clouded my thinking for a while, until rational thought returned. All that you hear or read in books about kidnappings tell how the victim's friends or relatives avoid going to the police, because they are frightened that the threat is not an idle one. That might make for a better story, whether it was true I didn't know, but I certainly agonised over what to do. I was sure I could get the money. The bank would lend it to me using the farm as collateral, wouldn't they? Should I phone Carter? Wiggins or Sandra or both of them were going to stop at nothing to get some money out of this. I had no doubt that he would kill Juliet if he found out I'd been to the police, but he might well do anyway. Sandra might even order it out of sheer spite and revenge for depriving her of her settlement. Her hand was evident at every turn of this crisis. It wasn't just a step she was ahead, it was now a leap.

The appalling attempt to murder Giles and his current condition lurked as a backdrop. Juliet's and my deteriorating relationship, worsened by her attitude to me, was already costing me sleep every night. Now, her uncertain fate and Tina's brutal death had pushed my stress levels to a point where I was beginning to act unreasonably. If I wasn't careful I would do something stupid.

I had to face up to this situation and keep control of myself. Carter had more resources at his disposal and could call in specialists to deal with a kidnapping if he wanted to. At that moment I didn't even know where to start other than with Sandra herself, and raging at her would only meet with denial and make the situation worse.

'It's Alastair Forbes here, Inspector.' Carter had answered on the third ring.

I heard him sigh. 'Yes Mr Forbes? I'm sorry, but we haven't found Wiggins yet.'

'I know, he's just kidnapped my fiancée!'

'What?'

'You heard me.' I heard my own voice rising, 'He's killed my dog and Juliet is missing. There's a ransom note – one point five million, and a threat to kill her if I speak to you.

I'm calling you on a pay-as-you-go phone, because I think my normal one is compromised.'

'All right. Please stay calm and listen carefully. Let me think a moment … We need to see the scene as soon as possible. Call me back on my mobile number using your normal phone …'

'But I've just told you …'

'Please listen to me Mr Forbes. I know what you're saying and I'll do all I can to get Miss Meredith back safely, and I'll call for expert help. Now, call me back on my mobile and ask for Knight Security. I'll play along in case they're listening, and you'll ask me to come and look over your house to install a security system. I'll come out in a white van with a couple of SOCOs and they can go over the place while you and I talk this through, all right?'

I agreed and felt a little calmer; action was being taken.

'While you're waiting for me, I suggest you make appropriate calls using your normal phone and make attempts to get that sum together. If they are listening, then it'll help to reassure them that things are going according to plan.'

Fiancée? What had made me say that? I had not even asked Juliet to marry me, and in her present mood such a prospect was completely out of the question. One's subconscious never ceases to amaze.

I spent the next few minutes shouting stupidly and futilely at the bank's computerised answering service. By the time a human being came on the line I was livid. I demanded to see the most senior manager. He wasn't available until the afternoon. I told the secretary it was an incredibly serious matter that was extremely urgent and demanded some attention. She was unfazed, but eventually relented and gave me a meeting time of three fifteen. I told her that if the manager I was to see was too junior to answer my query, I would take the matter to the very top of the bank and the newspapers as well. Afterwards I felt a bit ashamed of myself. It was no good taking out my rage on a secretary or PA or whatever she was, but her aloofness and the shielding of her boss were infuriating. If she gave me any more of that attitude in the afternoon I was going to remind her that it was my money that was paying her and her boss's salary.

A white van drew up outside about forty minutes later. It parked so that the front door could not be seen from the lane, and two SOCOs slipped from the van and went inside. Carter, who had dressed as if he had come to fix the drains, and I stood on the driveway for a short while, pretending to examine the outside of the house and pointing to the upper windows and generally putting on a show. It seemed ridiculous. I was impatient to start talking.

'I must first warn you, Mr Forbes,' He seemed to be warning me about an awful lot of things recently, 'that you are still under suspicion for the attempted murder of Mr Collins, and if this is a smoke screen, an attempt to confuse the issue and make you appear innocent, then I'll ensure that you're charged not only with the attack, but also perverting the course of justice and wasting police time.'

I didn't expected anything like that, and it only made me more angry. 'Bloody hell, Inspector, if you think I'm making this up then you can bugger off right now! I'm risking the life of my fiancée in coming directly to you because you're supposed to solve the situation, not throw accusations at one of the victims.'

'Calm down, Mr Forbes. I'm sorry, but I had to remind you that, from a police perspective, you are one of the people who could have assaulted Mr Collins. Now, let's go over this kidnapping. As with all these things, time is extremely important.' He pulled on a pair of gloves as I offered him the note. He looked at it for a moment then handed it to one of the SOCOs to put in a bag. He looked at poor Tina with an expression of anger and disgust. 'That was unnecessary,' he said. 'I'm sorry.' He sounded genuine.

We sat down at the dining room table. I naturally took the seat at the head, and Carter took one that left a chair between us. 'I can see you're very upset and I'm sure you're keen for some action, Mr Forbes, but I'm asking you to try and stay calm and do nothing that might jeopardise the result. I want you to do exactly as the kidnapper says. He or they have the whip hand and until we know where Miss Meredith is being held and who they are, we have to let them believe they're in control. If they feel they're losing that control they may harm her, and we may never find them.'

'I understand, but it's difficult, I'm not one for doing nothing.'

'I can see that, which is why I'm warning you to resist your natural instinct to do something that might endanger your fiancée. Now, give me your phone, the one they know you have. I'm going to put an app on it that will enable us to monitor your voice calls. May I use your wifi, please? It will only take a few minutes.'

I gave him the password and he set to work with his laptop. 'This app is completely undetectable and not visible on the phone.' He was talking as he manoeuvred around his screen. 'If your claim that they're monitoring your phone is correct, then this or a similar one may be on there already. Has this phone ever been in anyone else's hands? They would've had to have access to the instrument itself for a few minutes.'

It took me a moment to think about that while he tapped at his keyboard. 'Yes.' I recalled the first night with Sandra. She had left the bed for a short while, and she had gone, not to the toilet, but to the lounge where her computer was.

He finished the installation and gave the phone back to me. 'You're confident you can get that amount of money?'

'One way or another, yes. I wasn't able to make an appointment with the right person at the bank earlier on, but I'll go in this afternoon. Have you heard how Giles is? They asked me not to call, so you get the question.'

'As of yesterday, he remains in a coma. There's no change, he's in a critical condition, but is stable. I get the impression that unless there's some dramatic reversal for some reason, then he will recover. No one has actually said that, mind.

'On another subject, Mr Forbes: how did you know that Wiggins was going to be in Trident Park?'

I knew that was coming at some point, but had not decided how to answer it. In the end I stuck to the maxim that the truth was least likely to cause any harm and it could always be defended; one lie begets another. 'Is it possible for me to tell you something off the record?'

'I can't answer that truthfully, it depends on what you tell me.'

'Well, I'm not sure if I've broken the law or not. You see, I don't just suspect that Wiggins was responsible for that assault, I know it, and I had to prove it.' I went on to tell

Carter how I devised the letter, how I delivered it and about the plan to observe the result. I left Juliet out of the story entirely. 'You see, Inspector, Wiggins is impulsive and violent and he'll react quickly without thinking things through. I reckoned that by prodding him with a sharp stick, he'd make a mistake and prove that he was the guilty party, which effectively he has done by responding to the threat. Wiggins's aim was to identify 'Alice' and then to silence her, it wasn't to buy her off.'

'Blackmail is a serious offence,' Carter said, staring at me impassively, 'even if it is done against a criminal.'

'I'm putting myself at your mercy, Chief Inspector. You can't deny that it had the desired effect, even if it was wrong. After all, it was no different to a police 'sting' operation in principle.'

'We only do that sort of thing with authorisation from above.' He paused, thinking. 'All right, I'll put this information on a back shelf in my mind. But, and you must understand that I won't have any option on this, if it comes up in the investigation you must be prepared to face the consequences. On the plus side, Wiggins might claim you sent the letter, but he won't be able to prove it, and the court may not press the issue given the magnitude of the greater crime.

'However, and this is another word of caution, although you think your actions have had the desired effect, it probably led to him kidnapping Miss Meredith as an act of revenge. So maybe it wasn't a wise move, after all. My point being that you should not do anything other than what they tell you to do. If you do have to do something as a result of an instruction or you see an opportunity where you have to take immediate action, you must let me know so we can back you up.

And lastly, if and when he phones, keep him on the line as long as possible.'

We had kicked the hornets' nest, and now we were suffering the result. I wasn't proud of it. Then something else occurred to me. 'Isn't it curious that to meet the ransom I'll have to sell this farm? Sandra's the one who's done all the planning, not Wiggins. She's vengeful and has to be in control. She's saying, "I'm going to take you down, your fiancée, your house, everything. I'll teach you to mess with me!"'

Carter raised his eyebrows, shrugged and contorted his lips into a gesture of 'possibly'. He consulted his notebook. 'You have this John Knott working here in a rented barn?'

'Yes, and now there's another man called Harry Burbage, who's rented the smaller barn. I don't see either of them being involved, though. Neither are the type, even though Harry couldn't take his eyes off Juliet when he met her. He's more of a gentle giant, and I'm sure John Knott wouldn't hurt a flea.' That said, the lingering doubt about my conclusions over Sandra and Wiggins surfaced once again.

AS SOON AS the police had left, I phoned Mary on my pay-as-you-go. She had a right to know what had happened to her sister, and she would never jeopardise Juliet's safety by telling anyone. It was a traumatic conversation, but I promised to keep her updated with any news.

On Monday afternoon, I had a difficult time at the bank. The stuffy secretary who had tried to rebuff me on the phone was a middle aged battle-axe who, I decided, wore Harris Tweed underwear. While waiting for the appointed time, she glared at me and I glared back. I was seated in a green leather upright chair directly opposite the woman. If I had been her, I would have moved that chair so that the occupant did not have to look directly at me every time he raised his eyes, but she probably felt she could outstare anyone who posed a threat to her dominant position as the manager's PA. When three fifteen had come and gone by a minute on the wall clock, I confirmed with my watch and said, 'It's past time.'

'Mr Smythe is a very busy man and appointments can be delayed. Anyway, I don't see why you could not have asked to see one of the other managers. You would have been able to do that this morning.'

My face went hot with fury. 'My affairs are not your business, and it's not my practice to deal with under managers.' I don't think anyone had ever put her in her place before, because she went red and returned to study her screen again.

'Please remind Mr Smythe that I'm waiting.'

She pursed her lips in irritation, but did so. A moment later, he came out uttering empty apologies. I pulled myself together and tried to shed my anger which was threatening to scupper my attempts at a loan – Be pleasant, idiot!

Uninvited, I sat down in a comfortable chair at his expansive desk. There was a picture frame with its back to me, a polished wooden pen holder with a matching box full of business cards and another with a pad of notes. A computer monitor sat on the right side with a keyboard beneath, otherwise his desk was bare. Smythe himself was essentially a very sedentary man, flabby with three wobbling chins and a spider's web of fine veins that gave an unnatural flushed appearance to his pale skin. He would probably be panting from entering a lift, let alone climbing a flight of stairs.

There was no point in easing into the request with pleasantries. 'I need a loan of one and a half million pounds,' I said, and his eyebrows lifted slightly. 'I can provide my property, house and farm buildings as collateral, and they're worth much more than that. The matter is extremely urgent and has to be concluded by Thursday. I stress that this is highly confidential.' Any mention of 'life or death' was out of the question. He might guess what the reason was. It was going to be bad enough when I asked for the money in cash; he was bound to be suspicious then.

He swivelled his chair towards the computer and tapped away at his keyboard. 'Mr Forbes,' he said as he glanced through what was most likely my record, 'you're going to have to tell me the reason for such a large sum. The bank cannot put itself at risk through, er, shall we say, possibly suspicious dealings.'

'Mr Smythe, let's avoid wasting our time. Are you able to loan me one and a half million or not?'

'If you tell me the reason and answer a few other questions so that we can properly assess the risk, sign documents that will allow the bank to take your property (having had its value assessed, of course) then it's a possibility. I'll have to refer the matter to my superior, however, as I don't have authority for sums like that. All this will take time, of course.'

I sighed, it was obvious that I was not going to be able to get around this. 'It's a medical emergency. My fiancée is in need of urgent treatment and she's in Central America. The money is for the flight to the US, which is the closest place for the treatment, and for the treatment itself, of course.'

'What treatment is that? It's very expensive.'

'It's a specialised form of cancer treatment, it's new and not available on the NHS.' As I kept repeating to myself: one lie begets another and the grave I was digging from the inside was getting deeper. 'She's dying,' I added.

The suspicion in his eyes was clear. 'I'm very sorry to hear that, but you must please understand that we will need verification in order to proceed with the loan.'

Could I risk telling him the truth? It would expose the story, and if he or someone in the chain decided to go to the press, then it would be all over for Juliet. Carter had been emphatic about secrecy, not that I needed any reminding.

I stood up. 'I can see that this is going to take far too long. I told you that it had to be completed by Thursday, but your bureaucracy will not allow that to happen, and I don't think you can guarantee confidentiality. I have a couple of other options, I'll have to try them. I thought banks were supposed to help, considering they are operating using their clients' money.'

He steered clear of an apology, instead made a pointed remark. 'We have rules, I'm afraid. There is so much fraud these days, we cannot be too careful. If I just knew the real reason for the urgency then it might be simpler.'

'I'll try my other sources.' I picked up my bag and walked out, seething. I glared at the secretary in passing. She flushed and dropped her eyes.

Had I just sealed Juliet's fate through not telling him the whole truth? Please God, no. There was something impersonal and overpowering about a bank, though. How could they be trusted? How many people in this giant money making machine would be involved in granting such a large loan? What would they want to know in order to do it and, could such a massive institution move quickly enough to produce the cash in time?

To comfort myself, I reasoned that if I couldn't find the money by Saturday, then Sandra would extend the deadline. After all, it was the money she wanted, and she must have known that it would be extremely difficult for anyone like me to raise that amount in cash in five days.

THE REST OF the week passed with an agonising slowness. I didn't sleep well, disturbed by an awful recurring dream of Wiggins as a massive troll with a knobbly club. He was ten times his normal size and responded blindly and clumsily to orders from an indiscernible image with a sharp and humourless laugh. Juliet was there, though; her presence was strong, but I couldn't see her. I had other visions in the night. She was bound to a chair in a dingy cellar, ankles, hands and head strapped tight, a gag in her mouth, and her eyes wide with fear. She was wearing the same clothes as when she was abducted, jeans, soft shoes, a white shirt and her green jersey. Tina lay dead at her feet, more blood than she could ever have in her body seeping out in an ever expanding pool across the floor.

Then there was the living nightmare of the ransom. There was no way to raise one and a half million pounds without using the farm as collateral. The place was worth much more than that, but I didn't know for certain. My investments amounted to several hundred thousands; easily redeemed, but not even half the demand. I would bankrupt myself to find the money, but it was going to be damned difficult to achieve before the end of the week, that was certain. The bank's reaction had not been encouraging. The thought plagued me all through Monday night. Then at about four thirty in the morning, after the umpteenth time of trolling through a list of acquaintances who might have money to give away, I had a flash of inspiration. The trouble was I couldn't do anything about it until midday. In the meantime, there was another source closer to home that might be willing to help, but I had never met him.

19

AT SEVEN THIRTY on Tuesday I phoned Carter. It sounded as if there was a meeting in progress in the background. 'Chief Inspector, I'm sorry to call you so early, but you know how pressed I am. Please will you tell me how to contact Parsons, Sandra's last husband. I don't know him, but I know you've interviewed him. I think he might be sympathetic to my cause and, if he's suspicious, can I tell him to call you for verification?'

Carter grunted and said someone would call me back with the details. In five minutes they did, and at eight, when Parsons was likely dipping soldiers into his boiled egg before catching the train, I phoned him. He agreed to meet me as soon as I could reach the City. Although he didn't yet know what I wanted, he sounded pleased to help. With no Tina to feed or use as a sounding board for my troubles, I left straight away.

I loathe the Underground. I always feel like one of five hundred sheep crammed together on a truck on their way to the abattoir, but it is the quickest way to get around London. I bought Alan Parsons a coffee and a croissant in a café near St Paul's Cathedral. I explained the situation in simple terms, telling him only as much as he needed to know, but he was cagey. 'Look,' I said, 'I can understand that this appears to you like a bare faced con, but please phone Chief Inspector Carter, I believe you have his card, and he'll confirm that my need is genuine and very urgent. And, because of the urgency, please tell me right now if you won't help.'

He was a tall, heavy, well dressed man with thick, black framed glasses. He looked pleasant and honest but was obviously wary of me. 'It's not that I won't help,' he said. 'There's nothing I would like to see more than that bitch given her just rewards. And I would do anything to help, as long as I'm able to be there in court and she can see me laughing as she's taken down! Trouble is that she left me with so little that I really cannot help. When I came out of that divorce with nothing, I borrowed what I could to set myself up again. Friends helped and I'm eternally grateful to them. It's funny actually. That time, which was most traumatic for me, has made me into a better person. Previously I would have told you to sort your own problems out, but now I can understand and empathise with your situation. I would really like to help you, but the trouble is that I'm still paying off my debts. Look, I earn good money, and I'll be fine in a year, back on top, but now … I have to honour my commitments first. Do you understand?'

'Perfectly, Alan, and I respect that. It's how I would handle it. Thanks for your time anyway, and when we get to court, I'll be sure to let you know.'

'If there's anything else I can do, information, material assistance, anything except money, please ask.'

'Actually, there is. Can you provide me with a private telephone for a lengthy international call? I have someone else that might well help, but he won't be available until about twelve, our time. I'll happily pay for the call, but I can't use my mobile, it's compromised.'

He glanced at his watch. 'Of course, no problem there. Walk with me to my office so you know where to go, and then come back before twelve. There'll be no need to pay, we use our lines on overseas calls all the time.' He grinned. 'Besides, I'm the boss.'

In spite of his support, I felt flattened. I still had not sourced the ransom, and it was half way through day two. If the next call didn't produce results, then I'd be forced to go back to the bank.

THE PHONE RANG and went on ringing while I fidgeted anxiously, willing him to pick it up. I was in an empty office with nothing around to distract me, not even a window. Eventually a breathless voice said, '*Hola?*'

'Felipe, it's me, Alastair.'

'Alastair! *Mi amigo*, my friend, how you?' The delight in his voice was so typical. It lifted my spirits immediately.

'Felipe, have you time to talk? I have a very serious problem and I need help.'

'Sure, no problem, talk.'

'Felipe, first please understand that this has nothing to do with what you told me. There is no connection, and whether you help me or not, will not change what I promised. You owe me nothing.' I went on to explain what had happened, giving more detail than necessary, but that didn't matter. There would be no repercussions from Chile. I asked for anything he could find up to the full amount.

'Alastair, that is a lot of money. That is one and a half billion pesos!'

'I know, but I'm desperate.'

'My God! Okay, listen, you lucky, my uncle is staying in my house, we having a party tomorrow for my sister. Is her birthday. I ask him to talk to you, I get him now. Please wait.' There was silence, then voices in the background got closer and louder.

Mario Montano greeted me with his customary warmth. I explained my problem over again while he listened in silence. Eventually he said, 'Alastair, this is terrible. My deepest sympathy. I feel for you and your fiancée. Of course I will help. You have done so much for my company, and what are friends for? You can give your bank details to Felipe in a moment. When I have them I will instruct my bank in Singapore to transfer the funds to you, but it may take a day or two. Do not worry.'

'Mario, I don't have adequate words to express my thanks.' Relief virtually drowned me, and tears threatened to flow. Giles would have lent me that sort of money without a question. Juliet didn't have anything like a sum of that nature of course, but if she did, I knew she would lend it to me, even now in her present mood. Mario on the other hand, this man who really did not know me that well, not as Giles or Juliet did, was putting his trust in me because he believed I was a good person that needed help. I was touched, to put it mildly. 'You will get the money back,' I said.

'I trust you, Alastair.'

I misunderstood him. 'You will get your money back,' I repeated. 'I promise. If we recover the ransom, it'll be quick, but if the money is lost, then I'll sell my house and farm to repay you. In the meantime I'll raise the balance, but all that will take a little while. What you are giving me now is time, time to secure Juliet's release.'

'It is not the money, Alastair. Money is only money, it comes and it goes. Sure, the amount you ask for is very big, but still it is only money. What I value most is trust, and if trust is broken then a man's faith is destroyed. It is a great blow to the emotions, and then next time you want to trust another person it will be a little less, which is a great sadness for humankind.'

'You can trust me, Mario, I promise. Whatever happens, I will repay you.'

'Enough, my young friend. When are you coming back here?'

'Just as soon as this is all over. I'm sorry it has got in the way of our programme, but you understand. I hope to bring Juliet with me, so she can thank you.'

'I like that, I like it when pretty girls come to see me.' He laughed and handed the phone back to Felipe.

'*Gracias Felipe, muchas gracias,*' I said before putting down the handset.

ON THURSDAY MORNING I checked my balance, but the money had not yet reached my account. With nothing sensible to do, I drove to Oxford to look at Giles. To my surprise they let me into his room, although a staff nurse came with me and stood back watching. Carter must have cleared it, which gave me a measure of confidence that at least the police were no longer seeing me as a risk to Giles's life. He lay there, his head swathed in bandages with monitor leads from his chest to the screen behind him. He was breathing through a ventilator as a precaution, the nurse informed me, although he could probably do so without its assistance. His helplessness was quite depressing, and my anger at Sandra and Wiggins surged again.

The nurse was a middle aged, mousy haired woman in whose weary eyes all the trauma and sickness she had witnessed was reflected. Although she must have been toughened by the experience of trying so hard for all those she could not save in her years of caring, her compassion for those currently under her wing was not diminished. 'It could be weeks before we see any improvement,' she said.

I nodded. 'Thank you for doing what you've done and what I know you'll carry on doing.' She gave me a tired smile as she ushered me out of the door.

The next morning I was on tenterhooks as to whether the money would arrive. It was not visible with an on-line check of my account, but maybe it was in the pipe somewhere. There was just twenty four hours before I should receive instructions as to where to leave the ransom, and if I didn't have it … what then? I phoned Smythe, the manager, to try and secure his cooperation. With that sum coming into my account, he should be a touch more cooperative than before.

Which he was, confirming that a transaction was imminent. I told him that I had to withdraw the sum in cash in used notes before close of business. He promised that he would personally see that the money was issued to me and would hold the bank open late in order to facilitate the withdrawal. Smythe was as good as his word, and I had the plain wrapped parcel of cash in my grasp by six o'clock that evening. I put it in a blue holdall I had taken with me and left the bank with a huge sense of relief. With the ease with which that had gone, it was obvious that Carter must have had a word with him, and therefore the delay might have been due to the notes being marked for future tracing.

My phone rang when I reached home. A heavily disguised voice asked if I had the money.

I confirmed that I did, my words bitter and forced. 'But I want to know that she's alive before I hand it over.'

There was a short silence, then the same croaking voice snapped, 'Say his name, quick.'

'Alastair!' Juliet cried out, and was immediately cut off. Alive! She was alive, there was still hope. Her voice had been forceful, not weakened by captivity or abuse, but defiant and challenging, she was spirited and fighting. Good old Jules!

'Your instructions tomorrow,' the voice growled, and the call was cut.

20

I WAS UP at five on Saturday morning. The summer was receding, and it was still dark. A thin cover of cloud spread across the sky but ended just above the eastern horizon. There, a narrow bright strip heralded the sun's advance and left a fluffy red underside to the blanket.

I was up because I hadn't slept for hours, and it was a good time for coffee. My stomach felt empty yet heavy, weighing me down, and I had had a surfeit of that feeling recently. Today was the day I would get Juliet back – as long as nothing went wrong.

John Knott worked every day except Sunday, and even then he came in occasionally. Earlier than usual, I saw him drive past the house on the way to his workshop. Around nine thirty he knocked urgently on the back door. I was just opening it for him when Wiggins rang; well I assumed it was him, the voice was too muffled. 'Go to your pillbox at a quarter to. Not earlier, not later. Take the money with you.'

I turned back into the house away from John, hoping he wouldn't hear, but he followed me in and stood waiting, fidgeting and pushing a hand out to catch my attention.

I struggled to keep the tremor out of my voice. I had to come across as calm and cold. 'I'm not handing over any money unless I know she's alive.'

'You don't have a choice.'

'I most certainly do. If you want the money, prove to me that she's alive before I leave this house or you'll never get it.'

'Don't fuck with me!' he shouted.

God, it hurt to bargain over Juliet's life. 'Proof or there'll be no money.'

'Fucker! Get started, I'll ring you again.' He hung up.

I turned back to John. He had heard enough, too much unfortunately, and his eyes were wide with amazement and concern.

I was about to say something when Carter called me on the other phone. 'Good work,' he said. 'We've located his phone to be in the same area as yours. It's as close as we can get from the mobile mast signals.'

John was shifting his weight from one leg to the other and trying to talk to me. 'Hang on a moment Inspector, please. Yes, John? Good morning.'

'I just seen that bloke again.'

I quickly held the phone away from my ear so that Carter could hear what was said. John leaned towards it. 'I was having a smoke break outside when I looked up and saw him round the side of Harry's barn. I think he went off into the field.'

'Did you hear that, Inspector?'

'Yes thanks. Now listen to me carefully. Don't, … don't try to be clever. Do exactly as he says, remember Miss Meredith's life is at stake.'

'I'm not likely to forget that.'

'The chances are that the pillbox is not the final drop point. You'll probably get further instructions there. When you know what they are, call me if they weren't given by phone. I'll try to get some men to cover the drop point if possible in the time. And don't panic if Miss Meredith is not anywhere near. She'll be left somewhere or you'll be directed where to find her, but it's most unlikely to be where you'll be this morning.'

'Understood.'

He hung up and I turned back to Knott. 'John, I have to go. Thanks and please keep this to yourself, there's a life at stake. I'll explain later.'

'No worries, Alastair.' He lingered for a moment and there was genuine concern in his eyes. 'I hope it'll be all right.' He turned away towards his workshop, ignoring the light rain that had begun to fall.

It was nine thirty-nine; six minutes to get to the pillbox, and the vehicle track was a lot longer than the footpath. I grabbed the Defender's keys and the blue bag with all the cash and ran out of the door. At more than twice the speed I usually drove on that surface, the rough track threw the vehicle about. We were airborne once, landing with a hell of a crash just before I reached the end. There was a short uphill run to be made to the pillbox from where the track ran out. It left me panting heavily. It was raining harder now, and I had to wipe the drops off my eyebrows to see properly.

The door was shut. A new brass padlock glistened in the rain below a note stuck to the wood with Sticky Stuff; uncomplicated and typewritten.

7 mins hut in wood

Knocking on the door, I listened carefully for some sign of life inside. There was nothing but the twittering of birds behind me. It was probably nerves, but I had the distinct feeling I was being watched. Carefully, I removed the note and the plastic putty, thinking there might be something on them that the forensic people might use. This bastard was going to keep me running hard between sites before getting to the drop point; I could feel it. In the driving seat, I remembered to call Carter, but before I did my original phone rang.

'Yes?'

'Get over to the hut, now!'

'Do you mean the ruined hut in the woods opposite?'

'Don't fuck with me, you know where to go.'

'I want proof, I told you.'

He rang off. Had he called my bluff? I was dithering, should I go or insist on proof? Then the phone rang again. No one said anything at first. There was a pause, some muttering and scratching, then, 'Alastair?'

'Jules! Are you all right? We'll have you out of it soon.'

There was no reply, and the connection was cut. There was no need to phone Carter, he would have heard the next point was the hut.

The drive back to the house was the same as going out, fast and violent. Skidding to a stop at the yard gate, I yanked on the handbrake, took the keys, grabbed the blue bag and ran. I was inside the wood in five minutes from leaving the pillbox. I slowed to catch my breath, there was time in hand. Although I was now soaked, the rain was only just penetrating the tree canopy at that stage and the ground underneath was merely damp.

The green corrugated iron of the hut was visible through the trees. At the pillbox there was no cover, only open field all around, no one could have crept up on me without being obvious, but here in the wood it was dark and there was plenty of undergrowth. I was ever conscious of being stalked. Where was Wiggins? The likelihood of being attacked and relieved of the money before I could drop it was haunting me. That would be typical of him, attack savagely from behind, hopefully kill, and then make off with the cash. The thought made me hyper-alert. Scanning left, right and behind, I approached the hut. The door was still hanging on one hinge, but it wasn't as far open as the last time I'd been there. Every now and then a gust of wind shook the canopy, and the trees shed their burden of rain which plonked as heavy drops onto the iron roof. There was no note on the door, nothing white and clean against the grey, rotting wooden planks. He was forcing me to go inside, to be silhouetted in the doorway.

Instead of going straight to the entrance, I circled the hut and tried to see through the filth on the window from a distance; getting too close would give him the tempting target of my face against the pane. It was useless; nothing could be seen through the grime. Keeping the door between me and whatever was inside and aware that the last remaining hinge could fail at any time and allow the thing to crash to the ground, I eased it open. The dim interior was threatening. I was poised to leap back. A second note was stuck to the far wall. It was too dark to read it from that distance. I was to be lured in, my attention captured by the scrap of paper ahead of me.

To Wiggins, if he was crouching unseen in there, I was a silhouette in the doorway as my eyes adjusted to the gloom. It had to be done. With a quick glance left and right into the near corners, I stepped across the threshold.

Nothing happened.

More Sticky Stuff. It was barely holding to the mouldy surface and came away with the paper. Back outside, the rain dampened the note.

West 50 yds fallen tree put in stump hole go back to house

The wood ran almost due north away from the farm so, having come out of the door, I was facing back towards my house and west meant going to my right. From the hut, there was no indication where the trees ended, but the wood was not wide, so fifty metres would be very close to its edge.

Still moving slowly and carefully, I went west until the edge of the wood was immediately in front of me. There was no fallen tree. Moving first north and then south along the tree line, I eventually found it. It was a chestnut, blown down in the storms of the previous year. Ripped from the ground by a massive gust of wind, the trunk lay like a giant axle with its ragged wheel of earth covered roots standing almost vertically above the four foot deep crater it left behind. Another glance around and I dropped the bag into the hole. Was Wiggins watching? Were Carter's men watching and waiting?

Skirting the wood to avoid being pounced on, I kept to the field and trotted back to the farm.

I moved the Defender from the field gate back to the house, driving slowly. There was time now for some optimistic reflection. It was almost over. If Sandra kept her word, then Juliet would be back here later. Would she need help? Would she have to go to hospital? They would try to force counselling on her, which she would almost certainly resist. This was silly, I was getting much too far ahead. I should rather make sure that everything was in place for her return.

I parked the car and went to the back door. A remnant of Tina's blood still stained the paving. Before anything else I had to wash that away. If Juliet saw it, she'd be devastated, she might not even know that the poor dog was dead. That plan was dropped immediately when I saw the envelope that had been pushed under the door. The instructions for recovering Juliet, surely. Eagerly, I took the letter out and flattened it on the kitchen counter.

You disobeyed my orders. I promised to kill her if you went to the police. Change of plan. I will profit from her, and you will not get her back. She has been sold to a buyer in the Middle East. You will live with the consequences of your disobedience for the rest of your life.

That unforgettable memory: Peeling off the rock, falling. But now the pitons had all pulled out, and Giles was not there to save me. Tumbling over and over, the ground rising up in slow motion, knowing it would slam into me, break every bone and seal my doom. A mental scream. A vast emptiness. A vision of the end.

It took me a long time to calm down, and eventually it was only when Carter and Vale arrived that I subsided into what felt like a mixture of cold fury and despair, if such a combination is possible.

We were standing round the dining table. I didn't say anything, merely handed the letter to Carter. Vale read it over his shoulder. He did not look at me, but pursed his lips and stared out of the window. Carter's jaw muscles were working hard. 'This is not a good development,' he said. 'I'm really sorry. My men could not get to the drop site in time, but they did see a short stocky man running away with a bag. He disappeared downhill towards the main road.'

'I don't think it would have made any difference if they had caught him,' I said. 'This letter was not written by Wiggins, he doesn't use phrases like "consequences of your disobedience". This was written by his intelligent sister, Sandra. I told you, she has to have her way. I "disobeyed" her, which was a personal affront. It's also possible that she was going to sell Juliet on anyway, and my actions simply provided an excuse. What now?'

'This is a bloody mess,' Carter said, 'but it's not the end. We'll get her back, Mr Forbes.'

'How? Juliet's life is in tatters.' The admission weakened me, unsteadily I sat down.

'Well, now that they know we're involved, we can be more proactive. We'll publicise the case, alert all ports and airports and put customs onto anything that might be suspicious, such as a container for a human being, or a patient being repatriated or such.'

I pushed my despair away and forced myself to think rationally again. 'If a wealthy Middle Eastern man is involved, he'll not use a main airport. He'll have chartered an executive jet, or even have his own aircraft that can leave from a smaller airport such as Farnborough or Blackbushe. The security and customs at the VIP terminals at those places are not as tight. Or, he might have a private yacht leaving from one of a hundred smaller ports or marinas. Sail over to France or Holland, transfer to an aircraft and it's all over. Why don't you pick up Sandra Collins?'

Vale answered before Carter could reply. 'Because we have absolutely no proof that she's involved. It's only your suspicion that keeps the interest on her, you have no proof. We can't go around harassing people based on the suspicions of third parties.'

Carter did not agree. 'I'm going to do just that, Mr Forbes. If she is involved, then even an interview will slow down the process of abducting Miss Meredith.'

'Sir!'

Carter's look hardened. His reply was sharp. 'Later Sergeant, we'll discuss this later.' He had previously shown himself to be a quiet and well mannered man who felt little need to exercise his authority, but he had just signalled that there were limits to that side of him.

'Chief Inspector, Wiggins was in this area when he called me the first time today. He was able to get Juliet to say my name on that call. John Knott twice saw what might have been Wiggins, he hasn't seen anyone else, so at this end of the operation he appears to have been working alone. He would not have had time to go anywhere else to get her to talk. She was or maybe still is in the proximity.' I jumped up to start searching.

Carter had not sat at the table, but remained standing. Now, he started to pace the room. 'I know, which is why I have men searching the area already. Please relax and let them get on with the job. They won't be much longer.'

'John Knott is at work, so you'll have full access to the big barn, but Harry Burbage is away on holiday until … Monday, I think. However, I have keys to his barn and store. All the other stables and buildings are open.' I took the keys out of the drawer and gave them to Vale who left quickly from the back door.

When he was out of the room, I looked up at Carter. 'Inspector, do you believe me that Sandra Collins and the Wiggins are doing this, because it's obvious that Sergeant Vale thinks otherwise?'

Carter sat down at last. 'Let's just say it's a strong possibility, Mr Forbes. Sergeant Vale is right in that we have no hard evidence and, until we do, it will be difficult to make a case. We need to find Wiggins, but he's turned out to be a slippery chap.'

'I know I keep repeating this, but Sandra is orchestrating everything. She stays out of sight, removes herself from the action so she remains above suspicion. This whole thing, especially that letter, smells of revenge, spite and yet more money. Her brother Tony is the action man and his wife Mandy appears to be just a foot soldier.' I shrugged and added, 'However, Mandy might be playing a bigger role than we think.'

He drummed his fingers on the table a couple of times. 'You think, Mr Forbes. I don't think until I have evidence.'

'Excuse me, but that's rubbish. You're thinking hard all the time, and I don't believe that your thinking is very far from mine.'

Carter's dark brown eyes gave nothing away.

'In order for Wiggins to check on my movements from here to the pillbox and then to the hut, call me and get Juliet to talk, he had to be close and move extremely quickly without being seen. Thinking about it, he must have had help. It would not be Sandra, she won't be anywhere near here, it was Mandy.'

'Quite possibly.' Another bland, non committal statement.

Another thought sprang into my head. 'I'm wrong! Wiggins wasn't close to me all the time, but he was watching me, more than likely from the wood from where he would collect the ransom, because the pillbox is fully visible from the wood. He knew what I was doing. It was in his words. When I demanded proof out there at the pillbox, he hung up. I didn't notice the number, but the second call when Juliet spoke must have been from another phone. Wiggins had called someone else who was with her. If she wasn't with Wiggins then, she might not be anywhere near here.' I checked the recent calls on my phone. 'Yes, look, this was Wiggins and the next number when Juliet spoke was different.'

Carter made a note of the number. 'I hear you. Let's make sure your farm is clear first, then I'll go and see Sandra Collins.'

Vale came back in with a uniformed sergeant and gave me back the keys. 'Unless you've got a hidden room somewhere, she's not here,' he said.

'No hidden rooms.'

The police left and took with them my involvement. Abruptly, I was left with nothing to contribute. I was in a vacuum. A part of me had been ripped away and I didn't know how or where she was. What was Juliet doing, was she hurt, was she tied up, was she hungry, was she thirsty? Where was she? Fulfilment would only come when I knew she was safe. The frustration of knowing nothing and not being able to do anything about it was consuming me.

A generous measure of Scotch always helps, though. I sank the first one, poured a second, paced the room and fumed. This was not going to go unpunished. The trouble was that if I managed to find and deal with Wiggins to satisfy my rage, Sandra would continue with her plans for Juliet. It would be better to start with Sandra. But was Juliet held with her, or was it too late, was she somewhere else?

21

THE RAIN CONTINUED on and off all night, and it was still falling lightly on Sunday morning. There was a depressing greyness to the world which matched my mood. It reminded me of Aberdeen, grey granite buildings under leaden winter skies. On top of that, once again I had hardly slept.

Previously, before this nightmare, I would have dumped my woes on Tina to provide some consolation. She would have sensed my depression and nuzzled my hand, or sat comfortingly on my foot. Not now, though. She had been butchered in an act nothing short of barbarity. Previously, Giles and I would have drowned our sorrows over a beer or something, and I would have felt much better having shared my troubles with someone who genuinely cared and would think of ways to solve everything. Giles, however, was lying in a coma in hospital and would probably never be the same person again. Nevertheless, I needed to see how he was, maybe I could make a mental connection, unload to his subconscious and ease my worry in the process.

I had nothing else to do that day, there was nothing I could think of to do. Carter was going to interview Sandra, and I was sensible enough not to jeopardise that. There was no way I was going to stand back and let the police hunt for Juliet without taking some part, though. I needed to think about what options I had, and a drive to Oxford would stimulate some thought.

I never moved out of the left lane on the A34, except to twice pass very slow trucks on a hill. I was content with the pace; it meant that I could devote more time to thought. For a while my mind was far away, slave to all my problems, until at some point the unnaturally loud roar of the diesel broke my concentration. The rev counter was indicating almost four thousand – I hadn't changed out of third gear! I moved it straight into fifth. I was a pilot, for heaven's sake, it was my job to listen to engines, what was I thinking? Bristles scratched my hand, I hadn't shaved that morning – for God's sake, Forbes, get a grip!

Nothing had changed in the ward except the staff. I introduced myself to the Ward Sister who was a younger version of the last one I had seen. She smiled brightly and greeted me with a cheery, 'Good morning, Mr Forbes. There's no visible change in Giles, I'm afraid, but he is improving. He's more stable and out of danger, doctor says. The pressure on his brain is reducing very slowly and we're able to respond to that accordingly. If he continues to improve at this rate, then we'll be able to remove the respirator in a week.'

We stood looking down at him, the nurse on one side of the bed and I on the other. Monitors played out his heart rhythm, blood pressure, pulse rate, blood oxygen levels and more, while his respirator pumped rhythmically in the background, its tube to his mouth taped in position. He seemed comfortable, head still swathed in bandages, but he was pale and thinning compared to my friend that spent most of his home life out of doors, summer or winter.

'He's a fighter, love,' said the Ward Sister after a while. 'His spirit's still there. He'll come back, but we can't promise that he'll be the same person you used to know. Actually, we've grown rather fond of him. Daft isn't it? We've never seen him conscious, we don't know what sort of person he is, but to all of us here he's become our favourite patient. When we come on duty, the first thing any one of us asks is, "How's Giles doing?" She gave a little laugh at what she thought was their silly affection.

'I'll be with him throughout his recovery,' I said, 'and I'll make sure you know how he's doing at home when he gets there.'

She left me alone and, talking softly, I went over the whole dreadful saga with him. His future, whether Juliet would ever forgive me, whether she would ever come out of this current mess, Tina, Sandra, Wiggins, the ransom money, my potential bankruptcy, Mrs Potter and Henry, his house, everything. I talked myself to a halt. My psychiatrist slumbered. I wondered how different it would have been if he were able to help. We would have taken bloody Wiggins ages ago and Juliet would be free, that's what the difference was. There was no point in deliberating on what might have been, so my thoughts drifted back to Giles's future. The chances of him returning to normal were slim, he was bound to be scarred in some way or another. Would he even know me?

Would he recognise Juliet, his other great friend, the girl whose love he never won? I would have to wait and see, and deal with what arose to his best advantage.

I felt a little better for having shared my fears and problems, but also because I had seen him and hopefully given him support. Did his subconscious recognise that? A subdued peel of laughter from the nurses at the ward desk brought me back to reality, and I closed the door softly behind me.

By the time I left Oxford it was late morning and the roads were crammed with cars. Apparently a water main had burst and they had made a diversion, so progress leaving the city was slow. The traffic stopped for a while at one point. I was next to a park and idly watched an attendant picking up litter and putting it into a bin on a special cart. There was a small number of shiny little gas canisters on the ground as well as some brightly coloured balloons, now flat and lifeless. Just as Sandra had done in her flat a month ago, some idiots must have had a little nitrous oxide party the night before, inhaling the gas under control to get a high. It was dangerous fun, legal at that time, and it gave me a tantalising idea. It was something that had been sitting quietly at the back of my mind since Chile, ever since I had then recalled Sandra taking the stuff, but this reminder in the park triggered the formulation of a plan. Not to be done yet though.

22

EARLY ON MONDAY, the house phone rang. Henry said his car wouldn't start just when he was going out to buy some food for Giles's dogs. I told him I had a couple of bags that he could have. After all, I had no use them – *I'm going to kill Wiggins*.

The three Labradors sniffed at the food when I unloaded it, but only one expressed any serious interest. I told them that they were too fat anyway and that beggars could not be choosers and that they should be thankful for a good home. Then I helped Henry start his car which only proved to be a flat battery. We chatted for a while and he said that neither he nor Mrs Potter had seen Sandra since she had told them they had to go, and that things were as normal as could be expected under the circumstances.

On the way home, driving with my mind on Juliet, I was startled when my phone rang. Normally I would have ignored it and waited until I was back at the farm (after all, what could be so urgent I had to stop?). Maybe it was the whole situation, maybe intuition, but I felt it had to be answered. I pulled into a convenient spot. 'Hello Harry, how was your holiday?'

'Just back, mate. It was good and the missus enjoyed 'erself. Keep 'er quiet for a while now.' He laughed, then became serious. ''Ave you changed this padlock again, only I can't get into my store?'

'No, definitely not. I haven't even been in that barn. Hang on though, the police were in there and they might have swapped the locks over by mistake.'

'Police?'

'Yes. There's been a bit of trouble and they searched the whole farm. I gave them the keys.'

'Well, I tried all the keys an' none fit. What's goin' on?'

'Harry, I'm about fifteen minutes away. If you can hang on, I'll explain. It's nothing to do with you, though.'

'I've got to be off, mate. I only came round to get somef-ing. I'll find you later. Meantime fix the lock, will you?'

I put the phone away and carried on driving. What the hell was going on? Why were these padlocks being changed so often: the pillbox, Harry's store? The pillbox was Wiggins certainly, he might even have been sleeping in there, but with the store it must be that the police had muddled things up. I reached the lane which led past the farm and the phone rang again. John Knott. He could wait, I was almost there. The ringing stopped and started again almost immediately. Urgent! To hell with the law. I answered while still driving.

'Alastair, the barn's on fire. Harry's barn's on fire. Where are you?'

Christ. What's going on? 'Two minutes. Have you called the fire brigade?'

'No, I called you first. I'll do it now.' Daft bugger!

I chucked the phone back into the dash shelf and put my foot down. I think I killed a stupid pheasant on the way. As the car skidded into the drive, I saw the smoke rising in the yard. In the house, I grabbed the keys, the bolt croppers and an extinguisher; not much use in a building fire, but that didn't even occur to me. Gloves did, and there was a pair at the back door.

The fire itself was not visible from outside the barn. The only indication was the thick black smoke escaping through the roof tiles. The main doors were not locked; Harry must have left them open. John Knott was hovering around outside looking agitated. 'I called the fire brigade,' he said. 'What can I do?'

'Stay there. Show them the way, but don't come inside.'

John peered over my shoulder as the door creaked open and a draught of hot air hit us in the face. He stepped back quickly. Harry's cars were neatly arranged: the MG TC and Series 1 Land Rover were on either side close to the entrance, with the TA and the TF in the far corners at the back. The TF was ablaze, it was a wreck of bubbling paint, seat skeletons and smoking upholstery. The flames roared up to the roof where they had already taken hold of the beams. Bits of burning wood were ready to crash down followed by the tiles, and it would not be long before the other cars would be caught in the growing inferno.

Even now, I cannot say what was driving me. Why was I risking my neck to reach the store? It had nothing to do with me. For safety's sake I should have just stayed clear and let the fire brigade deal with it.

There was still a way to the back that was clear, behind the vehicles on the left side. I couldn't see the store through the smoke, but ran around the TC and then the TA to reach the back wall. The steel door was hot and I fumbled to use the key with gloves, in case it would work. It didn't. Sweat was already running down my face and I had to wipe my eyes to see clearly. The bolt croppers sliced through the padlock shackle with a bit of thrust, and the door swung open easily. It was like an oven inside. At first I couldn't see and groped for the light switch to find that it too didn't work. Claustrophobia raised its panicky head but receded with the crisis. The heat from the burning TF was frighteningly intense, but the fire's glow lit the dim interior enough to see something bundled in the far corner. Two steps forward. Her legs and arms and hands were bound with duct tape and there was a piece across her mouth. Her eyes were wild and scared. I was just a silhouette to her, a monster coming out of the flames.

'Juliet!' I had to shout over the roaring and crackling. 'It's me.'

Her eyes softened immediately. I started to rip the tape from her hands. Then she was no longer looking at me but behind me, her eyes wide with alarm. I spun round and leapt up in one violent move. The jemmy whipped past my ear. He was leaning forward, I came upwards and hit him with a full body blow. It had little effect, but I followed the charge through, knocking him back to the wall. He let out a lung full of air and dropped the weapon, which clanged on the floor. Wiggins was nothing if not tough. He was back at me in a flash with two hard punches to the chest and another to the face. They hurt. I recoiled with the force of them. I had to stay out of reach, he was much tougher than me and those iron fists would soon have me on the ground. I was never good at boxing which is why I learned to kick, and the first hit him in the ribs, the second in the crotch and he dropped. I turned back to Juliet, but he wasn't finished. He scrambled to his feet, and I kicked him in the face. Blood shot across the floor. Still he came for me. I had to finish this and get Juliet out of there before the fire took greater hold.

The flames were sucking the oxygen out of the air in that confined oven of a room, and I was panting as if at high altitude. After less than thirty seconds, the fight was already exhausting. There was a crash of something falling amid a shower of sparks outside the door.

I managed to dodge most of his blows. He was quicker and better than me, but my fury was greater than his. This man had wrecked the lives of too many people, and he had to be stopped. If I failed, Juliet would die, we would both die. We could not reach safety until he was put down. There is no honour in fighting cleanly, only in winning. I landed a stab with stiff fingers to his larynx and he recoiled backwards, choking. Another kick to his ribs and he cried out. He fell. I felt nothing but rage as I kicked the living daylights out of that destructive moron. I kicked him in the ribs again.

'For Giles.' I was shouting and aiming at his head. 'For Juliet!'

I felt nothing except the desperate need to immobilise him. Eventually he was still, but breathing painfully with little rasps. I turned back to Juliet and ripped the tape off her, only being careful with her face. She staggered to her feet and clung to me, too weak from immobility to move properly.

I pushed her gently in the tummy to buckle her over my shoulder and picked her up in a fireman's lift. As we passed Wiggins, I felt his hand grasp my leg in a final bid. I took a step to the side and stomped on his fingers. 'For Tina, you bastard!'

The heat outside the door was immense. The flames were following the draught, upwards to the hole in the roof, thank God. A piece of blazing wood crashed down from above, unheard in the roar. Sparks flew. I dodged it, paused briefly to see my way, then moved quickly to the side I had come in. A helmeted giant loomed in front of me, Darth Vader, a great hulking silhouette moving quickly and almost clumsily. The fireman put his arm round my shoulder and over Juliet, keeping his body on the fire side and herded us to the door.

Another alien appeared in front. I yelled above the roar of the flames, 'There's a bloke in there.' Why did I bother?

The barn door was open and welcoming, the air cool. Broad daylight flooded in, banishing the flickering orange glow behind. Helping hands tried to take Juliet from me, but I clung onto her until we reached the ambulance and I could lay her on a stretcher. I tried to stand upright, but she had her arms round my neck until the paramedics gently separated us. One looked at me, a tough looking woman with a kind face and a green overall.

'Let me look at you, dear,' she said. 'Sit down here. Anything wrong?'

'No, I'm fine.'

'Well, you don't look fine, you look a right mess, so I'm going to examine you. Sit still, please.' She started to probe. 'What's your name?'

The firemen had found Wiggins, and he was put onto a stretcher next to Juliet. That alarmed me. Sergeant Vale appeared, looking grim. 'What's happened here?' he said, his tone implying that it was all my fault.

I really did not need Vale's biased investigation techniques at that stage. With the climax over, I felt exhausted and answered his question sourly. 'That man is responsible for this destruction, and he kidnapped Miss Meredith. Right now, he's not restrained. If he wakes up, he'll be violent.' Although admittedly, it did not look as if Wiggins was capable of violence any time soon.

'Keep still, Alastair,' said the paramedic.

Vale ignored my attitude. 'Why is he on a stretcher?'

'He was caught in his own fire. Where's Chief Inspector Carter? Someone's got to take responsibility for Wiggins.'

Vale's look would have me crucified. 'Busy, he'll be along a bit later.'

'Alastair, you must keep still for me to examine you properly. Just turn your head left a bit for me, please.'

She deserved a smile. 'Sorry.' I looked at Vale, and in a calmer tone than I felt, said, 'Sergeant, will you please ensure that Wiggins is restrained. He's an extremely violent man, and he's lying right next to Miss Meredith.'

'He's under arrest as it is – for escaping from custody. You know that.'

'Even more reason to handcuff him to the stretcher. He's a tough bastard. He's not a victim here.'

'They'll both be off in separate ambulances in a few minutes, Alastair.' The paramedic interjected. She was tenderly feeling my shoulder and looking to see if I winced at her probing.

The detective did not like being told what to do, but he left in the direction of Wiggins. He came back a few moments later. 'Mr Wiggins appears to have broken ribs, a broken jaw and nose and two broken fingers. Did you do that?' Maybe it was my attitude that was at fault, but his tone implied that he would arrest me for assault given the slightest chance. I ignored him.

The paramedic had finished with me, although she said I had to go to the hospital for a check on the carbon monoxide level in my blood.

'You can go in the ambulance with her.' The medic smiled at me. It was a good idea, but there was much to sort out at the farm, and why clog the NHS? I accepted, but promised I would drive there as soon as things had settled down.

'No, Alastair,' she said. 'This is important. You've suffered smoke inhalation, and carbon monoxide poisoning is a very serious condition. You must be checked, and if the levels are high you'll be kept in overnight. It's not a joke, you must come with us now.'

The firemen had the blaze under control at last. The corner at the back of the barn was destroyed. The roof timbers were burned through and many tiles had crashed down into the building itself. The place was flooded with water and black with soot. There was a great burned hole in the wall, the edges of the wood cladding still smoking.

The cars, I had to see the cars before I left. I felt guilty that everything I'd tried to help Harry with had worked out badly and late, and I owed him something. The TF was destroyed, of course, but the rest had got off comparatively lightly. Since Harry had not yet started work on them, I did not think he'd be too upset. I rang him as I climbed into the waiting ambulance. He wasn't happy.

23

JULIET'S CONDITION WAS worrying. She had gone through a terrifying ordeal and had bruises to her face and arms where she had been pulled and shoved and hit. There was still a red weal across her mouth from the tape. Her normally clear hazel eyes were bloodshot with the dark rings of tiredness beneath them, and the right one had a vicious bruise which spread down into that cheek. Outwardly she seemed calm, though. I sat in a chair at the bedside. She was propped up on pillows and had on a pale blue hospital gown covered in a swarm of darker diamond shaped motifs. She did not want to talk about the experience at first, but then Chief Inspector Carter came in and she realised that she had to help him, so I learned what happened. He had brought a female officer with him instead of Vale who, maybe, was trying his luck with Wiggins.

'I was on my computer in Alistair's office when there was a knock on the door. I peeked through the window, but couldn't see anyone clearly. I thought it was you, actually,' she said, looking at Carter. 'I opened the door, but there was no one on the step, so I stuck my head out and suddenly there was a cloth over my face and … chloroform, I think. Anyway, everything spun around and I don't know what happened next.'

'Did you see the person?'

'Just a glimpse of a head with a balaclava, that's all. I woke up with a hood over my head and tape over my mouth and arms and ankles. I was in a chair in a cold damp place. It was a cellar, I found out later.'

'Can you remember any sounds or smells?'

'No, not then. It was just damp and awfully silent. Hours later, I heard someone come back into the room. He hauled me upright, and suddenly I was over his shoulder. He carried me up a few steps. Then there was a woman's voice. She said, "Put her in there." I was straining to pick up any clues as to what they wanted, or where I was, or what was going to happen. I didn't know if Alastair knew I was missing, I didn't know what time it was, day or night. It was quite harrowing.' She looked as if she were close to tears. Without thinking of her reaction, I reached out and covered her hand with mine; support for a friend in need. She didn't flinch or move away, but she didn't return my grip either.

'I'm sure it was very frightening,' said Carter. 'Are you all right to continue?'

'Yes, sorry. I don't know why I feel like crying, because I'm bloody cross.' Her voice rose. 'I'm pissed off, actually!'

I couldn't help grinning, she had not lost her spirit. She looked at my expression and saw the funny side for a moment, giving a short laugh.

213

Carter gave a relieved smile. 'And then?

'He threw me onto a couch. I knew it was a couch because it was soft, but my head hit the arm, almost stunning me. He just treated me like a sack of potatoes! They spoke in whispers and I couldn't hear properly, but I think they were deciding what to do with me, where to take me. I say they, but actually, just from the tone of voice, it was a woman who was making the decisions and giving the orders. Then he picked me up again, roughly, grabbing me by the arms and yanking me upright. He smelt unwashed and of cigarette smoke. As we went through the door, I suppose, he made no effort to steer me and my head hit the frame. There was no need for him to be so rough. I may be wrong, but it seemed to me then that he was deliberately hurting me, and all the time he carried me I kept wondering when the next blow would come. He climbed some stairs; quite a lot, he was panting when we reached the top.'

It must have been awful. Afflicted with claustrophobia, the mere thought of my head in a bag and being restrained like that brought on feelings of panic.

Juliet's lips pursed, trying to hold back the tears that glistened in her eyes. 'Then I ended up on a bed. I was petrified. I couldn't see, I couldn't move and I kept thinking of what that woman had said at the foot of the stairs. It was delivered with such venom.'

'What did she say?'

Juliet appeared not to hear. 'I heard him moving about, but I couldn't tell what he was doing. Then I heard furniture creak, and silence. I think he must have sat down in a chair. I was trying to breathe quietly, straining to hear. After a while,

I don't know how long, he went out.' She took a deep breath and fell silent.

Carter prompted her, 'Please go on if you can.'

The constable scribbled a note. Juliet looked up at her scratching with her pen. 'After another long time —I think I fell asleep during it – the man came back. He stank of cigarette smoke. He cut the tape on my ankles and yanked me upright. He pushed me to walk a few steps, steering me with his hands on my shoulders, then turned me round so that I faced him. I was trembling, I couldn't help it after what she'd said. He undid my jeans and pulled them down with my knickers. I thought, this is it, I'm going to be raped and I was powerless to even put up a struggle. But he didn't. He pushed me back, but there was something there, and I found I was sitting on a toilet. I realised this was an opportunity not to be missed, but I couldn't go even though I was desperate, I couldn't go with him standing right in front of me. He just stood there, saying nothing. Eventually I calmed myself and managed to go. When I was finished, he pulled me to my feet, hauled up my jeans and zipped them, put me back on the bed where he taped up my feet again, then picked me up without any violence and took me back downstairs. Then we were somewhere colder, outside I think, or maybe in a garage, and I was dumped into the boot of a car. He slammed the lid so hard. Brutal, always angry!'

Juliet was unburdening, releasing all her trauma in one full go, but there was still an unanswered question. Carter's voice was so soft it was almost a whisper. 'What did the woman say at the foot of the stairs?'

The back of Juliet's hand had been resting under mine, her palm on the bed. Suddenly she turned it over and returned my grip. Unaware, her nails dug into my skin, seeking strength. I swallowed, what the hell was coming next? Her voice broke suddenly, she no longer spoke calmly. 'Just before he started to climb, the woman came close, so close I could feel her breath on my ear. She said, "Fuck her, fuck her hard. That bastard is going to regret crossing me. Rape her till she screams for mercy!" Juliet looked at me, then at the policewoman, then Carter and cried, 'What kind of woman is that?'

No one answered her, I don't think any of us could. Carter said nothing, waiting for Juliet to calm herself. I gripped her hand and watched her face. The policewoman had her bottom lip in her teeth and was looking pale and tense.

We all, especially me, were waiting for an important answer. 'All the time in that bedroom, after her awful words, with him sitting there watching me, I was waiting for him to, to … but nothing happened. He ignored me, he didn't touch me or anything.'

I breathed a deep and silent sigh of relief. The mental trauma Juliet would have suffered from rape was not something that would go away easily, if ever, and I wasn't sure how I would have dealt with it either. Even if we never got back together, it would haunt me.

'Did you ever see anyone well enough to identify them? Did you hear any music, or animals, or traffic?'

'No, Chief Inspector. There was a hood over my head all the time I was in that house. Later it was removed when I was in the cellar, but he always had a balaclava on, and I never saw anyone else, only heard them. I thought I heard another woman, though. When that one said what she said, there was a titter, high pitched, which wasn't her or the man.'

'Mandy Wiggins giggles like that. If that was her, she didn't seem to be perturbed by what her husband was told to do,' I said.

'We come across some very strange and abnormal relationships in our business,' Carter said. 'What happened after that?'

'Well, they must have changed their minds, because after a short while in the car boot without going anywhere, he lifted me out and took me back to the cellar. He took the hood and the tape off. He put a plate of food in front of me and stood and watched as I ate with my fingers. I wasn't hungry, but realised that food might come infrequently so forced myself. When I'd finished he took the plate and went out. There were two blankets on the floor, a bucket in the corner and a bottle of water.

'I tried to sleep. Time passed, days, I lost track. I should have scratched marks on the wall, I suppose, but I didn't think it would last long enough for that. In any case, I couldn't tell whether it was day or night. Then, ages later there was a ray of hope when I was told to say your name, and I heard your voice.' She looked at me.

'That was on Friday,' I said, to give her a perspective of the time. 'The second occasion was on Saturday.'

'A long time later, maybe a day or more, he put the tape and hood back on me and pulled me to my feet. I was put back into the car's boot, and we drove for a while, maybe half an hour, not more. We stopped in the country somewhere, I could hear the sounds of nature and smelt the fresher air. The next place, I don't know for sure, but I think it was your pillbox. He carried me a long way to get there, and he stumbled a few times as if the ground was rough. The door creaked in the same way it used to, and there was a faint smell of fresh paint.'

'That could well be right,' I confirmed, 'the lock that I had put on that door had been cut when I was there last.'

'I wasn't there long, he took me at night to some woods. I could see enough light through the bag to know when it was daytime, but it was much colder and black on that trip. I could hear twigs snapping, and branches whipped my face.' She fingered her bruised right cheek gently, 'I think this scratch was a bramble.

'I'm sure then that he put me in the old shed. It smelt the same, mouldy and damp, and the floor was slippery, probably with moss. I was sitting with my back against the corrugated iron, I could hear it creaking and buckling as I moved. It became very cold and I couldn't stop shivering. He went away then and didn't come back until the morning. When he did, it was to take me to the store where you found me. He took the bag off my head and taped me to the chair and went out. He closed the door very quietly, but I heard him put the lock on. There was another wait, I don't know how long. Then I heard someone fiddling with the door, but it never opened. I wanted to shout to whoever it was, but the tape …'

'That must have been Harry before he phoned me. He said his key didn't fit,' I said.

'Then I heard crackling and it began to feel warmer. At first I was glad, then I realised there was a fire outside and the temperature went higher and higher until I was sweating.' She began to cry, 'Sorry, I'm being a real baby.'

I gripped her hand a little tighter and whispered, 'You're no baby. You're in shock. You've had an awful time, and that must have been terrifying. It was an oven.'

She nodded and sniffed hard. The policewoman stepped forward and handed her the box of tissues from the bedside table. 'Thanks,' Juliet smiled weakly at her. 'It was getting incredibly hot, and I was really scared. At that stage I thought I was going to die. I hoped I would pass out before I was burned. Then I heard clanging outside and Alastair broke in, followed shortly by Wiggins. I was still taped up and could only show Alastair with my eyes that there was someone behind him. It was a terrible fight. I could only watch, I was helpless. You know the rest.'

'Thank you for helping us with so much detail,' said Carter, 'if you think of anything else, I know you'll get hold of me. Oh, do you think you'd recognise the woman at the bottom of the stairs from her voice if you heard it again? Just a thought, it would never stand up in court.'

'I don't think so, not if she spoke normally. Then, she was venomous, it was harsh and horrible. She couldn't talk like that in normal conversation.'

Carter got up to go. As he ushered his constable out of the door, he turned. 'I got a warrant to search the Wiggins's house. I'm conscious of the very large ransom that's still not found, but there was nothing there.'

'Thanks. But what about Sandra's flat and Giles's house?'

'They'll be starting that search in about …' He glanced at his watch. 'ten minutes time. I'll let you know how it goes, one way or another.'

A nurse came in, cheerful and lively. 'Mr Forbes, you have a perfectly acceptable carbon monoxide count, so there's no need to keep you in overnight. Miss Meredith, your CO count is also low and you should be able to go home tomorrow, but we'll see if you're fit enough in the morning.'

Juliet said she was fit enough go home right there and then, but would rather sleep.

'I'll come back tomorrow and fetch you,' I said.

'Please bring my bag with you, I'll need fresh clothes.' She sounded utterly weary. 'How are we going to find the cash?' She had said "we"; that was hopeful.

'Well, the police will search the house and flat. If they don't find anything, and I bet they don't, then I'll have to try myself. I reckon Mandy has it, and …' Suddenly, the dinner conversation of a long three weeks ago sprang into my mind. 'The Wiggins have a portable home in a caravan park in Swanage. All I have to do is find it. I'll start tomorrow after you're released, but I'm not going to wait until Carter tells me that they didn't find anything. Sandra's too clever, she'll have anticipated a search, and it won't be where they'll look. Tonight I'll find out what caravan parks there are, do a bit of planning and take a trip down there tomorrow.'

Juliet's eyes were drooping, she was fighting to stay awake. I took her hand again and gave it a last squeeze before turning away, but she held my grip and smiled gently for the first time in days. 'Thank you Alastair, thank you.' And promptly fell asleep.

The hospital corridor, like any other, was clean and shiny, and reflected the light from the window at the far end. My shoes squeaked on the surface as I made my way to the single ward where they were holding Wiggins.

'You can't go in there, sir.' A very large constable was seated on a hard upright chair outside Wiggins's room and was already looking uncomfortable.

'Please,' I said. 'That man kidnapped and tried to kill my girlfriend, he also tried to kill my friend. I need to see him. You can come in with me and make sure I don't take revenge. I'm sure Chief Inspector Carter would allow it, because he knows I'm not stupid enough to attack a man in front of a policeman.'

He looked unhappy about that. 'I've orders, sir.'

'I won't be more than a minute with you right beside me. I just want to look him in the eye. Please?'

He did not reply immediately, deliberating on the risk he would be taking. Eventually, he opened the door and went in first. I followed and saw Wiggins turning his head with some effort. His eyes registered my presence and there was alarm in them. His right arm was bandaged and the fingers splinted, his jaw was bandaged shut and what was visible of his face was puffy and swollen. He was breathing painfully because of broken ribs and his left arm was also bandaged, from burns I was told. He was in a sorry state and wasn't going anywhere for a while, but his narrow eyes followed me across the room.

I walked up to the bed with the constable right beside me, nervous as to my intentions. 'That's close enough, sir.'

I stared down at Wiggins with contempt. He responded with hate. I didn't speak, but put my hand out to his jaw, staring him down. His eyes widened in panic. The officer reached out quickly and gripped my wrist. 'Time to go, sir,' he said firmly and twisted my arm away.

'It's all right,' I said to him as we moved to the door, but loud enough for Wiggins to hear. 'I wasn't going to do anything, I just wanted to see his fear.' Then in a lesser volume, as we went out, 'I won't tell the Inspector you let me in. Thank you.'

24

JULIET WAS READY and eager to leave when I arrived at the hospital to collect her, armed with her bag of clothes. She chose another pair of jeans and a navy polo shirt. Her eyes were still bloodshot, and the bruise on the right one had gone darker overnight and would be there for a while, yellowing gradually.

'You don't look so pretty this morning,' Teasing her might have introduced a bit of levity. Her mood after everything that had happened was uncertain.

'Thanks, that helps.'

Her sarcasm had no humour, and my hopes of a better relationship dimmed, but I couldn't resist retorting, 'Pleasure. The problem is mine though, I'm going to have to counter accusations that I beat you.'

Without rancour, she said, 'It's what you deserve, and I won't deny it.' Was comic relief in that, or not? I held out her boots, off which I had cleaned a fair bit of mud out of respect for the hospital. She noticed as she took them from me. 'Thanks.'

About halfway back to the farm, Juliet said, 'Alastair, I'm going to help you find your money. I'll come with you to Swanage, but if it isn't there and there are no clues as to where it really is, then I don't see how we're going to find it.'

'You don't have to do that. You've had a hell of a time and should rest. I can manage on my own.'

'I'm acutely aware that if you don't find the cash then you'll probably be bankrupt. You put up everything you have and took extreme risks to rescue me, so the very least I can do is help you find it.'

In another life, so long ago it seemed, we had always made joint decisions and each had respected the other's point of view if it proved to be the better option. Juliet was not doing that now, she was asserting herself. It was her decision to help, and she wasn't asking for my opinion. I didn't argue, I didn't wish to argue with her about anything. In any case, I wanted to prolong contact with her in the hope she would come to trust me again.

'If we reach a dead end today, then I must go back to Mary's. You won't need me to help you here, it will all be up to the police, and there's so much I have to do at home.'

Again, I couldn't argue, but that awful feeling of loss was creeping in again. More positively though, I knew it was an opportunity for Mary to support my case.

It was going to be a long day, and if her mood didn't lighten it was going to be a lot longer than it need be. 'Jules, in the past few days before you were kidnapped, you were becoming quite antagonistic towards me. I don't expect our relations to get better suddenly, but they were getting worse for no apparent reason. It wasn't as if I'd become a worse person than before, quite the contrary. I've been trying really hard to support you while maintaining the distance you need. So your increasing dislike has to be coming from within you. Please stop it. I'm not claiming any points for saving you from the fire. I don't need you to help me as a reward for that. I'd rather you returned to your normal feisty, fun loving self. So, if you're going to help me now and we're going to be together all day, it would really make life more pleasant if we worked on more amicable terms.' I told her that both she and Giles were my most trusted friends, and that was not something that I would ever relinquish. She might not wish to be my lover ever again, but I would always be ready to stand by her whenever she needed. I said she should respect that and try not to treat me as a pariah.

While talking, I took the odd glance across the car and saw her looking intently at me with an expression I could not read. When I finished, I looked across again and she nodded before turning away to her side window. It was an acknowledgement signifying, 'I hear what you're saying', but not of compliance. Still facing away from me, she eventually said, 'I don't dislike you Alastair, you ought to know that. It's just that right now I don't want to be here, I want to be with my sister.'

The trip down to Swanage was longer than it should have been at two and a half hours, due mainly to roadworks. On the way I told Juliet what I was going to do about Sandra, but limited it to retrieving the money because she would argue with me, and I wasn't going to be diverted from the plans I'd made. 'So on the way back we're going to shop for the gear I need. If you're up to it, that is.'

She did not speak much during the trip, but the atmosphere was less tense than before. Her moods had swung from antagonistic before her kidnap, to friendly in hospital, then less so that morning, and while we drove she was more withdrawn than anything else. I put it down to the stress and trauma she'd been through and tried to be cheerful.

The previous evening I had found nine caravan and camping parks in Swanage of which four were for park homes or caravans only. I noted the addresses, leaving out the field camp sites, and drew up a logical order in which to visit them.

We had no luck at the first two, but at Fossil End Holiday Homes the receptionist was a rather slow, past-middle-aged, lady with caked make up trying to hide the wrinkles. She said her name was Muriel and confirmed that the Wiggins family did have a caravan on the site.

Muriel was fascinated by Juliet's bruised face. She barely looked at me even when I spoke to her. 'Is Mandy, Mrs Wiggins, here at the moment?'

'I don't think so,' she said, her voice as crusty as the roll she was eating. There was a crumb sticking to the left side of her mouth, and I was tempted to point this out by touching my own face with a finger, but didn't want to alienate her, nor did I want to witness her make up flaking off if she scratched for the crumb, so suppressed the concept. 'She came in yesterday,' Muriel added, 'but went out again this morning. I didn't see her come back. She might have done, mind, I don't see everything.'

'That's odd,' Juliet said. 'We were due to meet her at twelve thirty for lunch, and she said to come anytime as she wasn't going out. Maybe she went to get some things to eat.'

She smiled sweetly at Muriel and asked, 'Do you think we could go and wait at their site, please? I'm sure she won't be long now.'

'Have you been in an accident, dear?' Muriel asked kindly, but looked suspiciously at me.

'Yes, I have actually, yesterday on the M4. I still feel a bit shaken up, but there's nothing seriously wrong with me. Umm ... may we go there? I'll call her and see where she is.'

'Of course dear. Number 74, just follow the road around to the left. The numbers are signed.'

Number 74 was on the left side against the hedge with a good view over the bay since the site was on the hillside above the town. No car was outside, in fact there was little activity in Fossil End generally, probably because it was not school holidays. The Wiggins's caravan was an old, plain, road type, while most in the park were fixed homes. It was a large model with a tax disc dated in 1998 and had more than likely been there ever since. The grass was thick around the legs and wheels, while underneath was bare earth. It had faded with time and there were patches of green algae in places. They probably cleaned it every time they came here on their holidays. It was going to be very green indeed before Tony Wiggins would next have a chance to scrub it.

Juliet stood back as I knocked on the door just to be sure Mandy wasn't inside. She wasn't. I went round to the rear of the caravan against the hedge and away from the road. The large back window was held in place by a rubber seal, like a car windscreen, but I knew from researching the internet that such old type seals were probably stapled in place and could not be pushed or prised out without damaging the surrounding shell. Thank goodness I had done the tedious research, because finding out how caravan windows could be replaced had helped me compile a set of tools that would be needed.

After a lot of muttered swearing and hard work, I had cut the seal round the bottom and two sides, and was able to prise the pane loose with a screwdriver. Juliet came to help support it, and we lowered it gently to the ground.

I pulled myself up and through the window onto a double bed. Juliet had another look around outside then followed me through the gap without my help. There was a musty, stale bedroom smell inside, but the interior was clean and tidy. We had no idea when it was built, but the cupboards and fittings were from a previous age, sixties or seventies maybe.

'You start there,' I said, 'and I'll tackle the other end. The money was in a blue and black holdall with "Sikorsky" emblazoned on the side. There's a little winged thingy as a logo as well.'

We opened every cupboard and possible hiding place, anywhere we could get access, but we didn't find the holdall. We worked towards each other, and I was beginning to lose hope when I reached Juliet who was struggling with a drawer. Just as I was going to yank it open for her, the drawer front came off in her hand. 'Odd,' she muttered, feeling around, 'there isn't a drawer here, but there's something.' She worked and tugged and pulled out a cardboard box that was wedged between the framework. Excited, she ripped open the top flaps. 'Yay!' she exclaimed. The box was packed tight with cash, but it wasn't anywhere near one and a half million.

'At least that proves we're on the right track. Have we covered everywhere?'

'I've done everything to here,' she indicated, 'including the other side, every crevice.'

'Me too, let's get out of here. We can count that later. It's not all of it by any means, but it looks a lot. We'll get the window back in and then look underneath this crate.'

We scrambled out and together lifted the pane back into place. I pushed it firmly until it was seated, then took some silicon sealant and stuck the rubber window seal back where it had been. It wouldn't pass close inspection, but from a distance it was not obvious that it had been removed. Juliet was crawling around underneath. 'Fantastic! There's wads here. It's tucked into the chassis members all the way along.' There was a grunt. 'On both sides!' She threw out bundles of notes wrapped in shopping bags, then crawled forward to retrieve more before worming her way out from under the vehicle. I brushed her down to get the worst of the soil and debris off her. 'This calls for a celebration,' she said, laughing with me for the first time.

We stopped at reception for Juliet to tell Muriel that Mandy wasn't going to come back as something had turned up. It was early afternoon and we still had to buy the kit I needed for my Witch Plot, as Juliet called it.

Our route home was via one outdoor and two diving shops. I found myself a summer wet suit in Bournemouth, Juliet bought me some wet suit boots in Christchurch, and I bought a neoprene hood in an outdoor shop in Southampton. I didn't get gloves because I already had a pair of black leather ones thin enough to provide a good touch yet tough enough for what I wanted. We considered using the cash from the caravan to avoid using a traceable credit card, but then re-membered that the money might have been marked somehow. It was a matter of choosing the least risky option. A credit card would provide an investigator with a direct link to either of us, but the cash could have reached the shops through any number of hands. We decided on the cash, thinking it would take a lot of police work to draw any conclusions from that trail of purchases by different people. There was still more to buy though, but I couldn't tell Juliet about that just yet.

We were both impatient to get back to the farm. Juliet because she was dog tired, and I because I'd just had enough of the day and felt like a drink. On the way, she started to count the money, but gave up because there wasn't enough space to separate the notes she had already counted. 'I don't really know, but if these are all the same, then from what I've done there must be around two hundred and fifty thousand here! Oooh! I've such a headache.'

'I'm not surprised. You need to rest and mend. It's been a long day for you. I'm going to tell Carter what we've found.'

'Really?'

'I've always, well almost always, been honest with him. It'll come out at some stage that we found some of the money, and I don't want him accusing me of hampering his investigation.'

When I spoke to him, Carter asked me about the caravan because he hadn't known of it. He said I should let him keep the money, because they would need to use it as evidence and it might have clues. I said I'd drop it off in the morning. He said he'd send an officer round to collect it immediately.

I told Juliet that there were going to be fireworks when Mandy found out about the money going missing. She would tell Sandra, and Sandra still had influence over us, because we could not predict her next move.

'When I get hold of Sandra, she's going to regret being born.' I had never heard such a harsh tone from her before. It was surprising and foreign to the character I knew her to be, but Juliet had never made a false promise in her life.

25

ON WEDNESDAY MORNING, Juliet slept until ten. It was most unlike her, but it wasn't surprising. I took advantage of the silence and privacy to research for my plan. I made a fresh pot of coffee and a few moments later there was a call from the little bedroom. 'I smell coffee!' Was it my imagination, or was there some cheeriness in her voice?

She came downstairs, her hair tousled and her face still bruised, but the colour was less intense and the swelling had reduced a little. Her left eye was clear, though the right was still bloodshot. She looked a mess, but a loveable one to me. I gave way to an internal sigh.

She left as soon as she was ready. I carried her bag out to the car and stood there while she arranged all the female stuff in the front for her long drive. 'I'll come back to help if there's anything I can do, and I'll come back when Giles improves. And I promise I'll keep in touch.'

I said nothing, but my sadness must have been obvious. Before she closed the door, she put a hand on my arm briefly. 'I'll keep in touch, I promise.'

I WENT INTO Reading after she'd gone, parked the car in a side street near the hospital then walked casually down to the A4 and headed east. It was a depressed area with many shops closed with boarded fronts and vacant terraced houses, some with rubbish and discarded furniture out the front. Yet, from previous experience of driving along that road, I knew that a black Range Rover or large Mercedes or BMW with tinted windows might emerge from the streets to the north. It didn't stretch the imagination as to why such expensive vehicles would be in a run down area like that, and it gave me a reason to be there.

I walked slowly, looking down every side street for … for what? Something that indicated drug use had to appear at some stage: addicts with vacant eyes stumbling about or lying in the alley, possibly? This was new territory for me, and I just hoped something would appear magically to give me what I wanted. After about twenty minutes of strolling, including down some likely alleys, there was a peel of hysterical laughter.

Four teenagers were sitting on the lower steps of a house, giggling stupidly. The faded red door above them should have been repainted five years earlier, and the torn lace curtains in the adjacent window were yellowed with age. A crushed beer can lay below the kerb along with sweet papers and a plastic punnet. Someone had dropped an ice cream on the pavement, its now-dry stain had run down to the road. I watched the youths for a moment, their laughter so infectious I almost felt like joining in.

It was obvious what they were doing. Empty by then, little shiny canisters of nitrous oxide had rolled onto the pavement and several deflated yellow balloons lent a rather sad touch of colour to the steps. One boy, his jeans torn at the knee and with a grey hoodie pulled up over his head, was trying to put a full balloon to his mouth, but he kept missing, which had the others in stitches. Every time he missed there was a farting sound as he let gas out, and each short fart had the whole lot of them rolling about in fits of giggles.

'Hey guys,' I called, 'that's happy fun.'

Hoodie looked up at me, pointed with a limp finger and burst out laughing again. This was going to take some patience. One of the others, who had a red beanie on his head seemed a bit more compos mentis. 'Wha?'

'I want some of that stuff, where did you get it?'

He waved vaguely in the direction of the main road, but he was facing away and his arm had to go back over his shoulder to do it, so he fell over. Hoodie thought that was so funny he let go of his balloon which shot up into the air with another long deep fart, and they all went completely helpless. Red Beanie was the first to recover. 'Wha' yer doin' 'ere?'

'I want to buy your stuff off you. Ten quid.' I didn't fancy going into a shop, they might remember me. Buying off these kids would be an easy way out; less traceable, but expensive.

'Twenny.' Red Beanie would go far in life, there were no flies on him.

I picked up their satchel and saw at least ten gas bombs and some balloons. There were also two crackers for controlling the gas outflow from the canister and into the balloon. One of them was the cheap common screw type, but the other was a harmless whipped cream dispenser. This had a trigger control for gas flow, which was ideal for my purpose. 'I'll take all of this.'

'Firty, then. We left with nuffin' if you take that.'

'Thirty it is.' I wanted to get out of there and stuffed six bombs and some balloons into my jacket pockets. 'You keep the satchel, a cracker, four bombs and four balloons. All right?'

'Bargin'. The others had put on serious faces as they realised what was going on. Hoodie said, 'He's takin' our stuff!'

'Shuddup! We got a good deal,' Red Beanie told him.

I left them arguing and giggling on the steps and headed back to my car, pleased with my very costly deal; I had ventured into unknown and rather scary territory and emerged better informed and unscathed. However, I still needed to buy another cream dispenser, which I found in a kitchen shop before heading home.

AS PREDICTED, THE police found nothing in Sandra's flat nor in Giles's house. It was now up to me, and I felt quite nervous over what I planned to do, which was to trick Sandra into telling me where the money was hidden. Was 'trick' the right word? Persuade, even force might be a better description.

It was well after midnight. The rain was swept around by a turbulent wind. Streaking drops flickered brightly in the orange street lights, sweeping first in one direction then another. The tarmac glistened and shed the deluge to the kerb. I parked a few hundred metres away from Sandra's flat and walked to the back of the building, coming out in the side alley from where the bathroom windows were visible. Several of them were open, Sandra's included. The waste pipes were that heavy cast iron type, screwed into the wall with solid cast brackets.

I was praying that no one would come around the corner, but then, hopefully, anyone that did was going to be drunk. They would not recognise me, of course, dressed in black leather gloves and a plain black wet suit with a hood. My mouth and nose were covered with a dark strip of material tucked into the hood on either side. I padded along silently in the rubber boots but, even drunk, they would surely remember such an odd outfit. A dark brown climber's haul bag that held the kit I would need was tied to a length of line which was fastened to my belt. The outfit was completely out of place and as foolish as a gorilla suit at a funeral. I was desperate not to be recognised and not to leave any DNA in Sandra's flat; no hair, no fingerprints, nothing. To encase my body in neoprene seemed a good way to achieve that.

Sandra kept her Porsche in the basement parking. I made sure it was there then peered cautiously round the front of the building. A security camera covered the main entrance whose light shone out as far as the road. I kept out of its field of view and had just turned away to go back into the alley when I heard the front door open and squeak as it closed.

Rain swirling in a sparkling eddy around him, Detective Sergeant Vale pulled up his collar against the wind, turned right and walked away down the street.

Well, well, well! That was a surprise. Vale conducting an interview with a beautiful and sexually supercharged woman at one in the morning? So this was how Sandra knew Juliet's whereabouts. This was how Wiggins had known that I was not at home but at the police station when he abducted her. This was how Sandra had known about my contact with the police after the kidnap, about other things such as when the police were going search her flat that kept her a step ahead of the investigation all the time. He must have been infatuated, and she had probably offered him a great deal of money in addition to the sex marathons. He had seriously jeopardised his superior's investigation and endangered Juliet's life. This one man with his greed, corruptness and partiality was complicit in everything that had happened to the woman I loved. Although furious, I had to smile, because an idea for influencing both their futures suddenly came to me.

A familiar hollow roar from a powerful engine echoed in the basement parking. The sound made me turn back to see the Cayman growl out of the building, pause at the road for a second then accelerate away to the left. Where was Sandra going at this time of night? Did she sleep at Giles's house sometimes? Was she going to retrieve the money from somewhere as the police had not found it in the flat? Now was the time to do that, after the search had proved fruitless.

There was no point in speculating. My plan to have Sandra tell me where the money was had now fallen through, and I would have to try again the following night. I could have gone in anyway to have a look around, maybe find something the police had missed, but the risk was too high and the reward probably nothing. I was a little wiser though, because I now knew that Vale was involved.

26

THE NEXT DAY I took stock, which is to say I moped around the house doing very little of consequence. It was Thursday and I could not try to get into Sandra's flat again until late that night. I had no clue as to where the money was, so there was no point in searching somewhere just for the sake of it. I could only deal with Sandra after dark when I was less likely to be seen and she was well under the weather. Given how much she drank, that would happen most nights. Additionally, I had to make sure that Vale was not around.

Once again, late that night, I dressed in my wet suit, checked the kit in my haul bag and threw the leather gloves into it for the moment. In the mirror, all I could see were my eyes. I put on a coat to cover the neoprene suit and found a hat that perched on top of the hood. I intended parking my car well away from the flat and would have to walk several blocks in public view, so I had to disguise my fish-out-of-water appearance.

For a moment I wondered how, if I ever had the chance, I would explain to Juliet what the real reasons were for doing this. She would never agree to it, even though she had been at the receiving end of Sandra's vicious nature. 'Two wrongs don't make a right,' she would quote, but I still held to what I'd told Felipe weeks ago in Chile – an eye for an eye, no more, no less. However, the way things had gone between us up to that point it wasn't likely that I ever would have to tell her.

FELIPE: MY YOUNG pilot friend who was far away in Santiago or maybe down south in the camp. The way he had ridden the world of a paedophile and salvaged some honour for his sister and his family had impressed me. It had been clever and almost undetectable as long as nothing had gone wrong during the event; and it hadn't.

We had sat together that night slowly downing a beer after a day's training. The other pilots had gone to bed in preparation for an early start the following morning, but we were off the next day and could afford to stay up late. The Porta-Kamp hut which was used as a crew room was insulated and virtually soundproof, and we were not likely to be disturbed. Even so, Felipe spoke softly and kept looking at the door.

He was finding it difficult to talk about it. The details came slowly, in bits, but it was clear how he had done what he felt he was honour bound to do. He called the paedophile Carlos, but told me it wasn't his real name. Carlos's death had to look like suicide, so Felipe ran through many ways to achieve that before settling on the easiest means, the one that suited him. Carlos could be thrown off a bridge, but there was always a possibility of Felipe being seen. Carlos lived in a single storey house, so throwing him off his own roof top might not kill him. He considered an overdose of sleeping pills combined with an excess of alcohol, or for Carlos to hang himself. Both of these could be done out of the public view, in the man's home, but would involve some element of violence or a struggle, which had to be avoided. Then he thought the easiest way to do it was to gas the man; have him sit in his car with a hosepipe from the exhaust stuffed through the window and he would die of carbon monoxide poisoning. The difficulty of how to get Carlos to sit in the car without a struggle which would leave tell tale signs of bruising remained, however. He would have to be unconscious before he was put in the car, and it was the way that Felipe had planned and carried this out that sowed the seeds for my idea.

First Felipe had to draft a letter from Carlos that showed remorse for what he'd done and that he could no longer live with the guilt. No names of the victims should be written down, Felipe decided, the note must remain vague enough to avoid identification. He completed this draft on a sheet of paper before he even went to the house, because it was carefully worded and he wanted to make sure he didn't make a mistake when he retyped it in the heat of the event. Because Carlos was supposedly a family friend, Felipe would be able to use the man's computer and printer to type the suicide note while he was there.

Felipe bought a new car every year because he enjoyed sampling different models and he had the money to do so. A new car was no good for his purpose, but he had a friend called Enrique who had WW2 Jeep which he used as a girl trap. It was considered really sexy, and Enrique could be seen on summer weekends cruising the corniche in Valparaiso with two or three girls, showing off and waving at the crowds.

Claiming he needed to impress a new find and managing to sidestep Enrique's probing questions, Felipe borrowed the Jeep. Over the course of a week, he assembled all the tools and equipment he needed: an empty gas bottle, an electric tyre pump, a length of garden hose, duct tape, some rags and a face mask with suitable tubing. He modified the tyre pump so that the air intake would accept the garden hose and he changed the outlet tube so that it fitted the head of the gas bottle. With the hose wedged into the Jeep's exhaust he opened the valve of the gas cylinder and switched on the pump. Slowly the needle on the pressure gauge began to rise until the pump slowed down and could not force any more of the noxious gas into the bottle. The pressure gauge read 18bar, close to the pump's maximum output. Felipe closed the cylinder valve, exchanged the hosepipe for the face mask and, nervously, put it on. 'I was very scared, Alastair. What if I became unconscious when I tried it out?'

The gas gave a low, rather hollow, hiss as it entered the mask. Felipe lost courage and ripped the deadly contraption off his face. Instead, he waited to see how long the cylinder would last, because the little tyre pump could not pressurise the bottle to anything approaching its normal level. It took about five minutes at the low rate of flow until the gas stopped. He summoned the courage and repeated the exercise, but this time held the mask over his mouth and nose and opened the valve. Apart from the familiar smell which made him want to choke, he felt nothing. Then he became unaware of how much time was passing and started to feel drowsy. Immediately, before he lost control, he dropped the mask and gulped in clean air. The gas was still hissing gently. Good, it meant that there was enough in the weakly pressurised cylinder to render Carlos unconscious.

On the night, Felipe put all his equipment into a holdall, grabbed a bottle of Central Valley merlot and went round to Carlos's home. He was a rich man, Carlos, and owned a rambling house with an attached garage, a door from which led into the kitchen. Fitting the climate, there was a veranda that stretched the length of the house from the kitchen, past the living room, the bar and on past three bedrooms to the end. Every room had access to the outside through its own door, and guests could wander out onto the veranda and join others at the barbecue on the adjoining patio, or go further down the path across the extensive lawn to the swimming pool, where there was another bar and shade. Carlos lived alone but entertained frequently, and often did not know whom he had invited. There was always a surplus of young women, Felipe told me. This night, however, he had asked to see Carlos alone.

Felipe took a long time to get around to telling me about the actual event. It was as if he could not bear to remind himself of what he'd done, let alone confess to it. He paced up and down the cabin in silence, picked up the bar book with its pencil on a string, opened it, closed it without reading anything and put it back. Then he opened the door and had a quick look around outside before continuing his story.

Carlos and Felipe had a good dinner and drank a lot of vodka and a lot of wine, although Felipe managed to keep his intake down without Carlos noticing. When the man started slurring and kept nodding off, Felipe said he was going to the bathroom, but instead took his kit out of the holdall, put on some gloves and went behind Carlos's chair. Carefully, he turned the tap and listened for the hiss of gas. He applied the mask very gently to Carlos's face, holding it just off his cheeks to avoid him fighting it. Carlos coughed at the smell but was too drunk to object to the exhaust fumes and didn't push the mask away. Felipe was sweating and trembling, he admitted, but he continued to hold the mask with an increasingly firmer grip as if his effort would accelerate the death. Eventually, after a what seemed an eternity but was probably just a minute or two, Carlos slumped to his left and Felipe had to lean right over the back of the chair to keep his hold. He pulled the mask away and heard the flow getting weaker, so he closed the valve, leaving some gas in reserve.

He opened Carlos's computer, took the suicide note he had drafted from his pocket and typed it out. He saved it to the desktop so that it would be easy to see, then switched on the printer. There was a whole page of confessions of abuse of unidentified young girls. In them, 'Carlos' admitted his carnal desires had ruined the lives of these vulnerable creatures. He understood their pain and their fears and loss of ability to have normal relationships. He expressed unlimited remorse and felt the only way to atone for his deviations was to take his own life. Felipe had written the letter in the long winded way that Carlos would talk, had gone over it time and again, convincing himself that it looked genuine.

Once again he opened the cylinder and put the mask back on Carlos's face. He wanted to exhaust the cylinder and make doubly sure this revolting paedophile was completely unconscious. Unconscious was all Felipe needed him to be at this stage, death would follow later. He was past the point of no return now, Felipe thought. There was no choice but to carry on, but he could not settle his nerves and continued to tremble.

The gas exhausted, he took the paper from the printer, read it again as it quivered in his shaking hand and took it over to the man himself. Carlos was still breathing, just. He pressed the limp fingers onto the paper to leave genuine fingerprints and put the sheets on the desk. The computer keyboard worked with Bluetooth, so was portable. Again, Felipe took Carlos' fingers and pressed them to every key and around the unit. Finally, he used his handkerchief to wipe where he had left prints and deliberately smudged the on/off switches on the computer and printer. He reasoned that a man about to commit suicide would not bother to shut down his machines, so he left them on.

Felipe went into the kitchen and opened the garage door. There were two cars there, a BMW X6 and a 1969 American Ford Mustang with a big, fat engine in it. The BMW would have a much cleaner exhaust with less carbon monoxide than the old gas guzzler which, like the Jeep, was made long before the days when catalytic converters were brought in. He turned the key in the Mustang and the engine churned over easily, but didn't fire. He swore, on the verge of panic, but at the third attempt it thumped into life with that unmistakeable rumbling of a V8. He left it running and the driver's door open. Carlos was fat and heavy, but Felipe was a big lad and managed to carry him through the kitchen and into the garage. Somehow, he fed him into the driver's seat, opened the right side window a little and went back into the house to fetch the hose pipe and rags. He folded Carlos's hands around the hose at both ends and a few random places then rammed it into the exhaust and wedged it in place with the rags before feeding the other end into the window gap.

Then the tidying up began, he went everywhere he had been in the house and wiped it clean of finger prints. He washed his wine glass and put it away in the cupboard. Had he touched Carlos's glass? Had he poured him a drink? No, he had avoided doing that for just this reason. The chair he had sat in was covered in leather, so a wipe was all that was needed there. If there was anything left which he had forgotten, and he was questioned about his presence, he could genuinely claim that he often went to Carlos's house.

Back in the garage, the car was full of exhaust fumes and Carlos was surely dead, but even if he wasn't, there was no doubt he would be by morning which was the earliest he'd be found. Felipe left the house unlocked, Carlos usually did, even though it was a stupid thing to do. He left by climbing over the garden wall beyond the pool and walked slowly down the hill to where he'd left his car. The enormity of what he'd done had not yet sunk in, but he was feeling a sense of accomplishment. There was relief it was over, of course, but a great mass of anxiety hung over him as well. 'Guilt, Alastair? Guilt? I don't think so. I was pleased, but I was scared. I still am scared, I don't want to be a murderer.'

There was nothing constructive I could add. 'It's a bit late to feel that, Felipe.'

THIS NIGHT, THURSDAY, was much the same as the one before, except the wind was much stronger and the rain was almost horizontal. Knowing that Vale might be there, I drove around the block as well as one on either side to see if his Vauxhall Astra was parked nearby. I could not see it so assumed he was either on duty or maybe he had left already. After all, it would take a great deal of stamina to keep up with Sandra on a nightly basis. I eventually parked two blocks away on a different road.

Once again I peered into the basement parking to make sure that her Porsche was there, but it wasn't. *Damn!* I waited around for an hour, but she didn't return. I went home.

I repeated the exercise on Friday night, but she still had not returned. Where was she? Was she staying at Giles's house or her brother's house? Had she taken the money and escaped, gone abroad perhaps? If so, I had lost. Then doubts as to the viability of my plan began to niggle at me. Was I being childish and hoping for too much, would it ever work? I put the negative thoughts behind me. There was nothing else I could think of doing, and at least I was doing something.

The next morning I phoned Giles's house. 'Hello Henry, how are things? Are you and Mrs Potter all right?'

He assured me that they were fine, but were frustrated at not knowing what was going on. I told him that Giles was improving slowly, so there was hope, then asked if Sandra was there.

'No, sir. We haven't seen her since she let us go.'

'Henry, please do me a favour. If she does appear, or contacts you at all, please will you let me know straight away. But it's quite important that she doesn't know I asked you to do that.'

I could almost hear him smile, pleased to be conspiring against the woman. 'Don't you worry, sir. We're on your side, we won't say a thing. I'll tell Mrs Potter.'

It was Saturday. I tried again with the rain pouring down for the third night in a row. Wherever it had been for the last few days, the Cayman was back in the basement. Good, I could now shake off my doubts and take action.

Leaving the haul bag on the ground, I shinned up the cast iron waste pipe. I had not done any climbing for a year, and was seriously out of practice. It didn't matter; the rubber booties, wedged between the wall and the pipe, gripped well, and the pipe was solid and provided a firm hold. Thank goodness for the gloves, the leather had good friction on the smooth wet pipe and it wasn't long before I reached the second floor. On my previous visit, Sandra had left the bathroom window open beyond the safety catch, there being no children, and it was still the same. I wedged my left foot into the crack between the pipe and the wall, held on with both hands and used the greater reach of my right leg to push the window as wide as I could. Then I leaned over, got a firm grip on the frame and pulled myself across. From there it was a simple job to clamber up into the bathroom.

The door was ajar, and light from the TV flickered through the gap. Canned laughter switched on and off with irritating and unrealistic precision. Pause, listen – there were no signs of movement. The rain was coming in the wide open window. I hauled the bag up with the line, unclipped it from my belt then pulled the window closed to its original position. A towel dabbed at the wet suit stopped any drips. Conscious that my boots were wet, I dried them with toilet paper as I didn't want to leave any debris from them on the towel or footprints on the carpet. The soggy bits of paper went in the bag.

I peered out of the bathroom into the living area. Sandra was watching the TV and facing away from me. There were two glasses on the table in front of her and what was left of a bottle of champagne. Two glasses? Where was the other person? Was Vale here after all? I waited a while, but there was still no sign of anyone else. Working as quietly as possible, I slipped a nitrous oxide canister into an empty dispenser and screwed the top on, puncturing the cylinder. Then I pushed the tubing from the mask over the nozzle and gave it a quick test. A hiss confirmed success, so I repeated the preparation with the second dispenser.

Slowly, and ever so quietly, I moved up behind Sandra and stood over her. She was so still I wondered for a moment if she were dead, but she gave a brief, unladylike snort and sagged over to her right. The TV quiz show had an orange stage setting, which lent a warming glow to her creamy skin. She was drunk and began to snore. Hopefully she would feel nothing but, very gently, trying not to touch her, I held the mask over her mouth and nose and released some nitrous oxide. No reaction, so I released some more. I wanted her totally pliable, unable to fight and with no signs of a struggle on her. This had to look as if it was self inflicted.

When inhaling from a balloon, the recreational user typically takes a breath of air in between hits from the balloon and so does not overdose. If a mask is used however, because it is stuck to the face, the user inhales the neat gas on every breath and so can quickly go unconscious. Over four minutes of this and death can occur, but in the latter stages of that time there will most likely be brain damage due to oxygen starvation. I had to be very careful that Sandra did not die. I did not want her to die, and I did not wish to be a murderer. No, Felipe.

Rather, I wanted her to be sufficiently compliant to tell me where the money was.

Her eyes opened slowly. At first they remained mere slits, then they widened and she looked around the room, dazedly taking in her familiar surroundings: the drinks cabinet, the TV, the white hairy rug, the chrome and glass coffee table, and finally the abstract pictures on the wall opposite, which held her attention for a while. She didn't seem to register me standing over her. I held the mask in place. She suddenly realised it was there, but was too fuzzy and, probably because she was used to breathing this gas, did not fight me. Instead she relaxed and closed her eyes again. I took the mask away and let her breathe to recover a little.

Trying to imitate Vale's accent, I whispered to her, 'Sandra, what are we going to do with our money? When do you want me to get it?' Her expression was puzzled, she didn't seem to understand. I pressed her, 'Sandra! Where's the money? We need to get it to launder it.'

Uncomprehending, she focused on the strange, unrecognisable character in black with only his eyes showing, but she could not register what was going on and started to giggle.

She squinted at me, curious and puzzled. 'Why…, why are you dressed like Ratman, or are you Bobin?' She laughed with a sudden 'Hah!' and collapsed giggling onto the floor, her body shaking with hysterics.

I moved quickly round the sofa and knelt beside her. Perhaps she needed to recover so she could talk sense, I waited for appropriate signs. She fell asleep. This was going nowhere, so I decided to conclude the other purpose of my visit and switched cream dispensers to use a full one then packed the mask to her face again, gently squeezing the trigger to let the gas flow. She didn't struggle, and I kept a close eye on the time. Three minutes and she had not moved. She was breathing steadily, though. Another thirty seconds was enough, any more and she could die. I took her hands and put them on the mask and around the creamer and then let her fall naturally back to the floor.

Her phone was on the table. I found Vale's number in her contacts and sent him a text: *I've had enough, I'm going to end it. It was a lovely time. S* That should summon him and implicate him by virtue of his fingerprints everywhere, his number in her phone and his DNA in the flat. If it worked, his future in the police would be over.

That was how I imagined it might go, loosely following my plan. Unfortunately for Sandra, it did not happen that way.

27

WHAT ACTUALLY HAPPENED was that I peered out of the bathroom and saw no one. There was a quarter of a bottle of whisky, a little jug of water and one glass on the table. Other than the TV which, as I described, was illuminating the room in a flickering orange glow and emitting canned laughter at a low volume, there was no sound.

I had to find out where she was before fetching my kit, I couldn't lug that around and bump into her somewhere. A quick glance into the kitchen proved fruitless, the hall too. Was she drunk behind a couch? No. There were two bedrooms, naturally I went to hers first.

Very softly I pushed on the door which was ajar. It opened without a sound. Peering through the crack, the first thing that came into view was the cupboard opposite, then her dressing table. In its mirror I could see her bare feet, heels down, at the end of the bed. *Stop.*

She was lying on her back, which meant she would see me as I entered the room unless she was asleep. If I startled her there would be a fight, and all my efforts to convince the police that no one else was involved would be wasted.

I couldn't go through this again, this dressing up for the occasion and entering through the bathroom window. The more I were to do it, the more the likelihood of being discovered. I would have to hope she was asleep and try to administer the gas as she lay there. I went back to the bathroom, quickly prepared the two nitrous kits and took my bag, putting it down outside the door. On my knees, keeping low, I pushed the door a little wider. From this height I was below the level of the bed.

Always ominous, The Scream watched over her. Whereas before, the painting had symbolised a troubled past, now the tortured figure, fleeing before a bloody sky and deafened by its own shrieks, tried to shut them out– the horror before it being too much to bear.

She was completely naked. Her wrists were cuffed and tied to the bed head. That much I could see, but there was more. There was something wrong with the scene. Cautiously I stood up. Sandra was staring at the ceiling, her eyes wide open and unmistakably devoid of life.

I could only see those eyes by viewing them from the top, because they were almost covered by the enormous testicles of an oversized replica of male genitalia, the silicon penis of which was rammed between her stretched lips. Sticking out between her legs was one end of a thick, violet coloured, double ended dildo. I stared, stunned at the obscenity of the scene.

In this flat illegally, a dead body in front of me, taking a huge risk, I was ultra sensitive to surprise. The front door closed with a sharp clunk. I jumped. Was it closed from the inside or the outside? Was the murderer still there, or had he just left? It was only seconds since the lock had clicked. Very quickly, I went round the flat, ready for anything, but there was no one there. I cautiously opened the front door and saw the lifts. The indicator switched from 1 to G to B, the parking. He was gone, whoever he was, and he'd left me with the corpse and looking as guilty as hell.

From carefully parted curtains, there was no sign of anything moving outside. I went back to Sandra, whipped off a glove and felt for a pulse just to be sure, even though it was easy to recognise the absence of life from the vacant eyes. She was still warm though. There was no apparent cause of death, but it must have happened a very short time ago. It was imperative that I get out of there immediately. I had wanted to search the place, but there was no time.

My plan to have her tell me where the money was had been foiled, but there was another aspect that I could still do. A quick rummage around and I found her phone in the bedside drawer. Vale was in her contact list. "Help" I typed and pressed Send. I left the phone on top of the cabinet, but then saw the keys in the open drawer. One was the type that might fit a locker. It had an orange coloured tag on it and an inscription that was mostly worn away, only "..orage" was legible with the number 1142. A luggage locker? The other key was on the same ring, and looked as if it would fit a padlock. I debated whether to take them with me or leave them for Carter's boys to find. Rather leave them, they would find the locker, or lockers, much quicker than I could. Vale would probably come first in response to the message, so the keys should not be left in full view. I put them back in the drawer under her other things, gathered my stuff, checked I had not disturbed anything or left any incriminating evidence and left the way I had come in, closing the window behind me.

28

SUNDAY MORNING AT about half past three was when I got back to the farm. After leaving Sandra's flat I drove around a bit, too wound up to go to bed. The vision of her in that state was not going to let me sleep, not because I was horrified so much as because of the implications that her death held. There was going to be a weighty fall out from it. So I sat in a lay-by looking out at the rain and contemplating my future. It didn't look bright. Unless the keys could be traced to a locker or something I was effectively bankrupt and, pessimistically, in Juliet I had lost the only bright star in my universe.

The Defender's lights shone on a car outside my house. The police already? No. It was Juliet's Volvo. Again my imagination ran riot. Was she back so soon to tell me she had had enough, and that she had found someone else? No, surely not, not in such a short space of time. She would realise that any man could have done the same as I did and she would be far too suspicious of a new relationship. She would need a lot of time, so it wasn't that. Maybe she had just made up her mind that she was going to cut me out of her life altogether – that was possible. But maybe, just a very small maybe, she had come to restore things between us.

I opened the door slowly and listened. Nothing. I called her name softly, not wanting to wake her if she was asleep. No answer. Then I had an awful feeling of déjà vu. The last time I had come home and called her name, she had been kidnapped. I had to find out where she was and listened at the door to the little bedroom. She was snoring so quietly I could barely hear her, but at least she was all right.

I might have slept for an hour, but was up at seven and put some coffee on. A few minutes before eight, the floor-boards above creaked – Juliet was up. I waited apprehensively. She appeared on the landing, showered and dressed in a dark knee length skirt and her green jumper.

'Good morning, Did you have a good night?' Her words had all the menace of a suspicious wife. 'Where were you?' she said as she came down the stairs.

I had no chance to reply, to dispel what I assumed was her disappointment in me; out on the town as soon as she had left. My actions giving the lie to how I cared for her, my false and pleading words, reinforcing her decision to sever relations with me. I could easily have reassured her on all of that, but was interrupted. There was a heavy knock on the door. I knew it had to come, but not so soon.

'Good Morning, Chief Inspector, what news? Found the money?' I tried to be cheerful.

'Not yet, Mr Forbes. May I come in?' he said, moving forward anyway. He looked serious. Following him was a female officer. 'This is Detective Constable Phillips.'

Phillips held up her warrant card. She was a tall, heavy young woman with a rather stern face under yellow hair. She did not return my smile; a tough no-nonsense girl who's narrow, blue and permanently suspicious eyes told a story of harsh experiences and hard knocks.

'Coffee?'

'Thank you, that'll be welcome.'

'Where's Sergeant Vale today?' I waved at a kitchen chair on my way back to the coffee machine. 'Have a seat.'

'Sergeant Vale has been taken off the case, he's needed in another enquiry.'

It was obvious that was all the information he was going to impart on the subject, but it seemed that my scheming had worked. I gave Carter and Phillips the coffees I had already made for us and started on another two. I waited patiently for him to ask the questions that had to come.

'Where were you between midnight and one last night, please?'

'Here, with Juliet. Why do you ask?' I gave her a quick pleading glance as I put her coffee down. She looked surprised at my reply, but said nothing.

'Will you confirm that you were both here last night,' Carter said to her. Phillips had taken out a notebook and was scribbling in it as we spoke.

I didn't dare look at her again. I did mutter 'Please' to myself, but Juliet didn't hesitate. 'Yes.'

'Watched TV?'

'No. We just talked mostly about what Alastair's going to do if the money isn't recovered. We went to bed about midnight. What's the matter?'

'Did you reach a conclusion?'

'No, we just went round and round in circles, I'm afraid. If there's no chance of getting the money, then he'll be forced into a decision, but until then I suppose procrastination will hold sway.'

Carter nodded his understanding. 'There's been a development on that score, but first I must tell you that Sandra Collins was murdered in her flat last night.'

'What?' Feigning genuine surprise is not as easy as it's made out to be, especially when you are being scrutinised by the police. 'How? Who? When? Oh, between twelve and one as you asked, I suppose.'

Juliet had her hand up to her open mouth, but she said nothing, her eyes wide.

'We don't know who yet, but I—'

'Have to eliminate you from our enquiries.' I gave him an innocent grin.

He smiled for the first time since he'd arrived. 'A hackneyed phrase, but apt. Yes, I have to do that, and I must warn you that an alibi from two people who might have the same motive will be treated with caution.'

'Chief Inspector, I'm not sure what I feel about her death at this early stage. Good riddance certainly, but mainly regret, I think, because she hasn't told us where the money is. Which leads on to a motive on my part: if I were going to kill her, do you really think I'd do it before the money was recovered?'

He acknowledged that, while Phillips continued to jot down notes.

Juliet came out of her shocked trance, her voice soft. 'How was she killed?'

'We don't know yet. There are no obvious signs, but the pathologist is working on it.'

'How do you know she didn't just die of a heart attack or some other natural cause?'

'She had been sexually assaulted. I'll spare Miss Meredith the details. I have some news for you, though. When the lads were searching the crime scene, they came across two keys, one of which appears to be from a storage locker. We think it's possible that the money is there, and I'll have men working on the location of that locker this morning.'

'Fantastic! Thanks, but come on, Chief Inspector,' I said, 'we're not children and we're heavily involved as you well know. What does "sexually assaulted" resulting in death mean?'

'It means she had a dildo stuffed in her mouth and another double ended one in her vagina.' Phillips was less inhibited than Carter and issued the news with force and evident disgust. It earned her a look of rebuke from him.

'I can't tell you the cause of death, I really can't at this stage. We'll have to wait for the pathologist.' Carter was not going to debate the situation. He picked up his jacket, 'Thanks for the coffee, we'll be in touch as soon as we hear about the lockers, one way or another.'

'What does this mean, Chief Inspector?' Juliet put out a hand to his arm. 'Where does this leave us?'

'I'll be in touch as soon as we know something, as I said.' Carter led the way out followed by Phillips who seemed to have mellowed slightly.

'THANK YOU. YOU have no idea how grateful I am for you covering for me,' I said. 'You have nothing to fear from lying for me, but it was a very loyal thing to do, especially without knowing what the implications would be.'

'I want a full explanation, now!' She her hand down on the table. 'Did you have anything to do with that witch's death? Or were you out socialising last night?'

'Slow down, Jules. Calm down, please. I did not kill Sandra, and I wasn't out having a good time in the pub or night club or anybody else's bedroom, which is obviously what you think. Sit down and I'll tell you everything. Would you like more coffee?'

I told her the whole story, everything that had happened since she left. I told her of Vale's involvement and how I'd sent the text message to incriminate him. I only left out my true intended method of revenge on Sandra. It wasn't necessary to tell her that.

'That double ended thing, that's used between two women, I suppose?' She got up and began to pace around the room.

'It must be, although with a stretch of imagination I can see how some others would find a way to harness its attractions. I don't know – not my scene.'

'What to you think, Mandy or Vale?' Juliet picked some eggs out of the basket for scrambling.

'I just don't know.' I put two slices of rye bread into the toaster. As I did so, it struck me how normal our breakfast preparations were. She didn't have to ask if I wanted eggs, and I knew she would have hers on rye. In spite of everything that had passed, we still reacted as the couple we should have been. 'The sexual nature of the crime could mean that it was an act of jealousy, and if she and Mandy were into each other then Mandy could have taken exception to the visits by Vale; amongst plenty of others, of course. And it could just as well have been Vale for similar reasons, or even someone else we know nothing about. Was this a lesbian murder? Surely Sandra wasn't that way inclined? But, I suppose, given her voracious carnal appetite she might well have been bisexual. Maybe this has nothing to do with our case at all.'

'Vale knew about the money, if that had something to do with it.'

'So did Mandy, but I'll bet no third party did.' Something else that should have been in the frame much earlier occurred to me, but a lot had been going on. 'Just a minute, I sent that "Help" text to Vale with Sandra's phone. That evidence will still be there on her phone and Vale's too if he hasn't deleted it.'

'You said you sent the message shortly after she died, and a guilty Vale would know that and would know that someone else must have sent it. If it was him, I wonder if he knew someone else was in the flat when he left.'

'If he murdered her, he would want to get her phone as soon as possible and destroy it to remove that evidence of his connection with her. If he didn't kill her, he would presumably respond to the text and he'd want to preserve the phone, because that would be evidence that he was not the murderer – she's not going to ask her killer for help. Either way he'd be in trouble, something he would not be able to avoid in any event with his DNA all over the place, but better to be accused of anything other than murder,' I said. 'Why don't we take Carter out for a drink? I like the man, and I think it's reciprocated. I was thinking of doing it anyway when the case was over, but why not now?'

'D'you think he'd come? The case isn't over and you might still be a suspect.'

'Maybe not. We can only try.'

A minute or two passed in silence. I couldn't wait any longer. 'Jules, why are you here? And why did you give me a false alibi?'

She gave me a very short smile and took a deep breath. 'There's only one answer. I've been lectured by Mary. She convinced me that I shouldn't throw this relationship away. She reminded me of everything about us before you did what you did. About how good we were for each other, how we had a positive effect on other people, how much fun we had … She said I would be daft to cut ties with you. So, I'm here to say that I want to return to being your best companion, your best friend along with Giles, so the alibi was a gut reaction to old loyalties.' She put her hand up as I opened my mouth. 'Wait, I haven't finished. So, that's what I am, your best and most loyal friend, but I'm not your lover. I may never be, I just don't know, I can't think about it. I'll have to come to terms with it and forgive you first, and I don't know how long that will take.'

Then she did something I'll never forget. She stood up, came close and kissed me hard and passionately on the lips. I started to put my arm around her, but she stood back and gave me one hell of a slap across my cheek. It knocked me side-ways off my chair and it stung too; such power from such a small person! I was on one hand and my knees on the floor, picking myself up. The other hand was massaging my cheek. She stood there, looking down at me without malice and said,

'That sums up how I feel; love and anger. I'm confused, but I'll muddle along until it sorts itself out in my little brain.'

'You can carry on beating me up if it's going to help.' The shock of her blow had transmuted into humour, and she laughed. What a wonderful sound, one I hadn't heard in, how long? An absolute tonic.

CARTER WAS RELUCTANT at first, but after a little persuasion agreed to meet us at The Mandolino. The weather had passed through and the autumn sun was warm, so we chose a table outside on the pavement. The area was not decorated and homely like the inside, of course, but it was more pleasant to be in the fresh air when conditions allowed. To my left, through the window, was the table I had occupied when Sandra barged into my life. It seemed that the wheel had almost turned its full circle. The Mandolino was where it had all started, and it was here that we were about to discuss what were hopefully the closing phases. I made a silent prayer that Carter would not ask when we were going to be married. That would lead to my use of the word 'fiancée' and bring down more trouble on my head.

A border collie, which was lying under another table, was watching us from between its front paws. I gave it an encouraging look and it wandered over to be petted, bringing back a brief sense of loss over Tina.

There weren't many people in the restaurant at that time, so it didn't take long for the drinks to arrive along with one of those little dishes with three compartments: one with green olives stuffed with a slice of chilli, one with green olives stuffed with a slice of garlic and one with black olives. Carter and I had a Peroni each and Juliet had a ginger beer. 'I'm driving,' she said, as if she were proving something to the policeman.

'Woman's lot, seems to be anyway, although my wife and I take turns, which I think is pretty generous on my part!' He laughed at his own expense. 'I'll walk home, it's not far.'

A bus drew up at the stop across the road to let some passengers off, but there was no queue to get on this time. A red Ferrari waited in the traffic on our side of the road, almost abreast of us. The driver kept blipping his engine, either loving the howl of power at his command or showing off; whatever, it was noisy.

'Chief Inspector, is Alastair still a suspect?' Juliet asked when the car had moved on, 'Am I a suspect as a beneficiary in Giles's will?'

'Officially? We have not found Sandra Collins's murderer yet, and we've not had a confession from Wiggins for the assault on Giles Collins. Both of those are still open, and Mr Forbes is still in the frame. Privately, sticking my neck out further than I should do, I don't see either of you being guilty of anything serious – yet. Things might change, though. I still have to maintain an open mind.'

'Fair enough,' I said. 'This is mostly a social occasion because I think you and I have a mutual respect for one another, and Juliet and I are both trying to calm down after all this and thought it would be good to get an off the record opinion; if you can, of course. In that light, may we call you Jim?'

His mouth twisted into his lop sided grin. 'Of course, Alastair, and Juliet.' It seemed that he too was happy to relax for a while at least. Maybe too, he thought we might let something slip to complete his picture of the case.

'I'll tell you where we are,' he said. 'Tony Wiggins is out of hospital and safely locked up in jail.'

'Will he get bail?' Juliet's concern was plain.

'I will certainly oppose it, and it's unlikely given the large amount of cash available to him to enable an escape, and the fact that he's such a violent man. If he is granted bail we'll be keeping a very close watch on him, so there's no need for you to worry.'

'That's a relief, anyway. We were thinking it was probably Mandy that killed Sandra, given the type of sex toys used?' Juliet said.

'Possibly. Forensics have examined the dildo and found traces of vaginal fluid on the end that was not inside her. It doesn't match her DNA, so another female was involved.' He paused and sipped his beer, a cautious drinker. 'We're looking for Mandy Wiggins, including at her caravan, but apparently she hasn't been there since Tuesday, according to the receptionist.'

Juliet stabbed an olive with a toothpick. 'And how did Sandra die?'

'Pathologist says it was a massive dose of pentobarbitone, injected into the abdominal cavity.'

'Pento what?' I said.

Juliet pulled the olive off the stick with her teeth. 'Pentobarbitone is a drug used by vets as an anaesthetic and also to put animals to sleep.'

'How do you know that?' I realised immediately that it was a stupid question and bound to be used against me.

'I thought that after all these years you knew all about me.' She thrust her toothpick towards me. 'In case you haven't realised it, I work with animals and every so often meet the vet.'

Jim Carter watched this teasing exchange with amusement. He seemed to be thinking of past pleasures of his own. 'Now, on the matter of the money.'

'Oh yes?'

'It was quite easy to find the locker actually, the key was marked with a storage company name, so all the lads had to do was find out which branch it was. There was no money in it though. It appears she was ready to travel somewhere, and as it was close to St Pancras station, it's possible she was thinking of the Eurostar to Paris, or … ?' He flapped an open hand. 'There was a large suitcase containing clothes, toiletries and so on. There was also a current passport in the name of Sandra Parsons, her maiden name.

'The other key is for a padlock and that could be anything, anywhere. However, if Sandra used a storage company for one bag, it's not unlikely that she used one for the other, and we're still searching. Logic says it must also be close to St Pancras if she wanted to make a quick getaway. It could take a long time to find it, I'm afraid.'

There was a muffled sound of a phone, and Jim dug it out from his jacket pocket. He stared at me as he listened. 'Yup,' he snapped and stopped the call. 'You didn't tell me you'd cut out the rear window of the caravan to get in.' The pleasant, relaxed look had left his face.

I was silent for a few seconds, and he said, 'Well?' with a raised eyebrow.

'Sorry, you didn't ask and I wasn't going to volunteer that I broke in. It was stupid of me, I should have told you, I suppose.' I was still stroking the collie and the owner, who was wearing a thick dirty jumper and wellies, gave me a friendly nod.

'I warned you before about taking matters into your own hands, and I ignored it before.' He was undoubtedly cross. Perhaps he felt I had betrayed his trust in me, or perhaps it was merely that I was meddling in his investigation. 'Again, because your actions are perfectly understandable, even if they do muck me about, I'll leave you to the mercy of the Counsel for their defence, and he or she may well have a go at you.'

'Thanks. Sorry, it won't happen again.' It already had of course, in Sandra's flat, but I was never going to admit to that.

'Let's hope not.' He tapped his glass and waved at the waitress. 'Another?'

'Please. Thanks.' We fell silent for a while, and I struggled to think of something to lighten the mood again, but failed. 'I have to say I'm glad that Sergeant Vale is no longer working on this, I found him a confrontational and difficult man.'

Jim didn't answer as the girl was on her way back to the table with the beers. He handed her some change. 'I suppose you'll find out at some stage,' he said when she'd left. 'Vale was sleeping with Sandra Collins, and—'

'What?' Juliet and I both uttered. She thought for a minute and said, 'That means he could have been telling her everything that was going on. It means his loose mouth could have resulted in my kidnap!' She was flushed and angry. 'And everything that followed!' It was a brilliant performance.

'I'm afraid so.' Jim avoided our looks and stared into his beer, perhaps feeling some guilt on behalf of the force which might even have mitigated his anger at my behaviour. 'I can do little else but apologise. Looking back, I realise there were signs, but I missed them. When we went over Sandra's flat after her murder, evidence of his presence was everywhere. Until we found that another female had used the dildo, he was seriously considered as being guilty of the murder. He's been suspended of course, he's not completely cleared of murder, but even if he didn't kill her he'll never remain in the force.'

'THINK ABOUT IT,' Juliet said later when we were back at home. 'If I were Sandra and was going to catch the Eurostar to some far off destination, I'd be worried about being followed. I'd store my go-away kit in a suitcase in a locker, aiming to change in the toilet and emerge a new person. I'd jump on the train immediately and reappear in France before anyone following me had worked out that I'd changed clothes.'

'What about the money?'

'Well, because I would want to spend as little time as possible in England in my new clothes, I'd have to have the money with me before I changed.'

'Fair enough, but where will you pick up the money? There must be several hundred lockers, even thousands within reach of St Pancras.'

'I know. This thinking doesn't get us any further forward, does it? It's so frustrating. And, even worse is that there's no reason why Sandra Parsons didn't store the money close to home and travel to London with it.'

'Parsons, Parsons. I've an idea, a flash of genius!' Excited, I picked up the phone and dialled Carter's number. 'Jim, sorry, it's late I know, but there's a lead you should consider following. Parsons, Sandra's last husband, told Giles that he'd met her at a storage facility where she was a manager. She might go back there to leave the money.'

'Good thinking, leave it with me.' It sounded as if he was lying down.

'I'M FOR BED. Goodnight.' Juliet gave me a slight smile. I think she was content that we were maintaining a more amicable relationship.

29

IT WAS AFTER eight when Jim Carter phoned us. He said they had sent an officer to Parson's house, but he wasn't at home. The neighbour seemed to think he had gone away for the weekend.

Juliet, the red apron on over her black jeans, had muttered something about making breakfast and was doing things in the kitchen. She had lifted the big cover off one of the Aga hot plates and put a frying pan down alongside it. She turned to me. 'You know, I can't forget Mandy laughing at the thought of my being raped by her awful husband. I can't get that silly giggle of hers out of my head. What's so funny about a woman being raped, and by your own husband! Some people are twisted.'

The unmistakeable click of a weapon being cocked behind us made me jump. It's an ominous sound, portending an end to life. I stood very still. Juliet did not recognise the noise, not so the high pitched voice that followed, though. She started and dropped her spatula.

'You needn't have worried about that, darling.' Mandy had opened the door of the walk-in pantry without a sound. 'You wanna know why I laughed? Because I knew that my pathetic husband couldn't ever get it up, and even if he did, it was so fucking soft it would never hurt you.' She giggled senselessly, then screamed, *'Where's my money?'*

She must have come in the back door and been hiding in the pantry. Her jeans were tight enough to accentuate the roll of fat round her hips, and an orange T shirt with an indiscernible logo strained to contain her chest. The tattooed tail of a reptile of some sort on her right shoulder snaked below her sleeve line. The gun was a six shot revolver, a .38 at a guess, because the cylinder looked too short to be a .38 Special. Thank goodness, because that would wreak much greater damage. The difference was almost academic, the hammer was back in the firing position, and the weapon quivered from the tension in her hand.

Juliet was by the cooker. I was in the middle of the room, now facing the pantry where Mandy had come in but hardly moved since. About three metres separated us; too far to go to tackle her, and she could hardly miss a shot at that range. Juliet was much closer, about half that distance. 'Don't do anything stupid, Jules,' I breathed to myself.

'Your money?' I said.

'The money you stole from my caravan, where the fuck is it?' She was quivering with rage, or was it? She might have been ill or drugged.

'That isn't your money, it's mine, extorted from me by Sandra, you and your husband. If it were your money, obtained honestly, it wouldn't have been hidden, it would have been in a bank. The police have it because it's evi—'

'*The police!*' Well, you're going to get it from them or I'm going to blow her fucking head open!' She waved the revolver shakily in Juliet's direction. 'She stays here, you go and get that money. *Now!*' She advanced, Juliet retreated. The counter stopped her, but she arched back over it, trying to get further away.

'I can't walk into a police station and demand to take evidence away. Use your head, Mandy.'

'*Bull!*' She was shouting again and turned the gun on me, 'It's your money, you say. They've no right to keep it, so go and get it!'

Uncontrolled, my anger flared and I took a step forward. 'Listen to me you deranged idiot. I've had it with you lot: you try to kill my friend, you kill my dog, you kidnap and try to kill my girlfriend, your stupid ineffectual husband tries to kill me on two occasions, you extort one and a half million pounds out of me, lose it, and now you want it back. Sandra plots and directs the operation, stupid Tony does the heavy work and you scurry around like a whipped assistant.' I paused to draw breath.

She jumped in, furious and red in the face. 'Sandra, that fucking bitch! She didn't plan it, I did. I came up with the ideas. Right from the beginning, from when we left school. I told her to use her looks and her body to suck money out of rich men. I found her first husband for her and told her how to turn it ugly and get a divorce. I did the same with your mate. And it was my idea to kidnap your bitch.' She waved the revolver in Juliet's direction again. 'And it was me that told Anthony to fire the barn. And I didn't only have the ideas, I watched for you at the airport, I followed you to the lane and told Anthony when it was time to kill Justin Giles.' She sneered his name. 'All bloody Sandra did was send you a message to meet him where you did. Meantime, she was out shopping, keeping herself well out the way.

'She thought out some details and did things her way, but it was my plans she was using. Then she cheated me. My ideas, my plan, most of the money should be mine, but she took it off her brother and has hidden it. She left us a fifth. A fifth for me and Anthony, while she walks off with one million, two hundred and fifty k!' She spat the words out. She was focused on me, forcing her version of events on me. Why? Did she expect sympathy for her position? Or was she simply letting off steam? There was no way of knowing if she was telling the truth or had talked herself into a leading role that did not really exist. Maybe they had sat down together and the ideas had been a joint effort.

My mobile phone rang and growled its vibrations on the table.

'Answer it. No, don't.'

Ring-ring, grrr-grrr.

'Suppose whoever's calling knows we're here, they'll think something's wrong if I don't answer.'

Ring-ring. With every 'grrr-grrr' the phone edged across the table.

'Answer it then, but be bloody careful or I'll kill her.'

Ring-ring, grrr-grrr.

'What if it's the police? What do I say?'

The constant ringing was breaking her down. Her face was tense. She was fidgeting and shifting from one foot to the other. I picked up the handset, 'Hello?'

Carter said, 'Good morning, Alastair. There's been a report that Mandy Wiggins is heading in your direction. We've not been able to confirm that, but assume it's true. Wiggins had a gun, it was licensed, but it didn't show up in his house when we searched it. There's a possibility that his wife has it, and she's a prime suspect for murder already, as you know.'

'Really? I didn't know that.'

He knew that wasn't true. 'Is everything all right?'

'No,' I said with emphasis, then injected some calm into my voice. 'No, we haven't seen her, Chief Inspector.' Mandy's face was not difficult to read. She didn't like this, she wasn't party to the whole conversation, couldn't decide what to do to control the situation and probably felt the world was closing in on her. I couldn't afford to let her get so desperate she would shoot.

'I get the message,' he said. 'I'll send some men out as soon as possible, we need to protect John Knott and anyone else on your property.'

'John could be here, but there should be no one else at the moment.'

'Alastair, none of your heroics or taking the matter into your own hands this time, all right? Cooperate with me and let us handle it. We'll be on site in about six minutes. Don't do anything stupid.'

'Wouldn't dream of it.' The kitchen clock showed twenty two minutes past, but there was no way to warn Juliet of Carter's intentions.

'What did he want?'

God, this woman was unhinged. I'd had enough of this yelling and screaming, but I had to keep the temperature down. 'Only if we'd seen you. You heard me say no.'

Mandy's jaw muscles were working constantly, her lips tight set. She had a hand on the counter top as if to keep steady, but could not hold the gun still. All it would take would be an unintended nervous reaction for a shot to go off. She seemed to get a grip on herself for a moment though, and decided that she could not manage two of us. 'You! Tie him up,' she yelled at Juliet.

'I'll try and find something to tie him with.' Juliet too was being deliberately calm. She must have been forcing herself to stay composed, given what she had been through because of this woman.

'Rope, get some rope, of course.'

'Mandy, Juliet doesn't live here and doesn't know where everything is, so please be patient. The only rope is outside, but I don't think you want all of us to go out and find it, do you?'

'Shut up, you! String, all kitchens have string. Find some.'

'In the top cupboard on your right,' I said to Juliet. I could not see any course but to help, and if I did this woman might calm down. To be confrontational would certainly be dangerous.

Juliet found the string, a great ball of it, certainly enough to prevent me breaking the bond. Following Mandy's orders, I sat down on a kitchen chair which had vertical bars down the back. It was already positioned sideways to the end of the table, which meant there was nothing in front of me. I put my hands behind me, and Juliet tied a loose knot round my right wrist and then wound the string round and round both wrists to hold them together. Mandy was behind me somewhere pointing the gun at Juliet's head.

'Tight, make it tight,' Mandy snapped, 'if he gets loose I'm going to start shooting.'

Juliet made a pretence of pulling and I forced my wrists apart against the tension. '*Ow*. That hurts, it's too tight, I'll lose circulation.'

'*Shut up*. Now tie his hands to the chair back.'

Claustrophobia. In me, being restrained leads to panic. If I can't undo a tight shirt button, I feel trapped. Now, I had a mental battle to get myself under control. I knew that once I had, I'd be all right unless threatened and unable to do something about it. Helping my fight was the knowledge that the bonds were not tight at all once I had brought my wrists together. I worked hard at slipping a hand free without any telltale body movements. Once one hand was out, the other would be easy.

'You.' Mandy looked at Juliet. 'call that bloody copper.'

'What do you want me to say?'

'Tell him that I want the money delivered here and a car full of petrol. I'll be taking you with me.'

'That's original,' I said. Stupid, because it was confrontational.

'*Shut up,* I said!'

Juliet dialled the last number that called. I could just imagine the Chief Inspector's gruff, 'DCI Carter' from the other end. Juliet passed the message, listened then held the phone out to Mandy. 'He says the money's in safe deposit, and it will take some time to get it. He wants to talk to you.'

'Well I don't want to talk to him, and I'm holding the fucking cards.'

'It's probably best you do talk directly, Mandy,' I said in as even a tone as I could. 'Misunderstandings often happen when a third party's involved.'

Surprisingly, she saw the sense in that and accepted the phone, but her gun remained aimed at Juliet. 'What do you want? Just do as I say and no one will get hurt. I want the money, I want a car full of petrol and you lot off my back.'

I could only imagine Carter's side of the conversation. He'd be trying to calm her, agreeing to give her the money and everything else she wanted, but explaining that she would never get away – the futility of it all.

Mandy put the phone back down on the table and sank heavily onto the chair facing me. She seemed to be a bit more relaxed now something was being done. There was a flicker of movement outside the window, far away down the drive. As if to confirm Carter's estimate, the clock struck the half hour, making her jump. Her eyes widened briefly with alarm.

Juliet kept a close watch on the ever pointing gun. 'Mandy, I want to sit down. I'm going to pull this chair out, okay?'

Mandy thrust the gun forward at Juliet, but she grunted agreement.

And so we waited. I was winning the battle to free my left hand and had managed to work some of the windings of string off the end of my fingers, but it was a long process.

I wanted to know if Mandy had seen me, albeit an unrecognisable me, in Sandra's flat the night she killed her. If she had, it would lead to a deeper investigation and some unwelcome questions. 'So why did you kill Sandra before you got the money from her?' Conversation would hopefully distract her, if she joined in.

She wasn't going to, but then, in remembering, started to shake again. Her hand was trembling, and there is no safety catch on most revolvers. 'We were good mates. I knew what hell her dad put her through. She hates men because of him, and she took revenge on every one she could. At school she took the boys and broke their hearts, then it was the turn of young men, now she rips off rich husbands. That was my idea, but always she was there in front, the beautiful image, the fantastic screw, while I was always second, always bloody second; Plain Jane to Sexy Sandra. We supported each other in the beginning, she was good to me and kind. It was only when she got all that money off Parsons that she got greedy. I love her though, I dunno why, because she never thanked me for my help. I just got the cast off men when they were too drunk to see the difference. She's rich, you know, rich from using my ideas, but I've seen bugger all of it.' She kept using the present tense with Sandra, as if in denial of her death.

'All I get,' she went on, 'is a pittance and sex with her when she's not working on a man.'

We needed to put her at ease, to speak softly and kindly and keep her talking. 'So why did you do it then, why did you allow yourself to be second?'

She let out a long breath, then with less tension, 'I dunno. I suppose because it gave me opportunities I wouldn't normally have.'

There was a glint of moisture in her eyes, was this regret for life or love lost? She was calming down having vented her feelings, but I had to hold her attention a little longer. I didn't need to try, however, she continued without prompting. 'So I boiled over – it was like the lid came off the pressure cooker, like a fucking volcano blowing. I'd had enough of sucking the hind tit, of being her bloody servant and sex slave.

'After Anthony was arrested, I reckoned I had to look after myself, go it alone. I stole some pentobarb' from the vet where I work and waited for the opportunity. With me, she liked to be tied up. It was something she would never do with a man. She had to dominate men. I suppose that was because of her perverted dad. Anyway, last night I tied her wrists to the headboard, pushed her plastic dick into her and sat on the other end. It was a vibrator as well, and while she was gasping away over that, I stuck her with the needle, right in the stomach. There was enough pentobarb' in there to stun a horse. It took longer than I reckoned for her to die, though. She bucked and heaved for a couple of seconds under me to get away, but I'm heavier than her and stronger than her, and her hands were tied. The stuff kills through respiratory arrest, so I helped her on her way by ramming another dildo into her mouth. How many real cocks had she had in there? Then I left that double stuffed where a hundred men had been.' She paused and began to shake even more. 'Bloody whore. I'm going to miss her. What will I do now?'

Loss and regret were tearing at her, but she had to justify herself to someone. Tears, laden with mascara, ran down her cheeks in ugly black rivulets. She began to sob, but her bloodshot eyes never left us.

The phone rang again, and Juliet picked it up when Mandy pointed at it. She put the speaker on and left the phone on the table within the woman's reach.

Carter's voice, tinny from the little speaker, said, 'Mandy, I'm just keeping you in the picture. We've got the car ready, and the authorisation to release the money will be signed very shortly. But you must realise that you will never get away. In the old days, you might have done, but not today with police cooperation across Europe and all the technology we now have. You're best course is to come out without your weapon and without harming the hostages. You don't want any further charges against you.'

'Switch him off.'

Juliet did as she was told. 'You must be hungry, would you like something to eat?' What was she up to with that caring tone in her voice?

Mandy nodded, and Juliet cautiously rose from her chair and crossed to the cooker. She was standing a single step away from Mandy who watched her all the time, ignoring me. Juliet fetched a bottle of oil, slid the frying pan onto the hot plate from where she had left it and moved the basket of eggs a bit closer to the Aga. Then she went back to the counter, opened a packet of bread and took out three slices, all normal calming actions. 'I hope you like wholewheat,' she said.

'Whatever,' was the sullen answer.

The phone rang again. This time Mandy picked it up and listened. I could just recognise Carter on the other end, but not the detail. She said, 'Nobody's going to get hurt if you do what I say and hurry up about it.'

Carter carried on talking and Mandy's concentration on Juliet faltered. Her left hand held the phone, and her right held the revolver which was lying on the table in front of her, ready to deploy. My own left hand came free at that moment, but the other was still attached to the chair back. Juliet picked the pan up off the hob.

'Mandy,' I said.

She ignored me.

'Mandy.'

She turned her head in my direction, away from Juliet, 'tell him you want a little aeroplane, you need to get out of the country.'

I swear I heard Mandy's flesh hiss as Juliet rammed the red hot pan against her shoulder, right on her tattoo. She screamed, whirled around and fired wildly. A deafening noise, a metallic clang and a clatter as the pan hit the floor. Juliet fell against the counter and crumpled into a heap on the floor. Mandy was up and swinging the gun down to Juliet who lay still. Was she hit? I panicked. No Jules, not you too!

The chair was still attached to my right hand. I leapt forward and crashed it down on the crazy woman. My left hand found the gun.

When you pull the trigger on a revolver, the same action rotates the cylinder to expose the next live round to the hammer. If you grip the cylinder so it cannot rotate, then the gun cannot be fired. The weapon was between us, the barrel forcing its way into my belly. I held that cylinder fast; to relax meant the end of me. Mandy fought like a tiger beneath me. She bit into my left arm. I felt nothing. I could not free my hand from the chair back, so I kept it rammed against her face, holding her down, a wood bar squishing her flesh and distorting her cheek. Juliet was deathly still on the floor. If you've killed Jules, I swear I'll turn this gun around to you.

There was another crash in the background. Suddenly there were armed police in the room, shouting at her to drop the gun, but she could not because I had my hand over hers and was not going to let go. Two automatic weapons were a foot from her head and still she fought.

'Let go of your gun!' The shout was repeated, and again, 'Let go of your gun!'

'The gun's between us.' My words came out as puffs of air from the struggle. 'She's got the trigger and I've got the cylinder.'

Mandy with me on top of her and the two officers pointing guns at her head and shouting at her formed a tight little group. I couldn't see Juliet, but one officer shouted, 'Stay back!'

Juliet ignored him. She came into my sight; unsteady on her feet. She had the pan in her hand again. She shoved it at the woman's face, stopping a finger's width away.

The officers' threats had no effect on Mandy, but the heat from the pan at her cheek, the blistering pain that was so close wilted her. She suddenly saw the futility of it all and stopped fighting me.

'Get up slowly,' one of the armed police tapped me on the back. 'Keep a grip on that gun.'

I struggled, as the chair was still attached to my right hand, but Juliet gripped my arm to help. I was on my knees, my left hand still over the revolver's cylinder.

The officer deliberately used a calming voice. 'Let go of the weapon.'

I thought he meant that I was to release the gun, and did so, turning away. I don't think Mandy intended to pull the trigger, it was just that she still had pressure on it and it went off when my hand was no longer around the cylinder.

30

I FELL. MY legs were out of control, quivering. My whole lower body was shaking. I felt nothing, yet was thinking clearly, puzzled. Why couldn't I move?

'Ambulance, man down,' an officer shouted.

Only then did I realise that I had been shot. It was supposed to hurt, where was the pain? I felt nothing at all. Hands freed me from the chair. Concern was written in Juliet's eyes as she tried to put me in a comfortable position. The trembling gradually subsided. My breathing was becoming rapid, shallow, strained.

The police had wrested Mandy over onto her front and cuffed her. The strength had washed out of her, and her bulk spread out like a seal on the beach. Her face was down on the floor, her cheeks flushed. A trickle of dribble escaped her twisted lips and formed a little puddle on the tiles.

The paramedics must have been close, because one was there almost immediately. He gently cut my shirt away and found the entry wound. Another medic appeared. A needle was stuck in my arm, an oxygen mask clamped to my face.

I had to talk to Juliet and pulled the mask off with my free hand. 'Are you all right Jules?' I paused for breath, panting. 'That was clever.'

Why couldn't I breath? Part of me was calm and rational, another part lacked understanding.

'Just dazed, my head hit the counter top.' She looked close to tears.

The paramedic put the mask back. 'Leave it,' he ordered.

It was getting cold. Breath was coming in shallow, brief pants. Somehow though, some thoughts were clear. I pulled the mask down again. 'Jules, … ask her to tell you … about finding Sandra's first … first husband.' My mind began to drift. Juliet's face was close to mine for a moment, her eyes begging me to be strong, to be replaced by a paramedic again. Vague recollections: lifted on a stretcher; an ambulance siren; unknown faces around me; fluid bags swinging as the vehicle lurched about. I didn't understand, felt no fear, just wanted to sleep. Far away, someone said, 'He's going!' Sleep at last. Woke again, more confused visions: the hospital ceiling passing above me; rushing through Accident and Emergency; many strong arms lifting me easily onto a theatre table; bright lights; things going on in the background; impersonal, un-known eyes alert, darting about over masks. Then a calm voice from an upside down head telling me to count down from ten. Did I even start?

Mandy's bullet had entered my left side just behind my upper arm when I turned away from her. It went through my left lung across my chest behind the heart and stopped in my right lung. I was incredibly lucky that it had been a light weapon. Neither my aorta nor my spine were damaged. Had that bullet been a larger or more powerful round or been a millimetre either side of its passage, I would have been either paralysed or would have bled to death. They told me that the shock wave from the round must have given my spinal cord a hefty thump, which is why my legs had given way.

My left lung collapsed as the bullet hole allowed air in to destroy the adhesion with the chest wall. I bled over three litres of blood from both lungs giving me a haemothorax in one and a haemo-pneumothorax in the other. The paramedics had been fantastic. Replacing the blood that was leaking into my abdomen and distending my belly, they pumped my heart to keep fluid circulating and forced oxygen in so my right lung could function as long as there was some real blood in the system.

Juliet was there when I came out of surgery. She was holding my hand. 'Hello,' she said tentatively, her face a picture of concern. I saw her and then passed out again. When I came round, she was still there and, through a haze of morphine, I tried to concentrate on what she had to say.

I started to speak, but was still intubated, the tube tied in place. I put my hand up to it, but she stopped me. 'I'll do the talking. News: before they took Mandy away, and in front of Jim Carter, I asked your question. She said they'd worked at the same place when Sandra met Alan Parsons. Mandy saw him park "a bloody great Bentley" and attended to him, and felt he was coming on to her. She said she wasn't stupid, she saw the bigger opportunity and went to fetch Sandra, gave her a quick word and left her to it. She said they'd already talked about how they were going to make money from men, so that was their first step. Here's the good bit, though; she said they worked at Porpoise Self Storage near Guildford. Carter's men went straight there, but I haven't heard from him.'

Then suddenly, 'Don't you ever do that to me again!'

'Huh?' All I could do was raise my eyebrows.

'You died in the ambulance, you went into hypovolaemic shock and had a cardiac arrest, but those fantastic men kept you going until you reached the hospital. Don't give me frights like that again! Ever.'

'Nh-nh.'

JIM CARTER AND his men tracked the ransom hoard to Porpoise Self Storage as we hoped. It was all there bar a few hundred pounds, which was an enormous relief. I had blithely convinced myself that, failing to get the ransom back, I could eventually get the money together to return to Mario Montano. Deep down though, I realised that it was going to be very difficult to do it in an acceptable time frame. To have the money back had lifted a heavy burden. I wouldn't have to sell the farm and, not least, Mario would see that his trust in me was justified. The police held onto the ransom until forensics had finished with it and the court had authorised its release.

SEVERAL DAYS LATER, I was off the ventilator and out of intensive care and becoming increasingly impatient with my physically weak state. When I say weak, I mean I hardly had the strength to stand and had to be supported when in X-ray. It was taking forever for my body to build up its blood supply again. Juliet visited me every day. This time her hazel eyes were serious. 'Alastair, I can't go on with this, with us like this.' She saw the instant pain in my face and clutched my hand in both of hers. 'When you so nearly died, I was frantic, I couldn't bear to lose you. If you never came back you would die unhappy, never knowing what I really felt deep inside of me but had repressed. I couldn't read my own mind after the shock you gave me. So, if you're still willing, can we go back to where we were before all this?'

I couldn't answer for fear my voice would break. Moisture blurred my vision. Tears trickled down her cheeks and into the corners of her mouth which was set in the broadest smile I'd ever seen.

A nurse came in and did a couple of things while we just stared silently at each other.

I cleared my throat. 'I have a confession to make.' I waited until the nurse left the room. I could hear the nervousness in my own words, my voice unsteady. The lift in her cheeks dropped, the smile in her eyes changed to worry, and her teeth held her bottom lip firm. 'When I first told Carter that you'd been kidnapped, my actual words were that Wiggins had kidnapped my fiancée!'

Juliet stared at me. Oh God! I had overstepped the mark, ruined our relationship again by putting it on a completely different footing, one that wasn't wanted. 'What on earth made you say that?' she said. 'Especially then.'

My mouth was dry, I stammered. 'It ..., it just came out in the stress of the moment. Sorry, I didn't mean to be presumptuous, but I couldn't retract it. In case it comes up in conversation with others, I thought you ought to know. Save embarrassment. Sorry.'

'Came out in the stress of the moment? Presumptuous? Damn right. You might have asked me first!'

I couldn't look her in the eye. Her reaction was far worse than I'd expected. You think you know people, and Juliet and I were so close. We were back together, perhaps not as strong as before, yet now, through a stupid slip of the tongue, I'd offended her and maybe, for the second time, destroyed another part of what we had. I took as deep a breath as I was able and decided that I really had to pull my socks up in the relationships department.

'Well, if that surfaced out of your subconscious, then should I consider it as a heartfelt proposal?'

I looked up. She was trying very hard not to laugh out loud. 'Got you! You deserved that, you silly man. Have you just 'subconsciously' proposed to me? If so, it has to be one of the weirdest ways of doing it.'

'Er, yes.' This was embarrassing.

'Well, er, *yes* to you too.' She laughed, tilting her head from side to side, emphasising every syllable. God, it was good to see her happy, but the moment overwhelmed me. I hadn't actually intended to propose. But why not? She assumed from my bungling approach that I wanted to marry her, and I couldn't go back on the words now. So why not? Why not indeed? I loved her, had done for ages. I knew that, but we were so comfortable in our distant relationship, and marriage might ruin some key part of that, it might not suit us. I also realised though, that it was unfair not to give her a future in a family. Someday she might drift away looking for just that, and that would kill me. I was conscious of her watching me patiently, but the smile was fading. It was too difficult for me to reach over, so I beckoned her closer instead.

Her head was buried in my neck. Her familiar scent overwhelmed me; not her perfume – her. My shoulders, my arms, my hands were useless in utter contentment. They were clamped around her, but immobile. I could not summon movement; I did not want to move from this euphoric state. It was over; all our troubles had blown away on a wind of togetherness.

'I need to think,' she said, her words pouring out as fast as her thoughts. 'I'll have to go home and close my business, sell the cottage, find someone else to look after the horses. Maybe I should bring the business down here? I love it up there on the edge of the moor though, it'll be sad to leave.'

'There's Giles to consider as well. He's going to need looking after for a while.'

Neither of us knew what to say with that sobering thought. She broke the silence. 'I almost forgot, here's a memento to hang on the wall.' She delved in the shopping bag she had brought with her and produced a frying pan. 'Mandy's pan.' She laughed. There was a ragged bullet hole through the bottom.

EPILOGUE

I CALLED MARIO as soon as I could after coming off the ventilator. He was appalled that I had been shot and spent a long time commiserating with me. Over the money, he was delighted of course, and readily told me where to transfer the sum once it could be banked. 'When are you coming back to work, Alastair?' he said, 'My company is going to the dogs without you around. Everyone is doing their own thing, and Felipe spends more time chasing the girls than flying.'

'Ha, ha. Your team have their hearts in the right place, Mario. They're not going to behave like that and as for Felipe, what do you expect? He's young, he's got *cojones!*'

The old man laughed. 'Of course, I joking. Felipe is working well, he's coming along great and as long as he doesn't have *bambini* before he's married, I don't care. When are you coming over?' he repeated. 'But only when you are well, of course.'

'Mario, I've been injured. It's going to take about six weeks before I'll be able to pass a flying medical again. I'll have to let you know later.'

'You take your time, my friend. Sort out your life and your health, there is nothing more important than your health.'

'Mario, I hope you don't mind, I'd like to bring Juliet with me? To see Chile and where I take my holidays!'

'Perfect, my friend, excellent! I look forward to meeting your brave lady, and I will lock up Felipe!'

IT WAS A little over seven weeks later that Juliet and I left for Santiago. I had passed my aviation medical and had full lung function, a factor the doctor focused on, as I would be spending time at high altitude. Our flight arrived at Co-modoro Arturo Merino Benítez International Airport before ten in the morning. Felipe, who was on time off from the southern operation, met us and took us to the hotel to freshen up before going to the office. Felipe told us that Mario was very keen to meet the lady at the centre of the struggle that he had help to win.

Mario was a short, stocky, roly-poly sort of man with a cheerful disposition. Life was fun for him and was there to be enjoyed. If you couldn't enjoy life, then you should go away and die quietly, ridding the world of another useless specimen was his oft-used announcement. Of course, he had the money to enjoy himself and not have any worries he couldn't laugh away. His callous words belied his great generosity though, for he gave significantly to worthy Chilean causes.

Felipe knocked on his uncle's office door. Mario himself opened it, a broad grin on his face and his eyes locked on Juliet. He stood there grinning with pleasure and held his arms out. 'Enter, come in, come in,' he called in his lightly accented English. He put one arm round Juliet's shoulder and led her into the office. Apart from a quick smile of greeting, I was ignored.

'You're on show,' I whispered in her ear, before she was whisked out of reach.

Felipe moved round to stand next to his uncle and they both stood looking at Juliet with undisguised admiration. Eventually Mario glanced briefly at me and, his hands flap-ping up and down in emphasis, said, 'Magnificent! My dear you are wonderful. Alastair, now I know why you spend so much money to rescue this lady. My congratulations, wonderful, wonderful.'

'You're embarrassing me,' said Juliet. 'If it wasn't for your generosity, I don't know if I'd be here. We don't know how to thank you for your support. Whatever we do will be inadequate.'

'It was nothing.' Mario dismissed the matter. 'Now, unfortunately today I am very busy or I would personally be your host in our beautiful city. But later, Felipe will collect you and you will come to dinner at my house and Alastair can start his work here in the office tomorrow, we have much to discuss. Today you must relax, and tomorrow my wife and daughter will organise your life to great satisfaction. We will discuss tonight.'

That set the tone for Juliet's time in Chile. She came south with me and saw what I was doing there. The only other woman in the camp was a surveyor for the electricity company. She spoke passable English and took Juliet out with her during the day. Juliet loved the mountains and the forests and over the rest of my contract period she moaned every time I went back there while she was left at home. At the end of that trip, we took some extra time and went south to Tierra del Fuego and then back up to see the enchanting city of Valparaiso before we went home.

The day after our arrival, as Mario had promised, his womenfolk swept Juliet away to see the city and entertain her. I worked with Mario and Felipe until mid afternoon when the old man left us alone. We had finished work and had the meeting room to ourselves. We both gazed silently out of the expansive windows at the view over the Rio Mapocho and the Parque de los Reyes that runs alongside it. Felipe fetched a couple of beers from the fridge and we stood in silence for a while, letting the business drain away.

'I want to discuss something with you Felipe. Actually, it's my turn to confess something. I kept your secret, I'm sure you'll keep mine?'

'Alastair! How can you even ask that? Of course. What is it?'

'Even Juliet does not know all of this story or what I really intended to do, so please … not even to her.'

'Of course, Alastair, of course.'

'When you confided in me, down there at the camp, I told you that I could not support you in killing that man. I realised that you had few options though, and you probably did the world a favour. I said that I supported the concept of "an eye for an eye" and thought that you had gone beyond that, remember?'

'*Si.*'

'Well I have a confession to make, and I hope that what I have to say will make you feel more at ease. You told me how you disguised Carlos's death as suicide. It was a clever and well thought out plan that worked, and you haven't been discovered.'

'*Si*, yes.' There was a remarkable intensity in his black eyes.

'At first I wanted to copy that idea and kill the woman that had organised the attack on my friend. It almost certainly left him brain damaged. Then I thought of what I'd told you, and my own words to you stopped me. I realised that I didn't want to kill her.'

Then I told Felipe how I had built the kit to gas Sandra with nitrous oxide. 'I climbed into her second floor flat with the absolute intention of holding that mask over her mouth and nose until she collapsed into unconsciousness. First though, I wanted her to tell me where she'd hidden the money, but she was incapable of doing that. Then I thought she might tell me if I gassed her to the extent that she wasn't in full control of her mind. To do that, I was going to hold the mask on her face for a few minutes more. That would have damaged her brain, but would not have killed her. I reckoned it would give me retribution for Giles as well as a lead to the money.'

He was still staring at me, riveted by this revelation from his mentor.

'When I reached her, though, she was dead. She'd been murdered already by, as it turned out, her school friend and lover, another woman. That's not the point of my story. The point is, Felipe, that I fully intended to reduce her to a cabbage to live out her life ever regretting her actions, if she could remember them. Can you imagine such a horrible existence?'

'But you did not do it. She was dead, you said.'

'Yes, but I was going to do it. I can't escape that fact. I was so angry at the hurt she'd caused. It clouded my judgement, I suppose, but I should never have let it. I should have remained cold and calm and let the police handle it. I now have to live with the knowledge that I'm capable of immense cruelty, and I thought I was a reasonable, kind and ordinary man. I can't disguise it with the fact that she was already dead.'

'Hey. So we are not different really, are we Alastair?'

I smiled at him. 'Huh! We're human, Felipe. There are hidden failings to all of us that may never come to the surface except under extreme provocation. I hereby withdraw my opinion of your actions, because I have no right to pass any judgement. I tried only to inflict a head injury for a head injury, but I'm not sure that killing her rather than letting her suffer would not have been a kinder option. I couldn't kill her though, that was a step too far. I just don't know, Felipe. Is there another beer?'

'Sure.' He turned from the window and crossed the room to the fridge.

'However, when I go to see my friend in a coma, I look at him and worry about his future. I get so angry at the waste of the valuable life of a man who not only meant so much to me, but also was so kind and philanthropic towards others. When I go home and my dog doesn't come to greet me, I get sad and then angry. When I saw the bruise on Juliet's face, I got angry; the burnt barn, the wrecked cars ... Those things make me feel my plans were justified. But deep down I know what I was going to do was not right. And, to make it worse, Felipe, I'm not sure she was the one to take all the blame. I could have damaged the servant and not the master.'

Felipe was lost in thought. 'Phila–? Ah, *filántropo*.'

We sat in silence for a while before he said quietly, 'Me too, Alastair, I also ask myself if I was right to do what I did. Then I look at my sister and get angry again.'

'*Salud*,' I raised my bottle. 'For your idea Felipe, *gracias*.'

WHEN WE RETURNED home, the first thing we did was to go and see Giles. The staff were buoyant. Two days previously he had opened his eyes for a brief while then again later for a longer period, and he responded to the stimulus of mild pain. Progress at last. When we entered his room, he was staring at the ceiling. Although the monitors were all there behind his bandaged head, there were no tubes attached to him.

I just looked at him, but Juliet took his hand and said, 'Hello Giles?' It was more of a question, really, attempting to see if he was capable of recognising us. He turned his head, but there was no reaction in his vacant gaze.

I tried. 'Giles, it's us, Juliet and Alastair. It's so good to see you again.'

His eyes tracked slowly over to me, but again there was no recognition. We stood and talked to him for a while until he closed his eyes once more. The same small middle aged ward sister was there with us. In a soft voice, she said, 'Don't worry, it takes a long time, but he'll recognise you eventually, I'm sure.'

As I write this, it has been eleven months since Giles was attacked, and his future still remains uncertain. Home with us in my house until we are confident of his ability to attend to his own basic needs, he walks with us and greets us and we think that our images are slowly coming back to him as the friends he used to have, rather than kind people who have appeared out of nowhere.

Mrs Potter and Henry are keeping his house in order and are looking forward to having him back permanently. He sleeps at our house, but we take him home almost every day, and on the first occasion his dogs were terribly excited to see him. Oddly, I think he recognised them immediately.

We don't feel insulted by that at all. Both of us are grateful that his memory is returning, no matter what shape that progress takes. And we are also very grateful that Giles has enough money for his full recuperation, even if it lasts a lifetime.

On the way home from the hospital once, Juliet asked me to go via Hamstead Marshall. 'There's someone I want you to meet,' she said as we turned in at the entrance to the Dog's Trust.

****

Before You Go

Thank you for reading *A Fitting Revenge*. Hopefully you enjoyed it. If you did and have a moment to spare, writing a short review on your favourite site would be greatly appreciated. Authors depend on reader opinions in order to produce enjoyable works. Reviews help authors to further their careers.

Amazon here: mybook.to/AFittingRevenge
All others here:

https://books2read.com/AFittingRevenge

To find out more about the author and his works please visit: https://www.helifish.co.uk where you have the option to subscribe to his mailing list.

You can also find him on Facebook:

http://www.facebook.com/casole75

Also by CA Sole

Thirty-Four

Ostensibly, Andrew Duncan is a fortunate, intelligent young man, but no one realises he's actually much, much older.

Andrew is aware that his condition has far-reaching implications and some potentially disastrous consequences for mankind. Big Pharma knows of his secret, though, and they will stop at nothing to learn how and why, because it will lead to massive profits.

While Andrew evades the tentacles of the giant corporation, he's framed for the savage murder of a reporter. But who really did it: the pharmaceutical company or the child trafficking gang the journalist was probing? To prove his innocence, Andrew assumes the reporter's investigation. But when he spots two of the victims, he's forced into making a critical decision.

Andrew must find the assassin and expose the depraved gang. But the police are looking for him, Big Pharma is after him and a pair of little girls depend on him.

Even worse, the assassin is closing in.

In *Scott's Choice* Cuthbert Jonathan Scott is a young man with a dominant adventurous spirit. He grew up being indoctrinated by his father into an approach to life that was completely at odds with his nature: take no risks, caution in everything, settle down while young, save your money, on and on. A random event results in a decisive moment. He is torn between two options: following his father's teaching or being himself.

Two personae emerge. One, Jonathan, begins a life following his natural instincts. His spirit of adventure predominates. His choice has consequences which bring several life-threatening events but also great rewards.

Jonathan's alter ego, Cuthbert, or Cuff, is the brain-washed youth who tries to adopt the more cautious approach. But his nature conflicts with this and leads him on a dangerous path to escape the mundane existence which was the consequence of his choice. It seems he cannot avoid risk. Indeed, danger appears to seek him out.

Two independent stories develop in *Scott's Choice*. The tales are linked only by his friends and enemies who continue to influence and react to events in Cuff's life in one way, and in Jonathan's life in an-other. However, certain events are common to both and fixed in the calendar.

Nature's Justice is the first sequel to ***Scott's Choice***. It traces Jonathan's life as he and Gudrun experience a horrific event in Southern Africa. Witnesses to the killing of a rhino and the sighting of the person responsible for the trade in horns, they are chased and hounded over a thousand kilometres from the Kruger Park through South Africa and Botswana to the Victoria Falls.

The Pilot is the second sequel to ***Scott's Choice***. Cuff Scott tries to follow a career to become an airline pilot, but his attempts to lead a stable and prosperous life are ruined by events.

At the flying school where he instructs, he becomes aware of someone smuggling illegal immigrants into the country by night. That's not his only problem. His student is being stalked by an increasingly dangerous man, and she thinks it's him.

It seems that trouble seeks him out and brings his inherent instinct for adventure to the fore. He is forced to question if he's really the persona he's trying to be.

The Author

CA Sole began writing in 1990 with a thriller titled Zahak's Breath. An agent took it on and, after a few not insignificant changes, submitted it to a publisher. The first rejection dented his ego and left its mark.- Colin took the extraordinary and foolish step of giving up his full-time job to write in 1995. His confidence took another hit, and he had to return to work for enough money to buy beer. He persevered, wrote a couple of short stories and about half a novel. That short manuscript has been incorporated into one of the sequels of the Scott series.

Colin's first published novel, *A Fitting Revenge*, came out in 2016 and quickly received 4- and 5-star reviews. His second book, CJ, was done through a small publisher and also received a small number of 4- and 5-star reviews. However, Colin's lack of enthusiasm (and plain laziness) over marketing resulted in poor sales. CJ has been rewritten and published in the summer of 2019 as *Scott's Choice*. It has two sequels: *Nature's Justice* and *The Pilot*. A fifth novel, *Thirty-Four*, was published in August 2021 and has received 5 star reviews.

Having been in the British Army, a professional helicopter pilot and an aviation consultant, his work has taken him all over the world to some 66 countries. He lived and worked in Africa – North, South, East and West – for 43 years before returning to England for good. It's therefore not surprising that the background to Colin's books is travel.

There is far too much of the less trodden world left to see.

To find out more about CA Sole's works and future projects, please visit: https://www.helifish.co.uk

Printed in Great Britain
by Amazon